Terry S[...]
Red-Dirt Ma[...]
Other [...]

"Terry Southern writes a clean, mean, coolly deliberate, and murderous prose—and in it we may have at last found the rightful heir (saints protect me from sacrilege) of Nathanael West."
—Norman Mailer

"Terry Southern is the most profoundly witty writer of our generation."
—Gore Vidal

"This is not your fey, bloodless, European wit. This is an ass-kicking, gang-stomping, chain-whipping, balls-to-the-wall Texas cage fight—mean as a buzztail and sharp as a cat-claw cactus. If there was a Mt. Rushmore of modern American humor, Terry Southern would be the mountain they carve it on."
—Michael O'Donoghue

"'The Blood of the Wig' is one of the funniest stories I have read in a long time and what with all this moving of hearts and brains from one place to another it could happen anywhere ... All in all a witty and profound collection."
—William S. Burroughs

"Terry Southern is a dirty Red and a marijuana head and one of the major American satirists of the twentieth century."
—Tony Hendra

"Terry Southern was one of the first and best of the new wave of American writers, defining the cutting edge of black comedy. It's a joy to have these wonderful works of his back in print."
—Joseph Heller

"[*Red-Dirt Marijuana*] contains most of the great short stories in English that are not by Mr. Hemingway or Mr. O'Hara."
—Robert Anton Wilson

"It is a large and amusing cast ... Several stories, including some reminiscences from Mr. Southern's Alvarado, Texas, boyhood, are almost Hemingway straight. The change of pace, or rather shock, is as refreshing as flower people coming out for hate."

—*Baltimore Sun*

"Southern has managed to lay a kind of prose on us that can perpetrate a complete hoax while telling a mother's own truth."
—*Chicago Tribune*

"Terry Southern has produced a remarkable collection of short stories. They reveal Southern not only as a master of dialogue but as a major talent in contemporary American writing, with an ability comparable to Scott Fitzgerald's to alchemize the essence of his times into literature.

"Appositely, Terry Southern is a great, refreshing shatterer of the American Dream; he jerks his illusion-prone, sham-intellectual public off their safe fences where facts are not cushioned by cliches. He casts the sacred cows of American society into a tumbling burlesque."

—*The Irish Times*

"Southern, in his savage sense of satire, seems a kissing-cousin of Nathanael West, while for sheer horror he compares favorably with Roald Dahl. He has an ear, a superb ear, for recording the way people talk and in that he's as good as Lillian Ross or John O'Hara. Southern has never learned the art of being dull."

—*New Society*

"Mr. Southern never loses his cool, for he has an incredible ear for speech patterns, and for the way in-crowds preserve their exclusiveness through in-vocabularies, and he is as much at home in Mexico as Paris and the Deep South.

"He is so perceptive about people that you begin to really feel what it is like to be a gun-happy bored boy called Howard, in Dallas, Texas, who just had to shoot the cat from next door, or a kid from the tenements of New York, growing up in a landscape utterly inhuman and de-humanizing.

"Mr. Southern has an astonishing talent. He *is* the failed bullfighter, the ticket collector on the Metro, the backstreet boy, the American in Paris, turning on, dropping out, making the scene, enjoying a mighty fine gage. *Red-Dirt Marijuana* sparkles like many jewels, clearly and brilliantly."

—*Evening Despatch*

"*Red-Dirt Marijuana* is a gripping, unflagging exercise in impersonation by a master storyteller, who can assume any identity from a gate-keeper on the Paris Metro to an American housewife. He seems to be not so much creating as listening and reporting with chilling and comic accuracy.

"Whether he is writing of hip culture or complacent bigotry in the deep South, his restraint is as astounding as his versatility. He knows the price of cool, the price of war, the price of living, but he is too clever to ram home his messsage. His victims speak for themselves."

—*The Sunday Telegraph*

& other tastes

Terry Southern

BLOOMSBURY

This edition first published in the USA
by Carol Publishing Group 1990
This paperback edition first published in the UK
by Bloomsbury Publishing Plc 1997
Originally published by The New American Library, Inc.,
New York 1967

'A Change of Style' (originally entitled 'Sea Change'), 'The Road Out
of Axotle', 'I *Am* Mike Hammer', 'Recruiting for the Big Parade',
'Twirling at Ole Miss', and 'You're Too Hip, Baby' were first published
in *Esquire* Magazine. 'Put-down', 'Red-Dirt Marijuana', and 'The
Blood of a Wig' were first published in *Evergreen Review*. 'The Sun
and the Still-born Stars', 'You Gotta Leave Your Mark' (originally
entitled 'The Panthers'), and 'The Night the Bird Blew for Doctor
Warner' were first published in *Harper's Bazaar*. 'Love Is a Many
Splendored' was first published in *Hasty Papers*. 'Apartment to
Exchange' and 'Razor Fight' were first published in *Nugget* Magazine.
'A South Summer Idyll' was originally published in *The Paris Review*.
'The Moon-shot Scandal', 'Red Giant on Our Doorstep', 'Terry
Southern Interviews a Faggot Male Nurse', and 'Scandale at The
Dumpling Shop' were first published in *The Realist*.

Bloomsbury Publishing Plc, 38 Soho Square, London W1V 5DF

A CIP catalogue record is available from the British Library

ISBN 0 7475 3487 X

10 9 8 7 6 5 4 3 2 1

Printed in Great Britain by Clays Ltd, St Ives plc

FOR NILE

Contents

Introduction

My earliest experience with Terry Southern was a discomfiting one. A story of his called "The Accident" (actually a part of his first novel, *Flash and Filigree*) was being prepared for publication in the initial number of *The Paris Review*. In those times (the early Fifties) the U.S. Customs was even more rigid and conservative than the U.S. Mails. As anyone who came through Customs would remember, a copy of Henry Miller's *Tropic of Cancer* or even Nabokov's *Lolita* could subject the traveler to confiscation of the book and fines. In 1959 the Customs in New York threatened to bond an entire shipment of *Paris Reviews* for a single line in a story (by Alex Trocchi) which read, "Give me that spike quick or I'll cut your fucking throat!"

The line in Southern's story was far milder. A policeman says to an irate motorist, "Don't get your shit hot." After much discussion, the offending word was changed to "crap" and at the last (I cringe to write this) the word was taken out altogether so that the line became feeble, and rather unlikely: "Don't get hot!"

Southern was properly incensed. He wrote a fifteen-page letter denouncing the magazine for its timidity and demanded that we publish it. It fell upon Peter Matthiessen, the literary editor of the magazine at the time, to try to reason with him. He pointed out that a fifteen-page letter would overbalance the contents of the next issue . . . it would take up about a quarter of the available pages. Southern was adamant.

Finally Matthiessen composed a short *erratum* which read as follows: "Terry Southern is most anxious that *The Paris Review* point out the absence of two words from his story 'The Accident.' The sentence 'Don't get hot' *should* have read, 'Don't get your *crap* hot,' an omission for which we apologize to all those concerned."

Art Buchwald, who at that time was writing a column for the Paris *Herald-Tribune*, felt that it was the funniest *erratum* notice he ever hoped to come across. He wanted to write about it in his column, but he knew his editor would never allow that word *crap* to appear. It was a problem that bedeviled everyone then.

In any case, Southern forgave us. Over the years we published a number of his short stories—some of which are included in this collection. Part of his novel, *The Magic Christian*, was excerpted. The selection won the Gertrude Vanderbilt Humor Prize, somewhat startling the donor since the novel concerns a tycoon with a Vanderbilt-like fortune who uses it, ten million or so a year, to mount extravagant and weird indignities on the public.

Then again, perhaps Southern only *partly* forgave us—mocking the staff's prudery by suggesting the reverse in a piece he wrote for the 25th Anniversary Issue: "...as I was entering the offices one afternoon, I caught a fleeting glimpse of two figures, in trench coats, atop one of our large editorial desks, writhing in what was clearly an impassioned sexual embrace—'going at it,' in point of fact, like a pair of maddened wart hogs. Their conduct in itself was not unusual. The *Review* offices were no stranger to excess in every form—indeed the great din and clatter, the flailing and thrashing, the ceaseless torrent of 'oohs' and 'aahs' emanating from the *Review* offices and audible to passersby and in adjacent shops, was a *vrai scandal* and a source of the deepest chagrin to many of us. Great God, when I think back on the number of *éclairs, Napoleons, frou-frous* and other *friandes variés* sent crashing to the floor of the neighboring patisserie, from the hands of the startled customer or *patronne* in response to the blood-curdling ecstatic shriek of one of the *Review* girls, 'LE VOILA! CA Y'EST! AIEE-EEE!!! which all too frequently echoed from one end of the rue Vernet to the other..."

One of the projects that Southern took on for *The Paris Review* was an interview with Henry Green, the author of *Loving* among other novels, who was very much admired by Southern and whose influence is discernible in his work. During the interview the two got into a mix-up over the word "subtle" which Southern had used in a question and which Green, who doesn't hear very well, had mistaken for the word "suttee"—the suicide of a Hindu wife on her husband's burning bier. "How dull," Green remarks when they finally get it straightened out. Green went on to imply that much of his work (which he calls non-representational) derives from such problems as deafness—misunderstandings, ambiguities, odd juxtapositions and the comic aspects that result ... and all that is very much a staple of Southern's work.

So are monsters. In the earliest of Southern's stories, belying the loveliest of titles, "The Sun and the Stillborn Star," a mysterious and indeed mystic monster emerges from the sea and engages a Texas dirt-farmer in a medieval-like duel in the melon patch. The monsters turn up in the Southern lexicon in any number of guises—brutes, hunchbacks, gynecologists, satanics, perverts (inevitably mispronounced by red-necks as 'pre-verts'), transvestites—if not monsters in the corporeal sense, certainly in their behavior. These are set against a beguiling cast of innocents—the first, of course, being Candy from the novel of that name written with Mason Hoffenberg and published under the swankish *nom de plume* Maxwell Kenton.* These principals play out their parts in wildly improbable and imaginative set-tos ... in which the abnormal is invariably treated as normal. All of this ("people striking sparks off one another" in Henry Green's phrase) is presented in what Normal Mailer once described as "clear, mean, coolly deliberate, and murderous prose"—appearing on the page in a plethora of italics, ellipses, off-balance emphases, exclamation points and other grammatical and stylistic oddities that would seem to be the obvious precursors of Tom Wolfe's distinctive style.

Somewhere in his interview Henry Green remarks, "If you can make the reader laugh he is apt to get careless and go on reading."

*The de Gaulle administration barred *Candy*. It was republished word for word under the title *Lollipop* when the obscenity laws were relaxed in 1957. *Candy* was published in the U.S. and rose to the top of the *Times*' best seller list. Its famous line, "Give me your hump!" was a greeting one heard around the cafes when it was first published.

Many would say that is Southern's greatest gift: the reader laughs despite the horrific goings-on and the fact that often he is writing about very serious matters. His targets are many. Perhaps one could encompass them by suggesting that what is poked at most consistently is what sappy ideologues refer to as the American Dream. A head-on photograph exists, which I cherish, of Terry walking across a bridge in Chicago on his way to the tumultuous Democratic Convention in 1968 flanked by his fellow iconoclasts—William Burroughs, Allen Ginsberg, and Jean Genet—all members of what was waggishly called the Alternative Establishment.

An interviewer once asked Southern how long his iconoclastic turn of mind had been part of his make-up. "I used to write a lot," he told her, "then show it to my friends—one or two of them anyway—with the idea more or less of astonishing or confounding them with the contents of the pages. I knew they had never seen anything like this before—I mean the weirdest thing they could possibly have read before was Poe or one of those little cartoon 'fuck-books,' as they were called, whereas my stuff was much more weird and immediate—using names of teachers, classmates, etc. These were well received by the two or three people—no girls—who read them, but finally I went too far, and alientated one of the readers—my best friend—by using his sister in a really imaginative piece, perhaps the best of the period ... and this slowed me down for a while—no daring. But finally I learned not to care too much, and would write wholly for an imaginary reader whose tastes were similar to my own. And this is, of course, the only way to work well . . . ."

Nothing about Terry Southern in person would suggest the good-humored savagery he is noted for. In appearance he is rumpled, soft-spoken, courtly and rather owlish. The distinguishing feature is his speech. Texas-born, he has developed a curious mock English complete with little harrumphs ("What? *What?*") delivered in fits and starts, with words often abbreviated in hipster style ("fab" for fabulous) and marked with qualifying endearments such as "Tip Top Tony" for Tony Richardson, the movie director ... very unique and not unlike how Goofy would sound if he were born an earl. All of this hides a quizzical and very sharp mind. I remember asking Southern once if he could make out what William Faulkner was up to in his novel *The*

Reivers. I was writing a review of it for *The New York Times Book Review* and had no idea where to start. "What?... doing a review of the Fab Faulk ... my word ... well, it's ... *what?* ... *dear* boy ... well, it's Faulkner's *Tom Sawyer!*" And of course he was exactly right.

During my bachelor days Southern came and stayed in my New York apartment on occasion. He never seemed to go to bed before four. Friends from his varied worlds would drift by—I could hear the murmur of their voices downstairs as I tried to sleep. Once I called from Los Angeles and in the background I could hear the bellow of a party going on, the clink of glasses, the piano ... At the time I had an elderly delicate, bird-like Finnish lady who came in three times a week and after a sigh or two fluttered a feather duster over the carnage from the parties. Terry called her "Katherine the Char," though the descriptive could not have been less charitable. She came to the apartment dressed as if she were on her way to a chamber music concert. She didn't know how to use the vacuum cleaner. She was a duster. I've forgotten how she came into my employ, but I suspect Terry was correct when he supposed that I supplied her only income.

In an interview with a friend of ours, Maggie Paley, Terry was asked what he would do if he had unlimited funds, very much like Grand Guy Grand of his novel, *The Magic Christian*. He thought of "Katherine the Char" and said as follows: "First I would engage a huge, but clever and snakelike, 'Blowing Machine' and I would have it loaded with one ton of dog-hairs each Monday, Wednesday, and Friday. It would be brought up East 72nd Street to the very end where it would poise like a great dragon. Then, exactly when Katherine the Char had finished one room, the powerful, darting snout of the machine would rise up to the 3rd floor windows and send a terrific blast of dog-hairs into the room—1/4 ton per room. I would observe her reaction—I have friends opposite—with a spy-glass—room by room. The entire place would be a foot deep in dog-hair, most of which however has not yet settled and has the effect of an Arctic blizzard. Then I would drop in—casually, not really noticing her hysteria, or that anything at all was wrong, just sort of complaining in a vague way, occasionally brushing at my sleeve, etc., speaking with a kind of weary petulance: 'Really, Katherine, I *do* think you might be more ... uh, well, I mean to say...' voice trailing away, attention caught by something else, a picture on the wall: 'I say, that *is* an amusing print—is it *new?*' fixing her with a deeply searching look, so there could be no doubt at all as to my interest in the print. If this didn't snap her mind I would give her several hundred thousand dollars—all in pennies. 'Mr. Plimpton asked me to give you this, Katherine—each coin represents the dark seed of his desire for you.'

Toward the end of the Henry Green interview the author tells Southern this: "... the novelist is a communicator and must therefore be interested in any form of communication.... We don't have to paint chapels like Cocteau, but at the same time we must all be on the lookout."

In 1960 Stanley Kubrick read *The Magic Christian* with considerable excitement, and feeling that the film he was preparing at the time, a cold war melodrama called *Red Alert*, needed the lunatic touch of Southern's novel, persuaded Terry to come to London ... to take on another "form of communication." The result was *Dr. Strangelove.*

Southern has always defended his move. He once told the critic, Francis Wyndham: "Films are a great medium; it seems to me that a thing should be a movie before anything else. It's like the difference between seeing someone hit by a car or reading about it. To see it is the next thing to experiencing it yourself. Reading about it is once again removed as you have to visualize it."

What he was saying was by no means a justification of movies over books but simply a qualification of his move from the "Quality Lit Game"—a descriptive incidentally I believe he first came up with. His contribution in Hollywood was considerable—writing or assisting in the scripts for *Dr. Strangelove, The Loved One, Barbarella, Easy Rider, The Cincinnati Kid, The Collector, Casino Royale* ... Concepts of his have left lasting impressions—the campfire scene in *Easy Rider* with Peter Fonda, Dennis Hopper and Jack Nicholson; Slim Pickins riding the atomic bomb to earth in the final scene of *Doctor Strangelove*, striking at his mount with his cowboy hat and shouting *"San Anntone!"*

No less lasting will be his contribution to the Quality Lit Game— this remarkable collection of his work. *Red-Dirt Marijuana* was first published in 1967. It was well-received, but never achieved the popularity it might have, except among Southern enthusiasts. The reasons for this are obscure. Bad timing has had something to do with it—public interest in what Southern writes about, or in his iconoclastic bent, having waned. Hollywood hasn't helped either. It absorbed his time, which was to little public notice: in films one remembers the scenes and perhaps the director for visualizing them, but rarely the writer who thought them up in the first place.

Perhaps the publication of *Red-Dirt Marijuana* will help redress the balance, and establish Southern as one of America's foremost writers, and not only in the tradition of the black humorists, or Nathanael West, with whom he is so often compared.

The Beatles put Southern on the famous album cover of *Sgt. Pepper's Lonely Hearts Club Band* along with others, alive and legendary, of the Alternative Establishment. Terry is tucked in behind Lenny Bruce and Edgar Allen Poe. What a fortuitous and telling placement—next to the master of the macabre on one hand and the great practitioner of black humor on the other. But Terry is barely visible. He should be down in the forefront. William Burroughs is also on that cover. He was once asked to write an appraisal of Southern's work. He scratched around, hoping to come up with some highfalutin verbiage, and finally came down to the nub of it all: "Terry Southern *knows how to write!*"

— George Plimpton
New York City
January 8, 1990

Red-Dirt
Marijuana

THE WHITE BOY came into the open-end, dirt-floor shed where the Negro was sitting on the ground against the wall reading a Western Story magazine.

In one hand the boy was carrying a pillowcase that was bunched out at the bottom, about a third filled with something, and when the Negro looked up it appeared from his smile that he knew well enough what it was.

"What you doin', Hal', bringin' in the *crop?*"

The white boy's name was Harold; the Negro pronounced it *Hal'*.

The white boy walked on over to one side of the shed where the kindling was stacked and pulled down an old sheet of newspaper which he shook out to full size and spread in front of the Negro. He dumped the gray-grass contents of the pillowcase onto the paper, and then straightened up to stand with his hands on his hips, frowning down at it. He was twelve years old.

The Negro was looking at it, too; but he was laughing. He was about thirty-five, and he laughed sometimes in a soft, almost soundless way, shaking his head as though this surely was the final irony, while his face, against very white teeth, gleamed with the darks of richest pipebriar. His name was C.K.

"*Sho'* is a lotta gage," he said.

He reached out a hand and rolled a dry pinch of it between his thumb and forefinger.

"You reckon it's dried out enough?" the boy asked, nasal, sounding almost querulous, as he squatted down opposite. "Shoot, I don't wantta leave it *out* there no more—not hangin' on that dang sycamore anyway—it's beginnin' to *look* too funny." He glanced out the end of the shed toward the big white farmhouse that was about thirty yards away. "Heck, Dad's been shootin' *dove* down in there all week—I was down there this mornin' and that damned old dog of Les Newgate's was runnin' round with a piece of it in his *mouth!* I had to git it away from 'im 'fore they *seen* it."

The Negro took another pinch of it and briskly crushed it between his flat palms, then held them up, cupped, smelling it.

"They wouldn't of knowed what it was noway," he said.

"You crazy?" said Harold, frowning. "You think my Dad don't know *Mex'can loco-weed* when he sees it?"

"Don't look much *like* no loco-weed *now* though, do it?" said the Negro flatly, raising expressionless eyes to the boy.

"*He's* seen it dried out, too, I bet," said the boy, loyally, sullen, but looking away.

"*Sho'* he is," said C.K., weary and acid. "Sho', I bet he done *blow* a lot of it too, ain't he? Sho', why I bet you daddy one of the biggest ole hop-heads in Texas—I bet he *smoke* it an' *eat* it an' just anyway he can git it into his ole *haid!* Hee-hee!" He laughed at the mischievous image. "Ain't *that* right, Hal'?"

"You *crazy?*" demanded Harold, frowning terribly; he took the Negro's wrist. "Lemme smell it," he said.

He drew back after a second.

"I can't smell nothin' but your dang sweat," he said.

" 'Course not," said C.K., frowning in his turn, and brushing his hands, "you got to git it jest when the *flower* break—that's the *boo-kay* of the plant, you see, that's what we call *that.*"

"Do it again," said Harold.

"I ain't goin' *do* it again," said C.K., peevish, closing his eyes for a moment, ". . . it's jest a waste on you—I do it again, you jest say you smell my *sweat*. You ain't got the nose for it noway—you got to know you business 'fore you start foolin' round with *this* plant."

"I can do it, C.K.," said the boy earnestly, "*come* on, dang it!"

The Negro sighed, elaborately, and selected another small bud from the pile.

"Awright now when I rub it in my *hand*," he said sternly, "you let out you breath—then I *cup* my hand, you put your nose in an' smell strong . . . you got to suck in *strong* thru you nose!"

They did this.

"You smell it?" asked C.K.

"Yeah, sort of," said Harold, leaning back again.

"That's the *boo*-kay of the plant—they ain't no smell like it."

"It smells like tea," said the boy.

"Well, now that's why they *calls* it that, you see—but it smell like somethin' *else* too."

"What?"

"Like mighty fine gage, that's what."

"Well, whatta you keep on callin' it *that* for?" asked the boy crossly, ". . . that ain't what that Mex'can called it neither—he called it '*pot*.'"

"That ole *Mex*," said C.K., brushing his hands and laughing, "he sho' were funny, weren't he? . . . thought he could pick *cotton* . . . told *me* he used to *pick-a-bale-a-day!* I had to laugh when he say that . . . oh, sho', you didn't talk to that Mex'can like I did—he call it *lotta* things. He call it '*baby*,' too! Hee-hee. Yeah, he say: 'Man, don't forgit the *baby* now!' He mean bring a few *sticks* of it out to the field, you see, that's what he mean by that. He call it '*charge*,' too. Sho'. Them's *slang* names. Them names git started people don't want the *po*lice nobody like that to know they business, you see what I mean? Sho', they make *up* them names, go on an' talk about they business nobody know what they *sayin'*, you see what I mean."

He stretched his legs out comfortably and crossed his hands over the magazine that was still in his lap.

"Yes indeed," he said after a minute, staring at the pile on the newspaper, and shaking his head, "I tell you right now, boy—that sho' is a lotta gage."

About two weeks earlier, on a day when C.K. wasn't helping Harold's father, they had gone fishing together, Harold and C.K., and on the way back to the house that afternoon, Harold had stopped and stood looking into an adjacent field, a section of barren pasture-land where the cows almost never went, but where there was a cow at that moment, alone, lying on its stomach, with its head stretched out on the ground in front of it.

"What's wrong with that dang *cow?*" he demanded, not really of C.K., but himself, or perhaps of God—though in a sense it *was* C.K. who was responsible for the stock, it being his job at least to take them out to pasture and back each day.

"She *do* seem to be takin' it *easy*, don't she?" said C.K., and they went through the fence and started towards her. "*Look* like ole Maybelle," he said, squinting his eyes at the distance.

"I ain't never seen a cow act like *that* before," said Harold crossly, ". . . layin' there with her head on the ground like a damned old hound-dog."

The cow didn't move when they reached it, just stared up at them; she was chewing her cud, in a rhythmic and contented manner.

"*Look* at that dang cow," Harold muttered, ever impatient with enigma, ". . . it *is* old Maybelle, ain't it?" He felt of her nose and then began kicking her gently on the flank. "Git up, dang it."

"Sho' that's ole Maybelle," said C.K., patting her neck, "what's the matter with you, Maybelle?"

Then C.K. found it, a bush of it, about twenty feet away, growing in the midst of a patch of dwarf-cactus, and he was bent over it, examining it with great care.

"This here is a *full-growed* plant," he said, touching it in several places, gently bending it back, almost caressingly. Finally he stood up again, hands on his hips, looking back at the prostrate cow.

"Must be mighty fine gage," he said.

"Well, I ain't never seen loco-weed make a cow act like *that*," said Harold, as if that were the important aspect of the incident, and he began absently kicking at the plant.

"That ain't no ordinary loco-weed," said C.K., ". . . that there is *red-dirt marijuana*, that's what *that* is."

Harold spat, frowning.

"Shoot," he said then, "I reckon we oughtta pull it up and burn it."

"I reckon we oughtta," said C.K.

They pulled it up.

"Don't gen'lly take to *red-dirt*," C.K. remarked, casually, brushing his hands, ". . . they say if it *do*, then it's mighty fine indeed—they reckon it's got to be *strong* to do it, you see."

"Must be pretty dang *strong* awright," Harold dryly agreed, looking back at the disabled cow, "you think we oughtta git Doc Parks?"

They walked over to the cow.

"Shoot," said C.K., "they ain't nothin' wrong with *this* cow."

The cow had raised her head, and her eyes followed them when they were near. They stared down at her for a minute or two, and she looked at them, interestedly, still chewing.

"Ole Maybelle havin' a *fine* time," said C.K., leaning over to stroke her muzzle. "Hee-hee. She *high*, that's what she is!" He straightened up again. "I tell you right now, boy," he said to Harold, "you lookin' at a *ver'* contented cow there!"

"You reckon it'll ruin her milk?"

"Shoot, that make her milk all the more *rich!* Yeah, she goin' give some Grade-A milk indeed after *that* kinda relaxation. Ain't that right, Maybelle?"

They started back to the fence, Harold dragging the bush along and swinging it back and forth.

"Look at the ole *root* on that plant," said C.K., laughing, ". . . big ole juicy root—sho' would make a fine soup-bone I bet!"

He had twisted off a branch of the plant and plucked a little bunch of leaves from it which he was chewing now, like mint.

"What's it taste like?" asked Harold.

C.K. plucked another small bunch and proffered it to the boy.

"Here you is, my man," he said.

"Naw, it jest makes me sick," said Harold, thrusting his free hand in his pocket and making a face; so, after a minute, C.K. put that piece in his mouth too.

"We could dry it out and *smoke* it," said Harold.

C.K. laughed, a short derisive snort.

"Yes, I reckon we could."

"Let's dry it out and sell it," said the boy.

C.K. looked at him, plaintive exasperation dark in his face.

"Now Hal' don't go talkin' without you knows what you talkin' *about*."

"We could sell it to them Mex'can sharecroppers over at Farney," said Harold.

"Hal', what is you *talkin'* about—them people ain't got no money."

They went through the fence again, silent for a while.

"Well, don't *you* wantta dry it out?" Harold asked, bewildered, boy of twelve, aching for action and projects—*any* project that would bring them together.

C.K. shook his head.

"Boy, you don't catch me givin' no advice on that kinda business —you daddy run me right off this place somethin' like that ever happen."

Harold was breaking it up.

"We'd have to put it some place where the dang stock wouldn't git at it," he said.

So they spread the pieces of it up in the outside branches of a great sycamore, where the Texas sun would blaze against them, and then they started back on up to the house.

"Listen, Hal'," said C.K. about halfway on. "I tell you right now you don't wanta say nothin' *'bout* this to nobody up at the house."

"You crazy?" said the boy, "you don't reckon I *would*, do you?"

They walked on.

"What'll we do with it when it's dried *out*, C.K.?"

C.K. shrugged, kicked at a rock.

"Shoot, we find *some* use for it I reckon," he said, with a little laugh.

"You think it's dried *out* enough?" Harold was asking now, as they sat with the pile of it between them, he crumbling some of it in his fingers, scowling at it.

C.K. took out his sack of *Bull-Durham*.

"Well, I tell you what we goin' have to do," he said with genial authority, ". . . we goin' have to *test* it."

He slipped two cigarette-papers from the attached packet, one of which he licked and placed alongside the other, slightly overlapping it.

"I use *two* of these papers," he explained, concentrating on the work, "that give us a nice *slow*-burnin' stick, you see."

He selected a small segment from the pile and crumpled it, letting it sift down from his fingers into the cupped cigarette-paper; and then he carefully rolled it, licking his pink-white tongue slowly over the whole length of it after it was done. "I do that," he said, "that seal it in good, you see." And he held it up then for them both to see; it was much thinner than an ordinary cigarette, and still glittering with the wet of his mouth.

"That cost you half-a-*dollah* in *Dallas*," he said, staring at it.

"Shoot," said the boy, uncertain.

"Sho' would," said C.K., ". . . oh you git you three for a dollah, you *know* the man—'course that's mighty good gage I'm talkin' 'bout you pay half-a-dollah . . . that's you *quality* gage. I don't know how good quality this here is yet, you see."

He lit it.

"Sho' *smell* good though, don't it?"

Harold watched him narrowly as he wafted the smoking stick back and forth beneath his nose.

"*Taste* mighty good too! Shoot, I jest bet this is *ver'* good quality gage. You wantta taste of it?" He held it out.

"Naw, I don't want none of it right now," said Harold. He got up and walked over to the kindling-stack, and drew out from a stash there a package of Camels; he lit one, returned the pack to its place, and came back to sit opposite C.K. again.

"*Yeah,*" said C.K. softly, gazing at the thin cigarette in his hand, "I feel this gage awready . . . this is *fine.*"

"What does it feel *like?*" asked Harold.

C.K. had inhaled again, very deeply, and was holding his breath, severely, chest expanded like a person who is learning to float, his dark brow slightly knit in the awareness of actually *working* at it physically.

"It feel *fine,*" he said at last, smiling.

"How come it jest made me *sick* that time?" asked the boy.

"Why *I* tole you, Hal'," said C.K. impatiently, " 'cause you tried to fight *against* it, that's why . . . you tried to *fight* that gage, so it jest make you *sick!* Sho', that was *good* gage that ole Mex had."

"Shoot, all I felt, 'fore I got sick, was jest right *dizzy.*"

C.K. had taken another deep drag and was still holding it, so that now when he spoke, casually but without exhaling, it was from the top of his throat, and his voice sounded odd and strained:

"Well, that's 'cause you *mind* is young an' un*formed,* you see . . . that gage jest come into you mind an' *cloud* it over!"

"My *mind?*" said Harold.

"Sho', you *brain!*" said C.K. in a whispery rush of voice as he let out the smoke. "*You* brain is young an' un*formed,* you see . . . that smoke come in, it got nowhere to go, it jest *cloud* you young brain over!"

Harold flicked his cigarette a couple of times.

"It's as good as any dang nigger-brain I guess," he said after a minute.

"Now boy, don't *mess* with me," said C.K., frowning, ". . . you ast me somethin' an' I tellin' you. *You* brain is young an' un*formed* . . . it's all *smooth,* you brain, smooth as that piece of shoe-leather. That smoke jest come in an' cloud it over!" He took another drag. "Now you take a full-*growed* brain," he said in his breath-holding voice, "it *ain't* smooth—it's got all *ridges* in it, all over, go this way an' that. Shoot, a man know what he doin' he have that smoke runnin' *up* one ridge an' *down* the other! He *con*trol his high, you see what I mean, he don't fight against it. . . ." His voice died away in the effort of holding breath and speaking at the same time—and, after exhaling again, he finished off the cigarette in several quick little drags, then broke open the butt with lazy care and emptied the few remaining bits from it back onto the pile. "*Yeah* . . ." he said, almost inaudibly, an absent smile on his lips.

Harold sat or half reclined, though somewhat stiffly, supporting himself with one arm, just staring at C.K. for a moment before he shifted about a little, flicking his cigarette. "Shoot," he said, "I jest wish you'd tell me what it *feels* like, that's all."

C.K., though he was sitting cross-legged now with his back fairly straight against the side of the shed, gave the appearance of substance wholly without bone, like a softly-filled sack that has slowly, imperceptibly sprawled and found its final perfect contour, while his head lay back against the shed, watching the boy out of half-closed eyes. He laughed.

"Boy, I done *tole* you," he said quietly, "it feel *good*."

"Well, that ain't nothin', dang it," said Harold, almost angrily, "*I* aw*ready* feel good!"

"Uh-huh," said C.K. with dreamy finality.

"Well, I *do*, god-dang it," said Harold, glaring at him hatefully.

"That's right," said C.K., nodding, closing his eyes, and they were both silent for a few minutes, until C.K. looked at the boy again and spoke, as though there had been no pause at all: "But you don't feel as good now as you do at *Christmas*time though, do you? Like when right after you daddy give you that new *Winchester*? An' then you don't feel as *bad* as that time he was whippin' you for shootin' that doe with it neither, do you? Yeah. Well now that's how much difference they *is*, you see, between that cigarette you got in you hand an' the one I jest put out! Now that's what I tellin' *you*."

"Shoot," said Harold, flicking his half-smoked Camel and then mashing it out on the ground, "you're crazy."

C.K. laughed. "Sho' I is," he said.

They fell silent again, C.K. appearing almost asleep, humming to himself, and Harold sitting opposite, frowning down to where his own finger traced lines without pattern in the dirt-floor of the shed.

"Where we gonna keep this stuff at, C.K.?" he demanded finally, his words harsh and reasonable, "we can't jest leave it sittin' out like this."

C.K. seemed not to have heard, or perhaps simply to consider it without opening his eyes; then he did open them, and when he leaned forward and spoke, it was with a fresh and remarkable cheerfulness and clarity:

"Well, now the first thing we got to do is to *clean* this gage. We got to git them *seeds* outta there an' all them little branches. But the *ver'* first thing we do . . ." and he reached into the pile, "is to take some of this here *flower,* these here *ver'* small leaves, an' put them off to the side. That way you got you *two* kinds of gage, you see—you got you a *light* gage an' a *heavy* gage."

C.K. started breaking off the stems and taking them out, Harold joining in after a while; and then they began crushing the dry leaves with their hands.

"How we ever gonna git all them dang seeds outta there?" asked Harold.

"Now I show you a *trick* about that," said C.K., smiling and leisurely getting to his feet. "Where's that pilly-cover at?"

He spread the pillowcase flat on the ground and, lifting the newspaper, dumped the crushed leaves on top of it. Then he folded the cloth over them and kneaded the bundle with his fingers, pulverizing it. After a minute of this, he opened it up again, flat, so that the pile was sitting on the pillowcase now as it had been before on the newspaper.

"You hold on hard to that end," he told Harold, and he took the other himself and slowly raised it, tilting it, and agitating it. The round seeds started rolling out of the pile, down the taut cloth and onto the ground. C.K. put a corner of the pillowcase between his teeth and held the other corner out with one hand; then, with his other hand, he tapped gently on the bottom of the pile, and the seeds poured out by the hundreds, without disturbing the rest.

"Where'd you learn that at, C.K.?" asked Harold.

"Shoot, you got to know you business you workin' with *this* plant," said C.K., ". . . waste our time pickin' out them ole seeds."

He stood for a moment looking around the shed. "Now we got to have us somethin' to *keep* this gage in—we got to have us a *box*, somethin' like that, you see."

"Why can't we jest keep it in that?" asked Harold, referring to the pillowcase.

C.K. frowned. "Naw we can't *keep* it in that," he said, ". . . keep it in that like ole sacka turnip . . . we got to git us somethin'—a nice little *box*, somethin' like that, you see. How 'bout one of you empty shell-boxes? You got any?"

"They ain't big enough," said Harold.

C.K. resumed his place, sitting and slowly leaning back against the wall, looking at the pile again.

"They sho' ain't, is they," he said, happy with that fact.

"We could use two or three of 'em," Harold said.

"Wait a minute now," said C.K., "we talkin' here, we done forgit about this *heavy* gage." He laid his hand on the smaller pile, as though to reassure it. "One of them shell-boxes do fine for that—an' I *tell* you what we need for this *light* gage now I think of it . . . is one of you momma's quart *fruit*-jars."

"Shoot, I can't fool around with them dang jars, C.K.," said the boy.

C.K. made a little grimace of impatience.

"*You* momma ain't begrudge you one of them fruit-jars, Hal' —she *ast* you 'bout it, you jest say it got *broke!* You say you done *use* that jar put you fishin'-minners in it! *Hee-hee* . . . she won't even wanta *see* that jar no more, you tell her *that*."

"I ain't gonna fool around with them jars, C.K."

C.K. sighed and started rolling another cigarette.

"I jest goin' twist up a few of these sticks now," he explained, "an' put them off to the side."

"When're you gonna smoke some of that other?" asked Harold.

"What, that *heavy* gage?" said C.K., raising his eyebrows in surprise at the suggestion. "Shoot, *that* ain't no workin'-hour gage there, that's you *Sunday* gage . . . oh you mix a little bit of that *into* you light gage now and then you *feel* like it—but you got to be sure ain't nobody goin' to mess with you 'fore you turn *that* gage full on. 'Cause you jest wanta lay back then an' take it *easy*." He nodded to himself in agreement with this, his eyes intently watching his fingers work the paper. "You see . . . you don't *swing* with you heavy gage, you jest *goof* . . . that's what you call that. Now you light gage, you *swing* with you light gage . . . you *con*trol that gage, you see. Say a man have to go out an' *work*, why he able to *enjoy* that work! Like now you seen me turn on some of this light gage, didn't you? Well, I may have to go out with you *daddy* a little later on an' lay that fence-wire, or work with my post-hole digger. Why I able to *swing* with my post-hole digger with my light gage on. Sho', that's you *sociable* gage, you light gage is—this here other, well, that's what you call you *thinkin'* gage. . . . Hee-hee! Shoot, I wouldn't even wanta *see* no post-hole digger I turn *that* gage full on!"

He rolled the cigarette up, slowly, licking it with great care.

"Yeah," he said half-aloud, ". . . ole fruit-jar be *fine* for this light gage." He chuckled. "That way we jest look right in there, know how much we got on hand at all time."

"We got *enough* I reckon," said Harold, a little sullenly it seemed.

"Sho' is," said C.K., "more'n the law allows at that."

"Is it against the law then sure enough, C.K.?" asked Harold in eager interest, ". . . like that Mex'can kept sayin' it was?"

C.K. gave a soft laugh.

"I jest reckon it *is*," he said, ". . . it's against all kinda law—what we got here is. Sho', they's one law say you can't have *none* of it, they put you in the jailhouse you do . . . then they's another law say they catch you with more than *this* much . . ." he reached down and picked up a handful to show, "well, then you in *real* trouble! Sho', you got more than *that* why they say: 'Now that man got more of that gage than he *need* for his personal use, he must be *sellin'* it!' Then they say you a *pusher*. That's what they call that, an' boy I mean they put you *way* back in the jailhouse then!" He gave Harold a severe look. "I don't wanta tell you you business, nothin' like that, Hal', but if I was you I wouldn't let on 'bout this to *nobody*—not to you frien' Big Law'ence or *any* of them people."

"Heck, don't you think I know better than to do that?"

"You ain't scared though, is you Hal'?"

Harold spat.

"Shoot," he said, looking away, as though in exasperation and disgust that the thought could have occurred to anyone.

C.K. resumed his work, rolling the cigarettes, and Harold watched him for a few minutes and then stood up, very straight.

"I reckon I could git a fruit-jar outta the cellar," he said, "if she ain't awready brought 'em up for her cannin'."

"That sho' would be fine, Hal'," said C.K., without raising his head, licking the length of another thin stick of it.

When Harold came back with the fruit-jar and the empty shell-box, they transferred the two piles into those things.

"How come it's against the *law* if it's so all-fired good?" asked Harold.

"Well, now, I use to study 'bout that myself," said C.K., tightening the lid of the fruit-jar and giving it a pat. He laughed. "It ain't because it make young boys like you *sick*, I tell you *that* much!"

"Well, what the heck is it then?"

C.K. put the fruit-jar beside the shell-box, placing it neatly, carefully centering the two just in front of him, and seeming to consider the question while he was doing it.

"I *tell* you what it is," he said then, "it's 'cause a man *see* too much when he git high, that's what. He see right *through* ever'thing . . . you understan' what I say?"

"What the heck are you talkin' about, C.K.?"

"Well, maybe you too young to know what I talkin' 'bout—but I tell you they's a lotta trickin' an' lyin' go on in the world . . . they's a lotta ole *bull-crap* go on in the world . . . well, a man git high, he see right through all them tricks an' lies, an' all that ole bull-crap. He see right through there into the *truth* of it!"

"Truth of *what*?"

"*Ever*'thing."

"Dang you sure talk crazy, C.K."

"Sho', they *got* to have it against the law. Shoot, ever'body git high, wouldn't be nobody git up an' feed the chickens! Hee-hee . . . ever'body jest *lay in bed!* Jest lay in bed till they *ready* to git up! Sho', you take a man high on good gage, he got no use for they ole bull-crap, 'cause he done see right through there. Shoot, he lookin' right down into his ver' *soul!*"

"I ain't never heard nobody talk so dang crazy, C.K."

"Well, you young, boy—you goin' hear plenty crazy talk 'fore you is a growed man."

"Shoot."

"Now we got to think of us a good place to *put* this gage," he said, "a *secret* place. Where you think, Hal'?"

"How 'bout that old smoke-house out back—ain't nobody goes in there."

"Shoot, that's a *good* place for it, Hal'—you sure they ain't goin' tear it down no time soon?"

"Heck no, what would they tear it down for?"

C.K. laughed.

"Yeah, that's right," he said, "well, we take it out there after it gits dark."

They fell silent, sitting there together in the early afternoon. Through the open end of the shed the bright light had inched across the dirt floor till now they were both sitting half in the full sunlight.

"*I* jest wish I knowed or not you daddy goin' to work on that south-quarter *fence* today," said C.K. after a bit.

"Aw, him and Les Newgate went to *Dalton*," said Harold, ". . . heck, I bet they ain't back 'fore dark." Then he added, "You wanta go fishin'?"

"Shoot, that sound like a *good* idee," said C.K.

"I seen that dang drum-head jumpin' on the west side of the pond again this mornin'," said Harold, ". . . shoot, I bet he weighs seven or eight pounds."

"*I* think we do awright today," C.K. agreed, glancing out at the blue sky and sniffing a little, ". . . shoot, we try some calf-liver over at the second *log*—that's jest where that ole drum-head *is* 'bout now."

"I reckon we oughtta git started," said Harold. "I guess we can jest leave that dang stuff here till dark . . . we can stick it back behind that fire-wood."

"Sho'," said C.K., "we stick it back in there for the time bein'—I think I jest twist up one or two more 'fore we set out though . . . put a taste of this heavy in 'em." He laughed as he unscrewed the lid of the fruit-jar. "Shoot, this sho' be fine for fishin'," he said. ". . . ain't nothin' like good gage give a man the strength of patience—you want me to twist up a couple for *you*, Hal'?"

Harold spat.

"Aw I guess so," he said finally, ". . . you let *me* lick 'em though, dang it, C.K."

Razor
Fight

THE CRAP-GAME STARTED at two o'clock that afternoon, when C.K. Crow walked into the Paradise Bar with a bottle of Sweet Lucy in one hand and $6 in the other. The white boy, Harold, was with him. "Smart nigger can double his money *quick,*" said C.K., "if he think I ain't comin' out on . . . *wham!*" and he threw the dice. " . . . SEVEN!" Then he lay his head back laughing and tilted the bottle of wine.

The place was jumping—funky wailing blues and high wild laughter. "Crow suck that bottle like it a big stick of tea!" "He do it like somethin' else I think of too! Hee-hee! Lemme have a taste of that Lucy, boy!" "You all *wise* do you celebratin' *'fore* you puts you money down," said C.K., " 'cause you sho' goin' be cryin' the blues *after* . . . where them dice!" Old Wesley stood leaning behind the bar, picking his teeth with a matchstick. "Drink of this establishment not *good* enough for you, Mistah Crow, that you got to bring you own bottle in here?"

"Never mind that, my man," said C.K., wiping his mouth, "you establishment don't carry drink of this particular quality." He slapped a quarter on the bar. "Gimme a glass."

Old Wesley put a large water-glass on the bar.

"Who you young frien' over there?" he asked, with a nod of mock severity at Harold, who hung back near the wall.

"An' my young frien' there have a *coke,*" said C.K., looking around at Harold as though he might have forgotten about him. "Ain't that right, boy?"

"Aw I guess so," said Harold, sullen, looking away, but aware of the two laughing together now.

In the Negro bar, C.K. affected an exaggerated superiority over the boy which, though it might sometimes be annoying, Harold didn't resent because he never felt enough a part of the situation to be vulnerable. He had been coming into the Paradise Bar with C.K. for about a year now, whenever they'd be sent to town in the old pickup to get feed, fence-wire, or whatever it happened to be. C.K. had started this thing of stopping off at the Paradise by saying that he wanted to call on some of *his people,* as long as he and Harold were in town, and this had first involved their crossing over into a section that was known on maps, town-records, and the like, as West Central Tracks, but was in fact spoken of simply as "Nigger Town"—and then driving through the absurdly bumpy labyrinth of dust and lean-to shacks, outside which great charred wash-pots steamed in the Texas sun above raging bramble-fires. Negroes sat hunched along the edge of ramshackle front-porches, making slow crazy-looking marks in the dust with a stick or gazing, with equal inscrutableness, at the road in front of them—driving through, and finally pulling in with the pickup, right into the dirt frontyard of one of these shacks.

Then at last they would be in the dark interior itself, seemingly windowless, smelling of kerosene and liniment, red-beans and rice, cornbread, catfish, and possum-stew; and Harold would sit in the corner with a glass of water given him and maybe a piece of hot cornbread, while C.K. sat at the table, in the yellow glow of the oil-lamp, eating, always eating, forever dipping the cornbread into a bowl, head lowered in serious eating, but laughing too, and above all, saying things to make the big woman laugh, she who stood, or sat, watching him eat, his aunt, cousin, girl-friend, Harold never knew which, nor cared. And after, on the way out of the section they would stop again, at the Paradise Bar, so that C.K. could "see a friend," while Harold, saying, "Goddang it, C.K., we can't fool around here all day," waited in the pickup, drinking a coke and eating a piece of hot barbecued-chicken or spare-ribs that C.K. had brought out to him. Then he too had taken to going inside, tentatively at first, either to get C.K. out of there or to get another coke for himself, only then perhaps to linger in watching the crap-game a while, or listening to Blind Tom sing the blues—so that in the end all pretense of calling on C.K.'s people or seeing a friend had been discarded; and whenever they were in town now, and had the time, they just drove straight over to the Paradise Bar and went in. And whereas Harold had in the beginning been merely bored by it all, even given a headache by the ceaseless swinging wail of the blues-guitar, and blistered lips from the barbecue so dredged in red-pepper that it brought both tears and sweat to his face, he had finally come to enjoy these interludes at the Paradise, or rather to take them for granted—sentiments which, in a boy of twelve, are perhaps interchangeable.

"*Well, who is it now? Seth Stevens' boy?*"

Sitting on a stool next to the wall near where Harold stood was a blind Negro of about sixty; he was barefoot and was strumming a guitar in his lap, he who turned his face, smiling, toward the boy at the sound of his voice, asking "Who is it now? Seth Stevens' boy?" And there was in this upturned face such a soft unearthly radiance as could have been startling—a wide extraordinarily open face, and the expanse of closed lids made it appear even more so, a face that when singing would sometimes contort as though in pain or anger, and yet when turning to inquire, as in waiting for the word, was lifted, smiling . . . even as in the way an ordinary man may cock his head to one side with a smile, this blind man would, but tilting his chin as well, so that with the light falling directly on his upturned face it seemed almost to be illuminated. It was an expression which on an ordinary person, would have resembled that kind of sweet Blakeian imbecility occasionally seen on faces along McDougal Street, but on this sightless Negro face now it appeared very close to being joyous.

"Who is it then? Hal' Stevens?"

"Yeah, it's Harold," said the boy, laconic and restless—accepting, yet half uncertain whether or not it was all a waste of time. He sat down with his coke in an old straight chair next to the stool. "How *you* doin', Blind Tom?"

"You voice begin to change, Hal'—I weren't sure it were you. How's you gran'daddy?"

"Aw he's awright. He's slowed down a lot though, I guess."

Blind Tom always spoke as though Harold's grandfather were still running their farm, even though the old man was eighty-seven now and had not been active for as long as Harold could remember. It was something which Harold had attempted to explain once, in one of their earliest conversations, and which Tom had seemed to understand, though gradually now the old notion had stolen back into his talk, and Harold no longer tried to dispel it.

"What kinda cotton you all goin' to have out there this year, Hal'?"

"Aw I reckon it'll be pretty good, Blind Tom—if the dang boll-weevils don't git at it again."

"What, he have some trouble with the weevil?"

"Aw they got into that south-quarter. Shoot, they ate up half-a-acre 'fore anybody knew it. We had to spray the whole dang crop."

"Well, you gran'daddy ain't lose no cotton-crop to the boll-weevil I tell you that!"

"Naw, we done sprayed it over now."

"You *'member* me to you gran'daddy now, Hal'. He 'member Blind Tom Ransom. I picked a mighty lotta cotton out there."

"I know you did, Blind Tom."

"He git good hands out there now?"

"Aw they say they ain't as good as they used to be—you know how they always say that."

"I use to pick-a-bale-a-day. I pick seben-hunderd twenty-three pounds one day, dry-load. He was down to the wagon hisself to see it weighed out. *He* tell you. They *say* it ain't never been beat in the county."

"I know it, Tom."

Leaning against the bar, C.K. was filling his glass, watching the bright red wine tumble into it.

"Big Nail back," said Old Wesley.

"Is *that* so?" said C.K., and with such smiling astonishment that one might have known it was false.

"Sho', he sittin' right over there in the *corner*—you see him?"

"Well, so he is," said C.K., partly turning around. "I *swear* I never seen him when I come *in!*" but he said this in such a laughing way, taking a big drink, too, that it was most apparent that he had.

"He lookin' fit, ain't he?" He laughed softly. "Old Big Nail," he said, shaking his head as he turned back around. He refilled his half-full glass. "I likes to keep a full glass before me," he explained to Wesley, "at *all* times." He did a little dance-step then, holding on to the bar and looking down at his feet. "How's business with *you*, Mr. Wesley?" he asked, coming back to his drink.

" 'Bout the same as usual I reckon."

"Oh? I would of said it was pickin' up a little," said C.K. smiling, looking at Big Nail.

"Can't complain," said Wesley.

"Remind me I hear a funny story today," said C.K., somewhat louder than before and half turning away from the bar; then he stopped to laugh, closing his eyes and lowering his chin down to his chest, shaking his head as though he were trying not to laugh at all.

"Oh yeah, it were ver' funny."

He had a loose uninhibited manner of telling a story, yet a certain restraint too, an almost imperceptible half-smile, as of modesty, even as if he himself were quite objectively aware of how very good a story it was.

"These two boys were *talkin'*, you see, and one of 'em say, he say: 'Well, boy, what you goin' *do* now you is equal?!?' And the other one say: 'Well now I glad you ast me that, I tell you what *I* goin' do—I goin' git me one of them *big* . . . *white* . . . *suits* . . . and a *white* shirt, and *white* tie, and *white* shoes and socks, and I goin' buy me a white Cadillac, and then I goin' drive down to *Houston* and git me a *white woman!*' And when he say that, the first one jest *laugh!* So he say, salty-like, he say: 'What's the matter with you, boy, you laugh like that when I tell you my *plans?* You so smart, you tell me what *you* goin' do now you is equal!' So the second one say: 'Well, now I tell you what *I* goin' do—I goin' git me a *black* suit, and *black* shirt and tie, and *black* shoes and socks, and I goin' buy me a black Cadillac, and then I goin' drive down to Houston . . . and watch them hang yoah *black ass!*' "

Though everyone had heard the story before, they almost all laughed, because of C.K.'s manner of telling it, the mock way he frowned and grimaced, and the short explosive way he delivered the refrain '*now-you-is-equal!*' making it nearly unintelligible.

"I *think* I know what he tryin' to say," said Big Nail, speaking to no one in particular, holding the dice and shaking them softly, close to his ear, "I jest wonder why he don't put his money . . . where his big mouth is!" And he threw the dice, saying: "Hot . . . SEVEN!"

So the game was joined, while on the stool against the wall where Harold sat, Blind Tom Ransom played his guitar—and as the crap-game got under way, his head was lifted, sightless eyes seeming to range out over the players, singing:

> "If you evah go to Fut Wurth
> Boy you bettah ack right
> You bettah not ar-gy
> An' you bettah not fight!
>
> Shruf Tomlin of Fut Wurth
> Cay's a foaty-fouh gun
> If you evah see 'im com-min
> Well it too late to run!
>
> Cause he like to shoot rab-bit
> Like to shoot 'em on de run
> Seen dat Shruf hit a rab-bit
> Wif his foaty-fouh gun!"

"Well, tell 'em 'bout it, Blind Tom!"

> "An' he like to shoot de spar-ry
> An' he like to shoot de quail
> An' dare ain't many nig-ger
> In de Fut Wurth jail!"

"Goddam, sing it, Blind Tom!"

"Yes he like to shoot de spar-ry
An' he like to shoot de quail!
An' dare ain't many nig-ger
In de Fut Wurth jail!"

The crap-game progressed through the afternoon; by four o'clock there were about fifteen shooters. Harold had seen C.K. cleaned out three times, and each time leave the bar, to come back a few minutes later with a new stake. The last time though, he had only come back with another 39-cent bottle of Lucy.

"Put this bottle aside for me, my man," he said to Wesley, "till I call for it later, in the cool of the evenin'."

"Who's winnin'?" asked Old Wesley.

"I wouldn't know nothin' 'bout *that* aspeck of the game I assure you!" said C.K.

"Big Nail winnin'!" said a boy about Harold's age who was picking cigarette-butts off the floor by the bar. "Big Nail hot as a two-dollah pistol!"

C.K. gave a derisive snort, and wiped his mouth. "I jest wish I had me a *stake*," he said. "Now I can *feel* it! Lemme have two-dollah, Mistah Wesley, I give it to you first thing in the mornin'—on my way to work! I ain't kiddin' you!"

"Where you workin' now, C.K.?" asked Wesley, winking at Harold.

"I ain't *kiddin'* you now!" C.K. said crossly, but then he sighed and turned away.

"Man, I can sure *feel it now!*"

He started snapping his fingers, staring at his hand, fascinated. "*Ump!*" He made a couple of flourishes, and his shoulders hunched up and down in quick jerks, as though through spasms outside his control. "Ump! Man, I'm hot now, I jest had me a goddam stake!"

"Here you is, boy."

The two bills, wadded together and soft with sweat, landed beside C.K.'s glass. He stared at them without looking up.

"Go enjoy yourself," said Big Nail who was standing next to him and appeared to be absorbed in counting and arranging his money, a great deal of it.

C.K. picked up the crumpled notes and slowly straightened them out. "Shee-iit," he said, and then walked over to the game, taking his bottle with him.

Blind Tom was singing:

> "De longest tra-in
> Ah evah did see
> Was one hun-red coaches long. . . ."

Back in the game, C.K. waited for the dice.

"I only bets on a *sure-thing* this time of day," he said.

"Here old Crow tryin' to make his *come-back!*"

"What you shootin', C.K.?"

"*Two-dollah?* My, my, how the mighty *have* fallen!"

"You jest git on *that,* boy," said C.K., "you be havin' all you want in a *ver'* short time!"

He rattled the dice, soft and then loud, he rolled them between his palms like pieces of putty—he blew on them, spit on them, rubbed them against his crotch, he raged against them like a sadistic lover:

"*Come,* you bitch, you hot mutha—*hit 'em* with it, SEVEN!"

"*Baby,* now *one* moah time hot SEVEN!"

He made five straight passes without touching the money, and across the room Blind Tom was singing:

> "An de only gal
> Ah evah did love
> Was on dat tra-in
> An' gone. . . ."

"What you shootin' *now,* C.K.?"

"You lookin' at it, daddy."

The $2, doubled five times, was now over $60—and mostly in ones, it lay scattered between them like a kind of exotic garbage.

During the delay for getting the bet covered, because no one wanted to fade him any more, C.K. kept whispering to the dice and shaking them.

"They tryin' to *cool* you off, dice, they's so afraid, they tryin' to cool you off you so hot! Lawd, I feel you burn my *hand*, you so hot!"

"Take all or any of it, boys," said C.K. "Goddamn, step back, we're comin' out!"

"Come on out then," said Big Nail, standing behind the first row of those crouched around the money, ". . . with *all* of it." And the bills fluttered down like big wet leaves.

"Shee-iit," said C.K., not looking up, shaking the dice slowly, ". . . you hear that, dice? Man from the *North* put down his money . . . man from the North give his money now to see you natural seven! Yeah, he want to see your big seven, baby," and he shook the dice gradually, and gradually faster now, near his head, rhythmically, as though he were playing a maraca or a tambourine, and he was humming along with the sound, saying, ". . . *yeah*, now you talkin', baby, now you gittin' it . . . *yeah* . . . *yeah* . . . now we comin' out, dice, goin' show 'im the seven, goin' show 'im the 'leven," and as he talked to the dice, his voice rose and his tone gained command until, as the dice struck the wall, he was snarling, "*Hit him you sonofabitch*, SEVEN!"

Two aces.

Most were relieved that C.K.'s run was broken.

"Don't look *too* much like no seven to *me*," said someone dryly, "look more like the eyes of . . . of some kind of *evil serpent!*"

"Hee-hee! That's what it look like to me too," said another, and then called out: "Turn up the light, Mister Wesley, way it is now C.K.'s natural-seven done look like *snake-eyes!*"

"You have to turn *off* de light 'fore *that* ever goin' resemble a seven!"

"Hee-hee! You *turn* 'em off, them snake-eyes still *be* there! Gleamin' in the dark!"

C.K. sat still for a minute while Big Nail gathered the money. Then he got up and went back over to the bar.

"Lawd, lawd," he said, shaking his head.

He filled his glass and took a big mouthful, swishing it around before he swallowed it. "Play the blues, Blind Tom," he said, "play the blues *one* time." But Blind Tom was playing a jump-tune; he was shouting it:

> "My gal don't go fuh smokin'
> Likker jest make her flinch
> Seem she don't go fuh nothin'
> Ex-cept my big ten inch . . .
> Record of de ban' dat play de blues,
> Ban' dat play de blues,
> She jest love my big ten inch . . .
> Record of her favorite blues

> "Las' nite I try to tease her
> Ah give her a little pinch
> She say 'Now stop dat jivin'
> An' git out yoah big ten inch . . .
> Record of de ban' dat play de blues,
> Ban' dat play de blues,'
> She jest love MY BIG TEN INCH . . .
> Record of her fa-vorite blues . . ."

After a few minutes, Big Nail returned to the bar; he was still counting his money and straightening out the crumpled bills.

"You know, I hear a right funny story today," said C.K. then, looking at Old Wesley, but speaking loud, "*I* had to *laugh*. There was these two boys from Fort Worth, they was over in Paris, France with the *Army,* and one day they was standin' on the corner without much in partic'lar to do when a couple of *o-fay* chicks come strollin' by, you know what I mean, a couple of nice *French* gals—and they was ver' nice indeed with the exception that *one* of them appeared to be considerable *older* than the other one, like she might be the great-grandmother of the other one or somethin' like that, you see. So these boys was diggin' these chicks and one of them say: 'Man, let's make a move, I believe we do *awright* there!' And the other one say: 'Well, now, similar thought occurred to me as well, but . . . er . . . uh . . . how is we goin' decide who takes the *grand-mother? I* don't want no old bitch like that!' So the other one say: 'How we *decide?* Why man, *I* goin' take the grandmother! *I* the one see these chicks first, and I gets to take my *choice!*' So the other one say: 'Well, *now* you talkin'! You gets the grandmother, and I gets the young one—that's *fine!* But tell me this, boy—how come you wants that old lady, instead of that fine young gal?' So the other one say: 'Why, boy, don't you *know*? Ain't you *with it*? *She* been *white* . . . LON-GER!' "

Finishing the story, C.K. lowered his head, closed-eyed as though he were going to cry, and stamped his foot, laughing.

"You ain't change much, is you boy?" said Big Nail.

C.K. leaned forward over his glass and seemed to consider it very seriously.

"Well, I don't know, they's some people say I ain't—then they's others say I just a little *faster* than I use to be, that's all."

"Now I wonder jest what do they mean by that, these people tellin' you you so much *faster* than you use to be."

"Oh they didn't say 'so *much* faster,' they jest say 'a *little* faster'— because I was *always* pretty fast . . . you may recall."

Big Nail finished his drink.

"I don't *think* I follow their meanin'," he said, "I wonder do they mean fast like *that*," and as he said the word, he brought his glass quickly forward against the edge of the bar, then held it, very steady, turning it slowly and regarding it, the base still firm in his hand, the edges all jagged.

Neither of them looked up at the other, and after a few seconds, Big Nail lowered the glass to the bar.

"Well, no," said C.K., "*I* would imagine—though, believe me, this is only a guess—that they was thinkin' more along other lines," and while he spoke, he gradually turned toward Big Nail, "I would imagine they was thinkin' more along . . . *smooth-cuttin'* lines," and he described a wavering circle in front of him, his hand moving from his own glass towards his chest and suddenly sweeping down to his coat-pocket and out with the razor—which he held then, open and poised, near his face, letting it glitter in the light, he who smiled now and looked directly at Big Nail for the first time that day. But Big Nail had moved too—had taken a step back, and he as well was holding his straight-edged razor there, just so, between two fingers and a thumb, like a barber. Smiling.

People suddenly began leaving the bar. The crap-game broke up. Harold watched them in pure amazement.

"They ain't goin' be none of that in here!" said Old Wesley, standing at the end of the bar near the door, holding a half-taped chisel in his hand. "You got differences, *git* on outside, settle you differences out there!"

"You stay out of this, old man," said Big Nail, backing out into the center of the room, "we jest havin' a private talk here."

Besides Old Wesley, Harold and Blind Tom Ransom, there were only four other people in the bar now, and they were carefully edging their way along the wall to the door. Outside, standing around the door and looking through the glass front of the bar were about twenty-five people.

"Ain't *that* right, C.K.?"

Sss-sst! Big Nail's razor made a hissing arc that touched C.K. just along the left breast, and part of his coat fell away.

"That's right," said C.K., "we jest havin' a friendly conversation." *Sss-sst!* "Big Nail tellin' me how glad he is to be going back." *Sss-sst!*

"Lawd God!" said someone.

"You stop it now!" said Wesley.

Outside, a woman screamed and started wailing, and one or two children began to cry.

"Make 'em stop it, Mister Wesley!"

"Somebody call the *police!*"

Inside, they circled like cats, now in one direction, now in the other, feinting steps forward and to the side, suddenly lashing out with the five-inch blade, and all the time smiling and talking with a hideous gentility.

"You lookin' fit, C.K."

Sss-sst!

"Well, thank you, Big Nail." *Sss-sst!* "I was about to remark the same of you."

"*You got to stop it now!*" shouted Old Wesley. "We done call the *police!*"

"Somebody git a gun!"

But they weren't listening any more. They were moving slower now, each one sagging a little, and they had stopped talking. Once they almost stopped moving altogether, standing about seven feet apart, their arms lower than before, and it seemed at that moment that they might both collapse.

"Reckon we might as well . . . do it up right," said Big Nail.

"Reckon we might as well," C.K. said.

So they came together, in the center of the room, for one last time, still smiling, and cut each other to ribbons.

Blind Tom Ransom, sitting on a stool inside the door, only heard it, a kind of scuffling, whistling sound, followed by a heavy swaying silence. And he heard the clackety noise, as the razors dropped to the floor—first one, then the other—and finally the great sackweight sound of the two men coming down, like monuments.

"It's all ovah now," he said, "all ovah now."

But there was no one to hear him; all the others had turned away from it towards the end. And they didn't come back—only Harold, and then Old Wesley to stand by the bar, his hands on his hips, shaking his head. He looked at Harold.

"Boy, you bettah git on home now," he said gently.

But before Harold could leave, a patrol-car slid up in front of the place, and Old Wesley directed the boy in through a curtained door behind the bar, as two tall white men in wide-brimmed hats got out of the car, slamming the doors and came inside.

"What the hell's goin' on here, Wesley?" asked one of them looking irately around the room and at the two bodies on the floor.

"Nothin' goin' on now, Officer," said Wesley, " . . . them two got into argument . . . there weren't no trouble otherwise."

"How *you* doin', Blind Tom?" asked the second policeman.

"Awright suh . . . who is it, Mistuh Kennedy?"

The first had gone over to the bodies.

"Put on some more light, Wesley . . . darker'n a well-digger's ass in here—no wonder you have so much goddamn trouble."

He turned one of the men over and put his flashlight on him.

"Goddamn they sure did it up right, didn't they?"

The other came over and gave a low whistle.

"Boy, I reckon they *did*," he said.

"You know 'em, Wesley?"

"Yessuh, I knows 'em."

One of the policemen crossed to the bar and took a small notebook out of his shirt-pocket. The other one went back out and sat in the car.

The policeman at the bar looked up at the ceiling.

"You still ain't got any more light in here than that?"

"Nosuh, waitin' for my fixtures."

The policeman gave a humorless laugh as he looked for a blank page in the notebook.

"You been waitin' a *long* time now for them fixtures, ain't you, Wesley?"

"Yessuh."

"Okay, what's their names?"

"One of 'em name 'C.K. Crow' . . . and the other—"

"Wait a minute. 'C.K. Crow.' Any *add*ress?"

"Why I don't rightly know they *add*ress. I think C.K. live out on the old Seth Stevens place, out near Indian River."

"You know how old he was?"

"C.K.? Why, he was thuty-five, thuty-six year old I guess."

"How 'bout the other one?"

"His name was Emmett—everybody call him 'Big Nail.' "

"Emmett what?"

"Emmett Crow."

"They both named Crow?"

"Yessuh, that's right."

"What were they? Brothers?"

"Yessuh, that's right."

"Well, how old was *he* then?"

"Why I don't rightly know now which one of them *was* the oldest of the two. They was always sayin' they was a *year older* than the other one, each one of 'em say that, that *he* a year older. Then Big Nail, Emmett, he was away, you see, up Nawth—in Chicago or New York City, I believe it was . . . but they was both thuty-five, thuty-six year old."

The policeman closed his book and put it in his pocket.

"They got any folks here?"

Old Wesley nodded. "We'll look after 'em awright."

The policeman stood staring at the bodies for a minute.

"What were they fightin' about?"

"Why now I don't rightly know. They got into argument, you see . . . between themselves. Wasn't nobody could *stop* it."

"What were they doin', shootin' craps?"

"Well, I wouldn't know nothin' 'bout *that*—they sho' weren't shootin' no crap in *here*, I know *that* much!"

The policeman stopped at the door, and looked down at Tom.

"Don't reckon *you* seen anything out of the ordinary goin' on lately, have you, Blind Tom?"

Blind Tom laughed.

"Nosuh, ah *cain't* say that ah have."

"You gonna gimme a *re*port on it though if you do, ain't you, Blind Tom?"

"Why *sho'* ah is Mistuh Kennedy, you *knows* that ah is! Fust unusual thing ah see, why ah be down at de station an' give a *re*port, *in full!*"

They both laughed and the policeman patted Blind Tom on the shoulder and left.

When the car had pulled away, Harold came out of the room behind the curtain, and people began coming back into the bar.

Blind Tom was singing the blues.

"I jest wonder how C.K. feel," said someone, "if he know he goin' to be buried on Big Nail's money. I bet he wouldn't *like* it!"

Old Wesley frowned. "C.K. 'preciate a good send-off as well as the next man. Besides," he added, "C.K. weren't never one to hold a grudge for *ver'* long." He looked at Harold. "Ain't *that* right, boy?"

"I can't listen to it again," said his mother, walking past the kitchen table, one hand raised to her head. "You'll have to tell him yourself—I'll tell your grandad; there's no use in him hearing it the way you tell it. But you'll have to tell your daddy."

"Well, that's the way it happened, dang it," said Harold, frowning down at the empty plate in front of him.

"Well, I don't care, I don't want to hear it. Now you tell him and then you go wash. We're goin' to have supper in a few minutes."

She walked out of the room and left Harold sitting alone at the table. Outside the dogs were barking, and he heard his father on the porch, stamping his feet, kicking the mud from his shoes; then the door opened and he came inside, still stamping his feet as though it were winter. He leaned the gun against the wall under a rack of others.

"I want you to clean that gun after supper, son," he said. "Where's your mother?"

"She's upstairs," said the boy.

"Looka here, boy," said his father, smiling now, holding up a brace of fat bob-white quail, "ain't they good 'uns?"

"C.K.'s dead, Dad," said Harold, as he planned, as gravely as he could, not feeling anything except trying to measure up to the adult type of seriousness he believed the words must have.

"What're you *talkin'* about, son?" demanded his father, scowling in anger and impatience, "didn't you and him take that calf in . . ." He stamped over to the sink and lay the birds down there to turn and face the boy and have it out. "Now what're you *talkin'* about!"

And for Harold it was only then, with the moment of his father's disbelief, that the reality of it fell across his heart like a knife, and something jumped and caught inside his throat and knotted behind his eyes. He looked down at the table, shaking his head, wishing only to say that it wasn't his fault—and then the thing inside his throat and burning behind his eyes broke loose, in a short terrible burst, and he stiffly raised one arm to his face to try and choke away the grotesque sobs, and the incredible tears—not the kind of tears he had known before, but tears of the first bewildering sorrow.

His father said nothing, frowning; then he came over and stood by him, and finally put one hand on his shoulder.

At the supper-table, no more was said about it, until once when Harold's father sat for a moment gazing distraitly at the knife in his hand. "Damn niggers," he said. "What did they git into a fight about anyway? A crap-game?"

"Drink some more milk, son," said his mother, raising the big pitcher.

"What was it they were fightin' about?" repeated his father.

Harold watched the glass in his hand, the white milk tumbling in.

"Aw I dunno," he said, "they got into argument—about one thing and another, and then they got to fightin'—wasn't nobody could stop it."

"Hadn't been a-shootin' craps?" said his old grandfather, wolf-lean, brown as leather, brooding forward over his plate toward the boy like a hawk.

"No sir," said Harold, "they weren't doin' nothin' like that."

The old man grunted and recommenced eating.

"I saw old Blind Tom the other day, Grandad," said Harold after a minute, ". . . do you remember him?"

"*Who?*"

"Aw, you know, old Blind Tom Ransom—he asked to be *remembered* to you."

"*Remember* him?" said the old man, wiping his mouth, "why hell *yes,* I remember him. Now there was a goddamn good nigger, no two ways about it. Best hand in the county before his sight failed him."

"Was he as good as they say he was, Grandad?"

"Picked a bale-a-day," said the old man gravely, "rain or shine, rain or shine."

"Did *he* sure enough pick seven-hun'red and twenty-three pounds in one day?"

"Sure as hell did! They got me down from the house to see it weighed in. Seven-hun'red-twenty-three pounds, dry-load. Damndest thing I ever seen. I always meant to write to the Association about it." His old eyes, glinting with brief challenge, moved swiftly around the impassive faces at the table. "Why, I'll bet it's a *goddamn State record!*"

The Sun
and
the Still-born
Stars

SID PECKHAM AND HIS WIFE were coast farmers and Sid was a veteran of World War II. They were eking out the narrowest sort of existence on a little plot of ground just east of Corpus Christi, about an eighth of a mile from the Gulf.

The cost of their farm was two hundred dollars. For one reason or another Sid had not been able to get a G.I. loan to buy the land outright, but he and Sarah had scraped together enough money for the down payment. Now, to meet the quarterly installments of twenty-five dollars, they depended entirely upon what could be raised there and sold for the vegetable markets of Corpus Christi, namely soft melons and squash.

Sid and Sarah were of a line of unimaginative, one-acre farmers who very often had not owned the land they worked, and whose life's spring was less connected to the proverbial love of the land than twisted somehow around a vague acceptance of work, God's will, and the hopeless, unsurprising emptiness of life. The only book in their little house was the Bible, which they never read.

For a time, before the war, they had lived on the even smaller farm of Sarah's father, sharing a room in the back and working most of the day in the melon patch. Then Sid was gone, in the Army, for three years.

They had one letter from France, but for all it said of what was happening it could have been written from Fly, two miles away, or even from his own family's place across the road.

> Dear Sari
> They told us all to write. Hope you are all well. I am fine. The place here and the food is all right. Rain yesterday here, and today. I hope you and the family are all right.
>
> > God keep you
> > Sid Peckham

In other respects, the letter was an epitome of their relationship. Speech between them was empty and hushed.

Only sometimes now Sid spoke of the *films* he had seen in the Army. Then he was more expressive than at any other time.

"That one were right good," he would say, "I seen it on the boat."

Sarah would listen. They had never gone to see films before. But since the war, every Saturday they walked the two miles into Fly for the new movie. The movie in Fly played once on Saturday night and once again on Tuesday afternoon. Sid and Sarah went to the Saturday night showing, and they always left the house well before sundown in order to get good seats. All the seats were the same price, fifteen cents. They saw comedies and mysteries, westerns, dramas and classic histories, one a week for seven years.

In the darkened cinema their faces were like a single wooden mask. Sometimes Sarah had difficulty in grasping the mood of a film at all. Then she would try to take her cue from Sid, leaning out to turn and peer at his face. But it never told her anything, and as soon as he noticed he would push her away again back down into her own seat.

Only, if Sid had seen the film before, Sarah might watch him from the side, how he covered his mouth from time to time, nodding his head at the screen. The way this happened though, it never failed to strike Sarah as being different from what was happening at the same instant on the screen. And Sarah's brow would go all dark furrowed, and she might draw her stiff fingers back and forth over the palm of her hand.

Later, in the moonlight, on the narrow dirt road as they walked back to their place, Sarah would stay a little behind Sid and stare at the back of his head. Or else she might shoot a furtive, intent look at him from the side.

"Nice film weren't it, Sid?"

"It weren't a bad film," Sid would say, and after a moment, "I seen it before now. I seen it in Englelan."

Sid Peckham had picked up one or two expressions in England. One of them was "piping" for hot, or more often to augment hotness. Only he had distorted it to "piper," so that now they sometimes referred to the coffee of a morning as being "piper hot." Or if Sarah simply asked, "How does this soup taste to you, Sid?" Sid might say, "It's a right good soup, it's piper hot." Curiously too, through his experience, perhaps from a chance overheard conversation between two barracksmates in the faraway past, Sid had come to use the word "realist" to describe certain films; but, instead of *"realist,"* it sounded as though he were saying *"reel-less."* And it was as if he might have somehow wholly confused the root stem of the word.

"How'd you like it, Sid?"

"It were good—it were one of them reel-less."

Or, perhaps, in the case of a musical or a cartoon:

"There weren't much to it—it weren't no reel-less film."

But somewhere behind this, the mask of each expressed life, deep under the dead wooden simplicity of their ever separate, unspoken awareness, little things were crawling alive, breeding and taking on great, secret shape.

During the day their labor was equally divided, until at last one Friday when Sarah was in the sixth month of her first pregnancy, it fell upon Sid to do most of the work in the patch. For her part, Sarah wondered if now, with the coming expense of the child, they would continue to go into Fly on Saturday for the movie. She wondered, too, how it would be after the child. And once, in a dream, she thought she saw the three of them sitting side by side in the darkness of the cinema, only their faces alight, as though she were seeing them from somewhere inside the screen. But she knew they had never, above the quarterly payments on the land, had money to spare at the time the payments were made. Moreover, with Sid working the patch alone, it was difficult to see how they would meet the next payment at all.

Saturday, and Sarah awoke from a dreamless sleep, in a summer darkness long before dawn. At waking, this darkness was pure, and except for the night wind, perfectly still. She sought, but no notion of time could form in her mind, and she knew as soon that beneath the swift softness of the wind the night was alive with sound.

She kept very still, her head straight against the flat cotton mattress. And, as out from the ceiling center, where the untrained vision lay, the room grew, like an image on a screen, slowly down around her to a vague, somehow familiar definition, she knew that he was awake too, and she touched his shoulder.

"What's that noise, Sid?"

"It's somethin' in the patch," he said without moving.

A dry electric rustling filled the room. They lay motionless for another moment as the rustling stopped, then started up again, and Sid got stiffly out of bed and went to the window.

"What is it?" asked Sarah. Sitting up now she could see Sid looking steadily out the window, but from the side, with his back almost flat against the wall. Then he was all crouched down, so that his eyes seemed at the level of the sill, peering out across the patch.

Sarah left the bed and knelt beside him. At the window the sounds were not the same as before. There was a scratching, a dry tinsel sound. Leaf against leaf, and leaf against vine. And these were of the night, but in the heart of the patch where the dark form lay moving, just there, were the different sounds, the heavy, wet-mouth breaking of melons and the sound of breathing. And while the rustling of the leaf and vine stopped, the breathing went on—yet somehow heard by Sarah as indistinct, so that she shook her head and turned it first this way and then that, out against the night, and at last even to peer into Sid's face.

"Where, Sid?" she asked. "What is it?" Because she saw that his eyes stared straight unblinking into the dark.

"It's a *critter* I reckon," said Sid. He stood up slowly and took his clothes off the chair. "I reckon it's a hog."

Sarah stayed hunched at the sill, looking out the window and back at Sid as he put on his clothes.

"It's bigger than a hog," she said.

"I know it," said Sid.

In the room she saw his back as he left the door, and at once, out the window, how he appeared at the corner of the house, a shadow in the darkness, creeping along the fence of the patch. Opposite the window he stopped, crouched peering out over the patch. And where the heavier shadow lay, there was nothing now except the still night and the breathing.

Then Sarah saw Sid rise, holding a large white rock. And she put out her hand, for in this light she saw him as though a film of oil lay stretched across the window. But in a sudden bound he was over the fence, throwing the stone and rushing ahead, as to Sarah at the window the two sounds were joined in a loud tearing sound of the breaking leaf and vine. And as quickly, the single shape was split, formed and reformed, and was lost twisting down through the darkness.

She stayed at the window while the sounds broke away, dying across the patch, down toward the sea. Then she went to bed.

Sometime after sunrise she awoke again, and was still alone in the room. When she was up and dressed, she made the bed and began to sweep the floor; but once, near the window, she stopped and stood there, staring out over the land. Across the piece of yard to the fence, over the patch and beyond the field, lay the dim sea, rising back high against the morning, and nothing stirred but the brilliant shooting patterns of the sun moving out across the land.

Sarah fixed the breakfast and Sid had not returned. Then she went out into the patch and chopped weeds until she was sick. She was lying on the bed when Sid came in at almost noon. His clothes were wet and torn; there were short deep cuts on his face.

"What is it, Sid?"

For a moment he stood motionless in the doorway.

"It was a hog," he said then, "a sea hog."

Sarah waited.

"I druv it back into the water," said Sid. And he took off his clothes and lay down.

In the late afternoon he awoke and got up hurriedly. Out in the patch he worked in a frenzy for two hours. Then he sat down on the back steps.

In the kitchen, mending the torn clothes, Sarah saw his head turned away from the setting sun, and always south to the sea. After supper they went straight to bed.

Sarah didn't wake until light. He was gone. She got up and dressed. Instead of fixing breakfast, she took the hoe from the back steps and went to work in the patch. By midmorning she could no longer feel her arms and shoulders. She tried to straighten up and something moved through her back like a burning knife.

She sat on the steps with her face in her arms. Much later, she got up, and under the hot sun walked down through the patch and the field toward the sea. Above the throbbing heat of noon she could hear ahead the constant play of the surf, and something more when she began to climb the dunes. But when she reached the top of the dune and looked down onto the vast mirrored sea below, she saw that he stood alone, in apparent dead fatigue, and Sarah could only follow the dull sweep of his eyes on the retreating darkness in the water.

She lay on the dune for a while after Sid left the beach, plodding past her, back up across the field toward the patch and the house.

When Sarah reached the house, Sid was asleep. He slept into the afternoon, then went out into the patch with his hoe. She saw as he passed how his mouth was fixed straight, like the breaking length of a black string. After an hour, he was sitting on the back steps.

From her chair at the kitchen table Sarah watched Sid with his pocketknife whittle off the handle of the hoe. He spent the rest of the afternoon there on the steps, sharpening the end of the hoe handle with his knife, so that finally what was left of the hoe was a sharp-pointed hardwood spear about three feet long. Then he went to bed.

And Sarah followed. She lay in bed, her eyes opened, turning ever again from where the ceiling spread above them like a veil, to Sid's face and back, and back again. Night. Night and the image of night.

She did not awake until late.

The land on the Gulf between Corpus Christi and Fly is a flat burning waste, with only the most gradual rise of dune above the surf.

At the still blaze of noon, there is a wildness here in the heat and light, and atop the dunes the air is overhung with a sound like water beating against some distant cliff, but this is the sound of the sun, which strikes and rises from the dead sand in black lined waves.

As Sarah climbed, crawling, she stopped, feeling the rise of sound and light, turned herself, her eyes, straight into the panic sun, and she slowly stood, her eyes strained to blackness. She was there, on the crest of the highest dune and she dropped to her knees at the sight of the endless sea stretched shorewise in an explosion of light. And below, deep in the burning surf, Sid Peckham fought for his life.

Sarah lay on the dune, half dazed by the flat crystal brilliance of the scene, as the two bodies heaved and pitched together in some heavy soundless purpose. Now one, now the other in ascendancy, they fell and rose, threshing, their rage a slowly desperate waltz.

Here from high atop the dune, she heard the muted scream and saw the lunge in the surf below, how the two fell grappling beneath the water, then rose wavering, fixed in heavy changing arcs of strength, leaning now toward the sea, now toward the land, but always flat under the burning sun. They gave no quarter except to fatigue when one beating arc would waver and fall, in favor of sea or shore.

And then to Sarah the battle seemed locked like a poised weight, and she sprang up from the dune and rushed down to the sea. The hardwood spear stood jutting aslant from the sand below the surf, and as the girl threw herself between them she wrenched the spear from the sand, and turning its point from shore to sea and back, and back again, all her knowing was struck dim by the terrible flux of weight, balance and change, her eyes blind to the tearing sun. Great cloudhead image on the silver screen . . . approach and retreat . . . *approach and retreat,* the growing approach, approach, approach, uncontained growing, swelling, swelling, swelling, to a scream. *"Stop!"*

Lilt. And the surf around them feathered out all white-edged rose, their motion faded to an end as gradual and even as the close of slow music.

For a long while Sarah stood in the surf seeing only where the water broke silver and red around the upright spear. Then she drew out the spear and facing the sea, she felt the tremor beneath her feet as the weight was dragged away along the sand, under the water. And she was alone.

Back at the house she worked in the patch until night, then she went to bed.

Before dawn she awoke, while the moon was still high and there was no sound except the stirring of the night wind in the patch. But beyond the patch and past the field, from down at the sea, she could hear something like the surf on rock cliffs, and above this, the listening that came up through the night.

She got out of bed and dressed, walked through the kitchen and out the door. Near the back steps, struck straight in the ground was the hoe handle that had been fashioned into a spear. Sarah would know as she passed, from the way its shadow fell under the moon, just how early or late the morning was.

She crossed the patch and was into the field before she could remember and touch the pocket of her thin dress. There were two coins there: a nickel and a quarter. She stiffened a little and stood still, holding the coins in her hand. A small cloud passed under the moon, and for an instant on the left the dirt road to Fly was only a twisting shadow. Then the cloud was gone, the road to Fly was clear. She realized that the man who sold the tickets would give her the change himself, and she started to walk.

She walked very slowly, her mind flowing a train of smoothly veiled thought as straight and dark as the narrow road before her.

The moon had waned and the sun risen by the time Sarah reached the square at Fly. Because she had never been to the Tuesday matinee, she did not know when it began, and so had come early as an assurance. Standing before the plain-front cinema, she saw at once that the glassed box was empty, and in place of the man was a sign reading:

SHOW—1:00

OPEN—12:30

For a long while she stood looking at the display stills that were attached to a kind of wooden bulletin board. Once, after glancing at the glassed box and around the desolate bleak-light square, she slowly raised her hand and touched one of the photographs. She drew her hard-pressing finger across the middle of it, then she went out to the curb and sat down.

She sat there until noon, then joined the line of children as it began to form.

When she reached the box, she gave the man the quarter and the nickel.

"Two?" he asked.

"One," said Sarah.

"Fifteen cents," said the man, returning her nickel and a dime.

She picked up the coins and turned aside. But when her eye fell again on the display stills, her brow assumed a crinkle of knowing and she turned back to the man in the glassed box, her face a serious frown.

"Goin' to be a *reel-less?*" she asked.

The Night
the Bird
Blew
for Doctor Warner

"I'LL HAVE TO BE A *HIPSTER*," Doctor Warner said leaning toward them from out of billowing dark leather while behind this great chair, where study lamplight softened to haze on a thousand grains of dullest panel, there danced in points of twos the refracted amber of glassed cubed-ice in the hands of his two friends opposite—danced, it seemed, on an opaque screen which could measure the wildness of thought and the tedium of conversation.

"A very *hip* hipster," he continued genially, and withdrew himself slightly, for emphasis, "if not, indeed, something *more*."

Dr. Ralph Warner was fifty-five, gray and distinguished, a man of remarkable vigor and personality. He was not a physician, but a learned man of music, who had received many public and institutional honors. An established author and critic, past conductor of the San Francisco, Boston and Denver symphony orchestras, he had become, because of his popular, progressive innovations in policy and repertoire, one of the most beloved and respected men in the musical history of the country.

"Something *more?*" said Professor Thomas, stressing his mock surprise with a sickly smile. He loathed strange jargon. "Don't tell me there's anything *more*, Ralph, than being a hipster!"

"That's right," said the younger George Drew eagerly, "how could anything be more *hip* than a hipster?" He *loved* it. "*En tout cas*, not semantically." He seemed to repress a spasm of delight, as though the prospect of sprightly argument could give him goose-pimples.

Dr. Warner allowed his own gaze to grow sober and formulative, staring down at the drink in his hand.

"Yes," he said evenly, "you might say that a *junky* is something more than a hipster."

Professor Thomas snorted politely. "Good Lord, from where on earth did they dig up that term?"

"From its not too earthy grave in Hong Kong harbor, I dare say," said George Drew coolly, finishing off his drink with a small effeminate toss of his head.

"Drugs again, I'm afraid, Tom," put in Dr. Warner, often their genial moderator. "Opiates. Heroin this time."

At home with every idiom, Dr. Warner gave himself as wholly to Alban Berg as he did to Tschaikovsky, as devotedly to Tanglewood as to the Juilliard String Quartet; and already, at fifty-five, he had been frequently called a "grand old man of music," and again, in other contexts, perhaps because his scope naturally tended at some points toward erudition, a "musician's musician."

Now more and more of his time was given over to writing. His work to date consisted of well-received one-volume studies of Brahms, Mozart and Schubert; hundred-page sections on Bach, Beethoven and Wagner; chapters on almost everyone from Palestrina to Schönberg; and a definitive little brochure on Bartók. Dr. Warner's writing bristled with information and tight parallels, in a style pleasantly fluid, sprinkled with humor, penetrating insights and anecdotes which lacked neither warmth nor sophistication.

Before the war, and since, he had toured Europe regularly and had guest-conducted every major orchestra from Blackpool to Copenhagen. He was mentioned with frequency and respect in the gossip sections of the weekly news-periodicals.

But now he had gone into hiding, or so it must have seemed to his biographers, though they knew in truth that he was away, working on his book. It was by no means the Doctor's only project at hand, though it was perhaps his most ambitious. Musicologists, critics, teachers in the colleges and academies, art-appreciation groups, cultured people everywhere looked forward to its release—a book which was to treat "the whole of Western Music, its origin and development to the present day," again touted by the publishers as being *definitive*. And while this claim was absurd, that the book would have certain value there were no doubts, because Dr. Warner, besides bringing to bear "the breadth of a versatile genius welded to almost unprecedented vitality and an all-embracing devotion to music," was known, in this world of music at least, to be relatively *fair*, or impartial.

"Heroin," said George Drew, pouring himself another. "Treacherous, treacherous."

"Amazing prevalence among them," joined Professor Thomas, unimpressed. "*Simply* amazing."

"Prevalent, Tom? Or standard?" asked Dr. Warner with a show of seriousness. "I'm really beginning to wonder."

"God knows!" wailed the Professor unexpectedly, raising his hands. "The whole thing is beyond me. In the first place, how you propose to—to get *next* to those people is more than I can see." There was heat and resentment in his voice, and it was only after a moment's pause that he could reassert a detached and amiable interest in the subject. "For my money, I think I'd stick, primarily at least, to the material already compiled. Lord, there must be a wealth of it." He exaggerated in a gesture the stack and assortment of books on the study table: popular histories of jazz, exposés and testimonials, confessional stories of reformed drug addicts, whores, and criminals—all of which had been somehow tied to the words "jazz" and "be-bop."

"Surface, Tom," said Ralph Warner. "Purely surface material. It's never been . . . really *lived* by anyone qualified to do it up."

"Ralph," began George Drew, "do you actually suppose you can, as Tom says, get next to them?"

"I think I can, George," said Ralph Warner. "I-think-I-can. After all, it's simply another viewpoint. A matter of language really. Vernacular."

"*Do you know*," said George Drew warming now toward the heart of it, "that you're *very* liable to be approached on this drug business yourself? I mean, they might ask *you* to take some. What do you do then, Ralph?"

Dr. Warner smiled a little, shyly it seemed. "Then? Why, then I suppose there would be only one thing *to* do—gracefully." And so saying, he leaned back in his great chair and slowly raised both hands. "The unhappy part of the business is," he went on, beaming helplessly, "I have an absolute horror of *needles*."

Before completing the book's section, "Dixieland and the Blues," Dr. Warner had meticulously sifted through all the written material on the subject, and had listened to some seven hundred graded recordings, many of them several times, taking copious notes the while. Then he had flown down to New Orleans for an intensive week of firsthand research. When he was not actually listening to music, he ferreted about the Quarter, poking into any narrow opening of whatever half-promise, prowling the blue haze of mid-night alleys, tapping carefully on every soundless, dawn-lit cellar door, as though each were his own oak podium.

He spoke to hundreds of people: strangers, drunks, unknown—and, most often, untalented—musicians, bystanders, children, blind men who touched their canes to the earth in some possible connection with the music. And if, in the bandstand's shadow of an afternoon session, a dog lay stretched in refuge from the heat of day, the Doctor might give it a pat on the head in passing. Then, at night, in the *boîtes* of the Quarter, instead of taking a table, he stood with his drink where the brass and the smoke were the bluest, at the left front corner of the bandstand, stood with one foot on the raised platform, tie loosened, an easy smile on his face which worked beneath half closed eyes on the blue, blue offbeat, while his free hand, at rest on his raised knee, raced the fingers in subtle and intricate tattoo. At the end of a number, if there was an empty glass on the bandstand, he had it filled, and when the men took a break, he was with them, the ones that hung together around the bar, to pay for the drinks and listen to the slow and easy talk of those who play the blues.

As soon as one place closed, he went to another, sometimes in the company of one or two musicians, and toward morning they ate together. By seven he was back in his room where he wrote steadily for two hours. Then he would go to bed and sleep until three in the afternoon, get up, dress, and eat again before resuming his tour of the Quarter. He did this for seven days, and during this time he was careful about three things: (1) never to request a number, (2) to talk with no more than one musician at a time about music, and (3) in doing so, to expose his own knowledge, not by dissertation, as the canyon openly yawns its vastness, but by remark, as a mountain will suggest fantastic untold depths through one startling crevasse. And he even had the gall and devotion, one time toward early morning in a booth gone blue-gray with the circling tides of smoke, when a sleepy-faced drummer passed him a sweet cigarette the thinness of two matchsticks, to hold it as he might have been expected, take quick deep drags, wink without smiling, and say in a low voice, *"Crazy, man."*

He never identified himself, but he was usually remembered as "an old guy who knew a goddam hell of a lot about music," or again, by such as the drummer, as a "pretty stuffy cat."

"Ralph," said Professor Thomas, "let me get this straight. Do you mean you're going to submit to drug injections?"

His hands clasped under his chin, Dr. Warner smiled, even sheepishly, though as one could see, with a certain secure pride.

"What sort of drugs, Ralph?" George Drew came in, having already chosen a side.

"Heroin, I imagine," said Dr. Warner easily.

Professor Thomas started to speak, but took a sip from his drink instead and pursed his lips.

"This may strike you as a bit old-fashioned," he said then, completely ignoring George Drew, "but isn't there a very real physiological danger in heroin injections—for a man of your age, Ralph?"

Ralph Warner shook his head. "I won't main-line," he said soberly. "Just skin-popping. Anyway, on single dosages, cardiac response is negligible. I've looked into it, of course."

George Drew, who was thirty-five years old, was beginning to resemble his undergraduate photographs at Princeton. He sat forward in the chair, spoke carefully and, as usual, seemed to put an emphasis on every other word. "Ralph, as I get it, 'main-line' is to take the stuff directly into a blood vein; and the other, 'skin-pop,' or 'skin-popping' is a muscle or tissue injection, right? But now, what exactly is the difference?"

"Flash," said Dr. Warner expansively, then paused to smile at Professor Thomas who had audibly scoffed over the question. "You see what I mean by language, eh? Well, the immediacy of effect in main-lining is called the *flash*. Something you don't get in skin-popping, where the effect is relatively gradual."

"Just what *is* the effect?" asked Professor Thomas, as though he were already bored with it.

George Drew shifted in his chair, impatient; and Dr. Warner waved his hands, vaguely protesting. "Oh, I'm sure it's very subjective, of course, Tom. A sort of will-less euphoria, I suppose. Sensations of security and general well-being. Wish-fulfillment. Self-sufficiency, if you like. Followed, I imagine, by depression, or letdown."

From Bach to Be-bop was, by publisher's choice, the title of Dr. Warner's book. And the Doctor sometimes told the story of how he had indulged them in this, only, of course, after stressing its obvious anomaly.

The book's opening plate was a diagram of the ear, and its second a sample of cuneiform writing; moreover, it was not until page fifty-one that there was mention even of Gregorian chant. And yet he would often end the story by admitting their point that, after all, three-quarters of the book was so concerned, with Bach and thereafter.

"What I tell them is this: 'I'll *write* it. You can *name* it, eh? And you can *sell* it!' " A well-received story. A funny story by a famous man, and the way the Doctor would laugh and shake his head gave the impression that he thought publishers like young women, dealings with whom called for, if anything, a slightly amused condescension.

"For one thing," said Professor Thomas at last, "it's against the law. Very much so. Against the law, *and dangerous.*"

"Calculated risks, eh Ralph?" said George Drew happily.

"Or, occupational hazards," replied Ralph Warner, glowing with modesty.

"Good Lord!" Professor Thomas finished his drink. "I'll stick to Scotch myself." He poured himself another and stirred in quite a bit of soda. "Drug poisoning. Addiction. An unclean needle and you could die of tetanus during your euphoria."

"Please," said Ralph Warner, half jokingly, "let's not speak of *needles*."

"Well, there you are," said Professor Thomas and took another sip, grimacing.

Shortly before the arrival of his two friends, Dr. Warner had begun the first draft of the book's final section. He had written:

> Life has always been a struggle.
> It is tedious to say again, that, through modern science and technology, our material horizons have been broadened, our physical burdens lessened. A badly worn phrase, and it is yet another to point up these gains as having not seriously affected the greater struggle . . . the quest for peace of mind and happiness, the search for security. For it is evident today, perhaps as never before, that we have. . . .

Here, he broke off and put in parentheses just below: "(greed, hate, war, moral and spiritual confusion, etc.)" and then a marginal note to himself, "break with humor—philosophic *doldrums* (?)" and to the list, "greed, hate, war, etc.," he added, "crime," after which he quickly resumed to write, lower on the page:

> Let it stand as living testimony to the fiber of our times that a musical idiom characterized by dissonance and atonality, by unpatterned time-change, and impassive distortion of popular themes, has gained wide favor. . . .

He took a second sheet and started at about the middle of the page:

> *Be-bop, bop,* or, more currently, (*modern*) *jazz,* has been defined as "variations on a theme which is never wholly stated," but which theme, it should be added, occurs (concomitant to the execution) in the mind of the performing artist (*and* the

good listener) and which, if expressed at any point, would, in the technical sense, harmonize with the improvization . . .

It is significant that the emotional nihilism, or again, the cold, satiric intent which has come to be identified with these interpretations. . . .

He skipped another space, and wrote:

Yet, beneath this cynical veneer, as beneath the chimera of strife and bitterness in everyday living, pulses a vital substance. . . .

Momentarily discarding this sheet, he went back to the first page, and where he had written, "Let it stand as living testimony to the fiber of our times," crossed it through, and rewrote, "Let it stand, a living mirror to the fiber of our times," and immediately below, in the margin, "reflection of, etc."

"Who's to say how you'll react?" Professor Thomas took it up again now. "According to all accounts, there's no foretelling the effect of drugs. You'd better be careful, Ralph. Damned careful."

"Ralph," said George Drew in an almost blatant interruption, "as, well, as an amateur *semanticist,* I'm very much interested in vocabularies and their physical correlations; that is, if and when they do exist. I mean, of course, in terms of the particular group mentality involved—"

"Careful," repeated Professor Thomas half aloud. "You'll have to be very careful." He was quite serious.

"Oh yes, Tom," said Dr. Warner, wearily, but added at once, as on an afterthought, and with a smile for them both, "yes, I'm hip that I will."

Coming up the subway stairs, Dr. Warner touched at his throat with an already damp handkerchief. It was a warm evening.

Dressed for the occasion, he was wearing a gray flannel suit and a soft dark shirt, buttoned at the collar. His shoes were suede and had heavy crepe soles. Clean shaven and hatless, his fine head erect, glinting silver beneath changing lights, he could have been an owner of horses, or a California surgeon. Or, he could have been a very proper junky, for his movements were listless, as without direction, and his face was in absolute blank repose, betraying nothing, except indifference and, possibly, a dull and distant contempt for effort. But his mind was still not under control. Why had he said he wouldn't main-line it? Of course, he *would have to main-line it*. What had he been thinking of? These weren't children.

At the top of the stairs he paused and brought the handkerchief to his face again. On the street it seemed even warmer. But he knew this would pass. Once he was moving, once he was functioning, it would be all right. He even managed to think: *then it'll be cool*. And he could have smiled at this, but his face wouldn't betray him. He had mastered his face. He had mastered everything but his thoughts, and his thoughts were of the order of those of famous actors in the seconds leading up to the big scene: *blood in the chamber . . . matches and spoon . . . you cut it, I'll cut it, won't cook up, will cook up, behind the knuckle, blood in the chamber, silence, . . . silence. Be cool.*

Leaning against an iron post by the subway entrance, Dr. Warner began to order his thoughts. He lit a cigarette, but the cigarette at once recalled the smoke-filled booth in New Orleans; and what he was about to do suddenly took on another irresistible importance. Marijuana was one thing, heroin was another. Heroin was *stronger*. He distrusted the word, but could think of no better one. Heroin *is* stronger, he thought. *There's something irretrievable . . . there's no emetic for a substance put straight into the blood stream. There's no turning back. And they say if you fight it. . . .*

At that moment, a cab passed very close to the curb, slowing for the changing light, and the Doctor's eye caught his own distinguished image framed squarely for an instant in the window glass. He dropped the cigarette and slowly ground his foot over it. And he knew he would be able to do whatever was required.

He crossed the street toward an alleyway opposite. At the head of the alleyway was a short-order place, its door and raised glass-front open to the summer night, where, because of a small neon MALTED sign, light lay upon light in soft transparent cubes, forming a great milk-green swath over the sidewalk and curb, violated by a flashing liquor brand across the way which moved in stabs of red as harsh as traffic noise. But from a juke-box inside came the sound of a singing tenor sax . . . leaping out raid-like through neon against the passing traffic, to flurry just above their heads, brandishing something there in sound so quick and serious before springing back again, it could only astonish them.

Standing around on the sidewalk, or leaning against the front of the short-order place, were three or four young men in different attitudes of listening to the music, or of just standing there. There was nothing in their manner or dress to relate them, and each seemed somehow alone, but all their faces bore the same stamp of extreme ennui and polite detachment that was due to something more than just civilization.

Walking very slowly, Dr. Warner paused when he reached the corner of the alleyway and the short-order place, and after standing for a few minutes listening, he leaned against the wall himself.

The person next to him was a boy of about twenty-five. He was as thin as an El Greco saint, with eyes like two black pins. He did not seem to have noticed the Doctor's arrival. After a few minutes, Dr. Warner spoke to the boy, not looking at him, staring straight ahead, his voice soft and without inflection.

"Hey, man," he said, "what's happenin'?"

The boy seemed to blink as he turned his head, giving the Doctor a slow, quizzical look, almost a smile.

"You tell me, daddy," he said finally, his lips scarcely moving, "know what I mean, like you tell me."

"Well, man," said Dr. Warner, "like I just got on the scene, dig, and I was wondering if anything was *happenin'* tonight. I'd like to make it, you know what I mean?"

"I'm afraid I don't," said the boy, as though from some incredible distance.

Dr. Warner gave him a tired, patient smile.

"Now don't jump salty, daddy-o," he said, "I mean like level with me 'cause I'm straight for loot, dig, and I got eyes, you know what I mean, like I got big eyes to get on and just fall out someplace where the cats are blowin'."

The boy turned his face away and was staring straight ahead.

"Like what?" he said at last.

"Well, like *Bird;* you *know?*"

The boy turned again and regarded the Doctor, slowly and vaguely. Then, and as though with considerable effort, he indicated a direction down the alley.

"Man, do you see that light? At the end? Yeah, well there might be something happenin' there."

Dr. Warner nodded with grave knowing. "Crazy," he said and then, with his slow wink of confidence as he departed, "Later, man."

The boy blinked with disinterest and sank carefully back against the wall.

The alley was narrowly lit and lined with a pure blackness from which rose huge dark piles of garbage.

As Dr. Warner walked, spiritedly now, he reproduced, whistling, almost exactly what he had heard from the juke-box.

Then he began to frame a sentence in his mind's eye: "As to progressional pattern, the atonal *riff* is invariably—" and he had just succeeded in freezing *riff* in italics when the word and the phrase exploded in a flash of blinding white, as an arm swung out from the darkness and laid a short segment of lead pipe across the back of the Doctor's head. As he staggered between two mountains of refuse, he was hit again, and the white light was shot through with coils and bolts of purple and gray, then flooded out on a heavy wave of blood-blackness.

One man took off the Doctor's watch and emptied his billfold, while the second went through his other pockets. They both wore gloves.

A South
Summer
Idyll

A SUMMER SATURDAY IN DALLAS and the boy Howard
sat out on the back steps, knees up, propping in between, an old
singleload, twelve-gauge shotgun. While he steadied and squeezed
the butt in one hand, the other, with studied unbroken slowness,
wrapped a long piece of friction tape around and around the
stock—for beginning at the toe of the butt and stretching up about
five inches was a thin dry crack in the old wood.

His mother came out, down off the back porch carrying an
enameled basin heaped with twists of wet, wrung clothes.

"You wantta be careful with that old gun," she said, making a
slight frown.

A squat woman and dark-haired, almost eastern in the intensity
she tried to bear on situations, her face was perhaps too open, eyes
too widely spaced, and the effect was never what she calculated. She
would not suspect, however, that within the block only a few could
take her seriously.

Her boy Howard did, of course, though if others were present he
might be embarrassed, or a little irritated.

"Aw now you're kiddin'," he said, wanting mainly to reassure her
about the gun.

She had just given him a dollar for the weekend, and before dark
he would have spent over half of it. Sitting now on the back steps he

could reckon exactly how it would go. And with her standing there talking, he was aware, too, that except for the show she had no idea at all how he would spend the money.

At the kitchen table his father treated it lightly.

"Where you *goin'* boy? Shootin'?"

"Aw just fool aroun'," said Howard, looking away, eating slowly at a piece of bread, buttered and covered with sugar.

"Who, you and Lawrence? What're y'all goin' *after*?"

"Ah I dunno," said Howard, "just fool aroun', I guess."

"Where're you and Lawrence *goin'*, Howie?" asked his mother, back at the sink again.

"Aw out aroun' Hampton Airport, I guess," he said.

"You wantta be careful out there at Hampton," said his mother, "with the planes comin' in and all."

Howard tried to laugh, even to catch his father's eye.

"They ain't any *planes* there now," he said, sheepish at having to be impatient with her, "they closed it down, didn't you know that?"

"I don't want you goin' up in that trainer-plane neither," his mother went on as unhearing, almost closed-eyed, packing faded dripless lumps of cloth into the basin.

"Aw now you're kiddin'," said Howard, "it don't cost but three dollars for fifteen minutes. Not likely I *will*, is it?"

At the table though, his father spoke about the gun, the danger, abstractly, as if he himself had never fired it. And yet, when he saw the box of shells on the table, he opened it and shook two or three out, holding them loosely, so as to appear casual, familiar, he who had not held a gun in thirty years.

"Look like good'uns," he said finally, "what'd they *cost*?"

Howard reached Big Lawrence's house by way of the alley. Stepping through an open place in the fence two houses before, and cutting across these back yards, he could hear Lawrence on at the house and he saw his shadow dark there behind a window screen.

"Ka-*pow!* Ka-*pow!* Ka-*pow!*" was what Lawrence said.

It was a small room.

Big Lawrence sat out on the edge of the bed, and all down around his feet the scattered white patches lay, fallen each as the poisoned cactus-bloom, every other center oil-dark, he cleaning his rifle, a 30-30 Savage.

Across one end of the bed, flat on his stomach looking at an old comic book, was Crazy Ralph Newgate, while Tommy Sellers sat on the floor, back flat to the wall. Tommy Sellers had a baseball and glove in his lap, and every so often he would flip the baseball up and it would twirl over his fingers like an electric top.

As Howard came in and sat down on the arm of a heavy-stuffed, misshapen chair, Lawrence looked up, laughing. Most of the time Lawrence's laugh was coarse and, in a way, sort of bitter.

"Well, goddam if it ain't old Howard!" he said, perhaps remembering a western movie they had seen the night before.

Somewhere, next door, a radio was playing loud, Saturday morning cowboy music from Station WRR in downtown Dallas.

Big Lawrence slammed bolt home, slapping it.

"You ready?" he asked Howard, and Howard nodded—but before he could get up, Lawrence had turned around on the bed and leaned hard across Ralph Newgate's legs, sighting the rifle out over the back yard. There across the yard, out about three feet from the back fence, so crouched half-sitting that the feet were drawn way under, was a cat—a black cat, rounded small and unblinking in the high morning sun.

Big Lawrence squeezed one out on the empty chamber.

"Ka-*pow!*" he said and brought the gun down, laughing.

On the floor, next to the wall, the baseball spun twisting across Tommy Sellers' knuckles like a trained rat.

"Goddam! Right in the eye!" said Lawrence. He raised up, and with some shells from his shirt pocket loaded the rifle; then he quickly threw out the shells, working the action in a jerky eccentric manner. One of the shells, as they flew all over the bed, went across the comic book Ralph Newgate was holding and hit the bridge of his nose. The other three boys laughed, but Crazy Ralph muttered something, rubbing his nose, and flipped the shell back over into the rest next to Lawrence's leg, as he might have playing marbles—and Big Lawrence flinched.

"You crazy bastard!" said Lawrence, "what if it'd hit the cap!" and he picked up the shell and threw it as hard as he could against the wall behind Ralph Newgate's head, making him duck. They left the shell where it fell on the floor behind the bed. Ralph didn't speak, but just kept turning the pages of the comic book, while Lawrence sat there looking at the book in front of Ralph's eyes for about a minute.

Then Lawrence reloaded the gun and drew another bead out the window. The black cat was still sitting there, head on toward the muzzle when Lawrence moved the safety with his thumb—and next door someone turned the radio up a little more.

In the small room, the explosion was loud.

The comic book jumped in Crazy Ralph's hand like it was jerked by a wire. "God*dam* it!" he said, but he didn't look around, just shifted a little, as if settling to the book again.

The cat seemed to have hardly moved, only to have been pushed back toward the fence some, still sitting there, head down, feet drawn under, as though staring at the screen.

But in the screen now, next to a hole made in opening the screen from the outside, was another, perfectly round, flanged out instead of in, worn suddenly, by the passing of the bullet, all bright silver at the edge.

Big Lawrence and Howard walked a dirt road along one side of Hampton Airport. It was a hot, dry day.

"What's a box of shells like that cost?" Lawrence asked, and when Howard told, Lawrence said, "*Sure*, but for how many shells?"

At crossroads, the corner of a field, a place where on some Sundays certain people who made model airplanes came to try them, they found, all taped together, five or six shiny old dry-cell batteries as might be used for starting just such small engines.

Howard pulled these batteries apart while they walked on, slower now beneath the terrible sun, and when Lawrence wanted to see if he could hit one in the air with the shotgun, they agreed to trade off, three rifle-cartridges for one shotgun shell.

Howard pitched one of the batteries up, but Lawrence wasn't ready. "Wait'll I say '*Pull*,'" he told Howard.

He stood to one side then, holding the shotgun down as he might have seen done on a TV program about skeet-shooting.

"Okay, now *Pull!*"

Lawrence missed the first one, said that Howard was throwing too hard.

Howard tossed another, gently, lobbing it into the sun, glinting end over gleaming end, a small meteor in slow motion, suddenly jumping with the explosion, this same silver thing, as caught up in a hot air jet, but with the explosion, coughing out its black insides.

"Got the sonofabitch," said Big Lawrence. "Dead bird goddam it!"

Howard laughed. "I reckon it is," he said softly.

Once across the field, away from the airport, they turned up the railroad track. And now they walked very slow, straight into the sun, burning, mirrored a high blinding silver in the rails that lay for five miles unbending, flat against the shapeless waste, ascending, stretching ablaze to the sun itself—so that seen from afar, as quite small, they could have appeared, as children, to walk unending between these two columns of dancing light.

With the rifle they took some long shots at the dead-glass discs on a signal tower far up the track, but nothing happened. When they were closer though, one of the signals suddenly swung up wildly alight. A burning color. Lawrence was about to take a shot at it when they heard the train behind them.

They slid down an embankment, through the bull-nettle and bluebonnets, to walk a path along the bottom. When the freight train reached them however, they turned to watch it go by, and at one of the boxcars, Big Lawrence, holding the rifle against his hip, pumped three or four rounds into the side of it. Under the noise of the train, the muted shots had no connection with the bursting way the dark wood on the boxcar door tore off angling, and splintered out all pine white.

As they walked on, Howard said, "Don't reckon they was any *hoboes* in it do you?" Then he and Lawrence laughed.

They struck the creek hollow and followed it in file, Lawrence ahead, stepping around tall slakey rocks that pitched up abruptly from the hot shale. Heat came out of this dry stone, sharp as acid, wavering up in black lines. Then at a bend before them was the water hole, small now and stagnant, and they turned off to climb the bank in order to reach it from the side. Howard was in front now, as they came over the rise, he saw the rabbit first. Standing between two oak stumps ten feet away, standing up like a kangaroo, ears winced back, looking away, toward the railroad track. Then Lawrence saw it too, and tried to motion Howard off with one hand, bringing his rifle up quick with the other.

The sound came as one, but within one spurting circle of explosion, the two explosions were distinct.

On their side, the half face of the rabbit twitched twice back and down even before it hit him, then he jumped straight up in a double flip five times the height he had stood and landed across one of the old burned out stumps like a roll of wet paper.

"*Goddam!*" said Lawrence, frowning. He walked slowly toward the stumps, then looked at Howard before he picked up the rabbit. "God*dam* it!" he said.

One side of the rabbit, from the stomach down, looked as though it had been pushed through a meat grinder.

"You must be crazy," Lawrence said, "why didn't you let me get him, goddam it, I could of gotten him in the *head.*" He dropped the rabbit across the stump again, and stood looking at it.

Howard picked up the rabbit, studied it. "Sure tore hell out of it, didn't it?" he said.

Lawrence spat and turned away. Howard watched him for a minute walking down toward the water hole, then he put the rabbit back on the stump and followed.

They leaned the guns against the dead grassed ground that rose at their backs, and sat down. Howard got out the cigarettes and offered them, so that Lawrence took one first, and then Howard. And Howard struck the match.

"Got the car tonight?" he asked, holding out the light.

Big Lawrence didn't answer at once for drawing on the cigarette. "Sure," he said then, admitting, "but I've got a *date*." In this sun, the flame of the match was colorless, only chemical, without heat.

"Where you goin'?" Howard asked, "to the *show?*"

"I dunno," said Lawrence, watching the smoke, "maybe I will."

The water hole was small, less then ten feet across, overhung only by a dwarfed sand-willow on the other bank, so that all around the dead burning ground was flushed with sun, while one half of the hole itself cast back the scene in distortion.

Over and on the water though, in and through the shadow that fell half across them, played wasps and water-spiders, dragonflies, snake-doctors, and a thousand gray gnats. A hornet, deep-ribbed, whirring golden bright as a spinning dollar, hung in a hummingbird twist just on the water surface in the deepest shadow of the tree, and Lawrence threw a rock at it.

Then an extraordinary thing happened. The hornet, rising frantically up through the willow branches, twisted once, and came down out of the tree in a wild whining loop, and lit exactly on the back of Howard's shirt collar, and then very deliberately, as Lawrence saw, crawled inside.

"Hold still," said Lawrence, taking a handful of the shirt at the back and the hornet with it, holding it.

Howard had his throat arched out, the back of his neck all scrunched away from the shirt collar. "Did you get it?" he kept asking.

"Hold still, goddam it," said Lawrence, laughing, watching Howard's face from the side, finally closing his hand on the shirt, making the hornet crackle as hard and dry as an old match box when he clenched his fist.

And then Lawrence had it out, in his hand, and they were both bent over in looking. It was dead now, wadded and broken. And in the shade of his hand, the gold of the hornet had become as ugly-colored as the phosphorus dial at noon—it was the stinger, sticking out like a wire hair, taut in an electric quaver, that still lived.

"Look at that goddam thing," said Lawrence of the stinger, and made as if to touch it with his finger.

"Be careful, you'll get stung," said Howard.

"*Look* at it," said Lawrence, intent.

"They all do that," Howard said.

"Sure, but not like that."

Lawrence touched it with his finger, but nothing happened.

"Maybe we can get it to sting something," said Howard, and he tried to catch a doodle-bug, crawling on a bluebonnet that grew alone between them, but he missed it. So Lawrence bent the flower itself over, to get the stinger to penetrate the stem at the bottom. "It'll kill it," he said, "it's acid."

Lawrence held the tail of the hornet tight between his thumb and finger, squeezing to get more of the stinger out, until it came out too far and stopped moving—and Lawrence, squeezing, slowly emptied the body of its white filling. Some of it went on his finger. Lawrence smelled it, then he let Howard smell it before he wiped his finger on the grass.

They lit another cigarette. Big Lawrence threw the match in the water, and a minute after it had floated out, took up the 30-30, drew a bead, and clipped it just below the burnt head.

"*Why?*" he asked Howard, handing him the rifle, "are *you* goin' to the show tonight?"

"I might," Howard said.

"Yeah, but have you got a *date?*"

"I guess I could get one," said Howard, working the bolt.

"I've got one with Helen Ward," said Lawrence.

Howard sighted along the rifle.

"You know her *sister?*" Lawrence asked.

"Who, Louise?"

"Sure, maybe we could get 'em drunk."

Howard held his breath, steadying the rifle. Then he took a shot. "Sure I know her," he said.

They shot water targets, mostly with the rifle, Howard using the shots Lawrence owed him. Once, however, after he dug an old condensed-milk can out of the bank and sat it on the water, Lawrence took up the shotgun and held the muzzle about a foot from the can.

"H-Bomb," he said, pulling the trigger.

They sat there for an hour, talking a little and smoking, shooting at crawfish and dragonflies, or underwater rocks that shone through flat yellow, or more often, dull dead brown.

Then they decided to go back to the house and drink some beer.

Near the stumps, Howard crossed over and picked up the rabbit, Lawrence watching him.

"What're you goin' to do with that damn thing?" Lawrence asked.

"Aw I dunno," said Howard, "might as well take it along."

Lawrence watched while Howard held it by the ears and kicked at a piece of newspaper, twisted dry and dirty, yellow in the grass. He got the paper, shook it out straight, and he wrapped it around the rabbit.

They started across the field, Lawrence not talking for a while. Then he stopped to light a cigarette.

"I know what," he said, cradling the 30-30 to one arm, "we can *cook* it."

Howard didn't answer right off, but once, as they walked back toward the stumps, he looked at the sun.

"I wonder what time it is anyhow," he said.

Using Howard's knife, Big Lawrence, once it was decided, sat on one of the stumps to skin the rabbit while Howard went pushing around through the Johnson grass, folding aside with his feet, peering and picking, bundling back, to build the fire.

At the stumps, Lawrence cursed the knife, tried the other blade, and sawed at the rabbit's neck, twisting it in his hand.

"Wouldn't cut hot niggerpiss," he said, but somehow he managed to get the head off, and to turn the skin back on itself at the neck, so that he pulled it down like a glove reversed on an unborn hand, it glistened so.

He had to stop with the skin halfway down to cut off the front feet, and in doing this, hacking once straight on from the point of the blade, the blade suddenly folded back against his finger. He opened the knife slowly, saying nothing, but he sucked at the finger and squeezed it between two others until, through all this heavy red of rabbit, sticking, covering his whole hand now, he could almost see, but never quite, where in one spot on his smallest finger, he himself, up through the blood of the rabbit, was bleeding too.

He went down to the pool to clean his hands, but he finished skinning the rabbit first.

When he got back, Howard was down, ready to light the fire.

"Are we goin' to the show or not?" Lawrence said.

"I don't care," said Howard, staring up at him. "Do *you* want to?"

"Well, we better get back if we're goin'."

Howard got the old newspaper from where he had put it to burn and wrapped it around the rabbit again, and he put this inside his shirt. He folded the skin square and put it in his pocket.

Lawrence had the rabbit's head. He tried to get the eyes to stay open, and one did stay open, but only the white showed when he sat it on the stump. He took a rock from the windbreak Howard had built for the fire and put this on the stump too, behind the head, and they started across the field. When they were a little way out, they took shots at the head, and finally Lawrence used the last of the shells he had coming to go up close and shoot the head, rock, and even part of the stump away with the old twelve-guage.

Before they reached Rosemont Street they could hear Tommy Sellers cursing and Crazy Ralph Newgate farther, yelling, "*All the way! All the way!*" and as they turned in, Tommy Sellers was there, coming toward them, walking up the middle of the street, swinging his glove by one finger.

Howard pulled the wad of newspaper out of his shirt and held it up to show, and Tommy Sellers stopped and kicked around at some dead grass piled in the gutter. "*Okay, all the way!*" Ralph Newgate was yelling halfway down the block, and Tommy Sellers found the ball with his foot. Then, bending over, in a low twisting windup from the gutter, never once looking where, he threw it—the ball that lifted like a frozen shot to hang sailing for an instant in a wide climbing arc.

Big Lawrence brought the rifle off his shoulder. "Ka-*pow!*" he said, "Ka-*pow!*" and the barrel-point wavered, sighting up the lazy wake of the ball. "Dead sonofabitch bird," he said.

Tommy Sellers was standing closer now, hands on his hips, not seeing down there an eighth of a mile where Ralph Newgate, with his eyes high, nervously tapping the glove palm, was trying to pick the bouncing throw off the headlight of a parked car.

"God it stinks," said Lawrence, making a face when Howard opened the newspaper. The paper now was like a half dried cloth, stiff, or sticking in places and coming to pieces. Almost at once a fly was crawling over the chewed up part of the rabbit.

"You know what it's like?" said Lawrence—"*goddam rotten after-birth!*" and he spat, seeming to retch a little.

"What was it?" asked Tommy Sellers, looking close at the rabbit, then up, away, not caring, dancing out to take the wild looping throw from Crazy Ralph.

They walked on. Howard wrapped the newspaper around the rabbit again and put it in his shirt.

"It's already beginning to *rot*," said Big Lawrence.

"Aw you're crazy," Howard said.

"*Crazy*," repeated Lawrence, "you're the one who's crazy. What'll you do, *eat it?*" He laughed, angrily, spitting again.

They were walking in the street in front of Lawrence's house now. Tommy Sellers and Ralph Newgate were at the curb, throwing their gloves up through the branches of a cedar tree where the ball was caught.

There were some people standing around the steps at Lawrence's front porch. One was a youngish woman wearing an apron over her dress—and a little girl was holding on to the dress with both hands, pressing her face into the apron, swinging herself slowly back and forth, so that the woman stood as braced, her feet slightly apart. She stroked the child's head with one hand, and in the other she was holding the dead cat.

They watched Howard and Lawrence in the street in front of the house. Once the woman moved her head and spoke to the fat man standing on the porch who frowned without looking at her.

Howard didn't turn in with Lawrence. "See you at the show," he said.

As he walked on, the fall of their voices died past him.

"How'd it *happen,* son?" he heard Lawrence's dad ask.

He turned off on a vacant lot that cut through toward his house. Halfway across, he pulled out the paper and opened it. He studied it, brought it up to his face and smelled it.

"*That rake'll reach!*" Crazy Ralph was yelling way behind him, "*that rake'll reach!*"

Put-down

HAVING PASSED THE LAST TABLE of the Fore as slowly as it is possible to walk, they stopped and half turned, standing uncertainly now—to appear surely as four Americans, wholly, typically, lost in the rich summer afternoon of Paris—but, in fact, so used to it, it no longer mattered.

"Want to turn on?" Boris asked, absent and polite.

Aaron tried to consider it, preoccupied, scrutinized the tables for a face.

Priscilla was a little breathless. "What is it?" she whispered, ". . . *tea?*" asking Violet first, and then Boris, who just stood there, barely smiling, only finally moving his head in the direction of the street where he lived.

"What *is* it?" Priscilla wanted to know.

"What difference does it make?" said Aaron, suddenly coming back to them, scowling as though he had already decided, and perhaps against her even then, ". . . it's *something*, isn't it?" He was nervous, in the slow, ponderous way of heavyweight-intellectuals.

"It's hashish," said Violet.

"*Hashish!*" Priscilla was delighted. She almost clapped her hands. "Baudelaire used to have it in his *confiture!*" she cried.

"Sure," said Boris, "you see?"

"There you are then," said Violet, all smiles from the very beginning.

Boris' room could have been large, but it was very dark. For there was a heavy curtain over the window, and in the center of the room, an electric light-bulb, suspended from the ceiling, was all wrapped in newspaper.

They sat on the bed. Near the bed, leaning against the wall, was a dark thin Spanish guitar, and Priscilla took this up, carefully.

"How lovely," she said.

Aaron snorted, as if he were that impatient with her now.

But Boris was there, hunched over the nightstand, rolling a cigarette. "Sure," he said.

Violet nearly laughed.

"*Listen* . . ." Aaron began, but then he dropped it.

"Train's at the station," said Boris, coming up with the cigarette at last, arab-shaped, like a white paper funnel, lighting it with care, turning it slowly in the flame, lighting all the cone-flat end of it.

When Boris had inhaled twice deeply, he handed the cigarette across to Priscilla. No one spoke now, Priscilla taking one big drag and passing it on, to Violet and Aaron, and finally back to where it had begun, to Boris. And where it had begun, too, as a simple paper funnel, looking hollow, having such a wide flat whiteness for an end, it was now all thickly mashed, misshapen, and half the size in whiteness—though what had been consumed remained in length, a sharp fiery ash, so hard it could not be flicked away. And it passed again to Priscilla, to Violet, and to Aaron, to each around once more, three times in all, until there was nothing left of it but a small piece of burning paper and some wet worthless tobacco.

Then Boris took the guitar from Priscilla's lap, and after just holding it for a while, he leaned his head very close, as if for only his own ear to listen while the hand picked softly at one silver string. So softly now, the sounds were separately soft, and far-spaced, as moving horizontally on a screen, or again, as in diffusion, from behind the screen in a straight-on stream, to strike the screen and feather out as might drops of pure purple reaching up through a surface of snow.

Priscilla listened, lay back on Aaron's arm, her eyes closed as, sometime after, it was Boris humming softly, hunched again at the nightstand, where, as if quietly toying, he made another cigarette.

Still Violet simply sat leaning out, for a long time looking just at that wallpaper nearest the bed; and Boris could have seen this, perfect host, for he gave her a nosedrop-bottle then, which held a small piece of mercury. And she poured this out into her hand, as a lump of wet mirror, small as the smallest silver coin, though with Violet being so close, it might not have been like that now, and even in letting it move across one palm and onto the other, and back, she must let it fall to the floor. So that while Boris slowly stood to adjust the newspaper light, Violet knelt down very close, as if she might have already made out what loomed there near in the half-light— which it did when the light came, like a soft silver moon, as big as a mountain against a black plateau, and all around, at different and precise distances, were its pieces, shattered, perched glittering and isolate on the same expanse, or down, glinting up half-hidden deep at the bottom of parallel fissures where the surface dropped sharply away, or yet again, over and beyond: one, two, three dark fields away.

Violet and Boris were each with a stranded piece nearby, to begin moving this piece towards the larger one: Boris, using as leverage a stiff segment of cigarette-tobacco, rolled and pushed from behind, while Violet had taken one of her own blonde hairs, and herself ahead, dragged the load in a loop. This arrangement, however, perhaps because of the weight of the mercury, allowed the hair to go under the load, to strain, and slip away.

"It nearly broke then," said Violet once, thinking obviously of the hair and the moment of strain before the tension broke, and how with that sudden snap of tension she could have fallen over, perhaps even into this near fissure, being near the edge herself and as high as she was.

"It's probably cooler to roll it," said Boris then, working close to the edge. And so saying, he drew his first load up sharp just before the silver mother, and around to one side, was pushing from behind, now with his fingernail, as they watched the great silent fusion: how these two surfaces touched, weighed heavily each against the other, arcs flattened, straining black in the silver, and then in an instant's quaver, bent one over one, and collapsed whole with the great slush of soft cold metal.

By the time Priscilla and Aaron came down, the center place had been cleared of all except the one big piece, and Violet and Boris were working away to the left, bringing, as was necessary now, the outlying pieces of mercury over one, two, and sometimes three wide cracks in the floor.

So that these two, in their turn, began working the other side, Priscilla facile with a bit of broom-straw, Aaron less so, yet very sure, with a matchstick.

But once now Priscilla stopped as speaking to them all, and said:

"If you merge several small ones so they make a large one, then you can take them all in one trip."

And she sat so erect in the silence while the others went on, heads down, even as unhearing, so engaged was each, that she had to say:

"Don't you agree?"

And only then could someone speak, as from another room:

"What's the hurry?"

"Well, no," said Priscilla, even scowling, "but I mean there's no sense in being irrational about it, is there?"

"Forget it," said Aaron with four pieces lined up on the brink of an adjacent crack, driving them across like golfballs. Still the last one failed to clear, rising early in flight, taking the most gradual arc to strike the opposite wall and fall, so slowly, to the bottom of the chasm. And Aaron leaned on his stick there, sullenly, looking after it.

"*See,*" said Priscilla, who had watched, almost wringing her hands, "if you had put them all together, it would have rolled right over!"

"I topped it," said Aaron.

"Now we'll never get it," the girl went on, hopeless.

Violet, lying on her stomach, put her head down, laughing.

Yet Aaron heard only Priscilla, seeing her face very close for an instant. "*Why not?*" he said, his voice tense, but at once lighter, as if perhaps in what he had seen there then he had somehow been mistaken. "Of course we'll get it," he said, ". . . come on, I see it already."

And for the moment they worked together, but then Priscilla had to say repeatedly: "You've got to pull it! You've got to pull it!"

"It's actually cooler to roll it," said Aaron, distant, as though to himself, ". . . that way you're behind it."

"In case anything goes wrong, that is," said Violet without raising her head.

Priscilla stopped short. "What do you *mean?*" she fairly hissed; but when Violet didn't answer at once, she turned back, haughty, speaking rapidly, as though really unconcerned: "There's another advantage to merging the small ones," she said, "they'll roll right over the crack."

Now that all the apparent pieces had been returned to the great mother piece, what they continued to do individually took on the nature of a treasure-hunt—with occasional discoveries, in the fissures or behind a nailhead, which excited the attention of the others. Yet once, as perhaps was sure to happen now, Priscilla sat singly, simply staring for a long while down.

"What is it?" asked Aaron when he saw, quietly this time, so as not to involve the others.

"Down there," the girl said, pointing, while Aaron peered, not really seeing it, not as she did, there in the fissure, as crouched deep dark, glinting in a false-promise of silver blue, gray as death through the snarl of lint.

Then he did see, though surely never as she saw, and he moved to go down with her, yet stopped. "What's the matter?" he asked gently, nudging her, meaning simply that she should lean over with him.

"Nothing," she said, *"you* go," and she laughed, a little nervous.

Aaron snorted. "Come on," he said, "we'll both go."

And so, heads together, they leaned over, to stare down into this crack in the floor, eyes like diamonds, to see what the girl had found.

It was dark there, and it was narrow—so narrow that Aaron could not use his match, but must take Priscilla's straw and poke into the very heart of the thing.

"Not like that," she said, breathless, touching his wrist in something now beyond alarm.

Aaron shook her away, yet would work the straw more gingerly now, less deep, nearer the tangled edge—while Violet, risen to one elbow, watched as mesmerized, and Boris frowned once and shook his head. "You shouldn't let it bug you," he said, for it seemed that then, at the point of the straw, just where it disappeared into the gray, there was a sudden treacherous movement, as of the angry living thing inside, and Priscilla screamed at the top of her voice.

Violet and Boris frowned terribly, and for a moment Aaron sat agape, like a stricken mute—but then it was he who had to put Priscilla, sobbing now, onto the bed, and to move around and around trying to calm her and tell her not to worry, baby, that it wasn't anything, baby, wasn't anything at all.

"I know, I know," said Priscilla.

"You shouldn't let it bug you," said Boris from the floor, where very high on a heavy straight ledge, he was at that moment bringing two minute pieces together, merging them.

"I know, I know," said Priscilla, whimpering her gratitude—for she probably thought he was talking to her.

You're Too Hip, Baby

THE SORBONNE, where Murray was enrolled for a doctorate, required little of his time; class attendance was not compulsory and there were no scheduled examinations. Having received faculty approval on the subject of his thesis—"The Influence of Mallarmé on the English Novel Since 1940"—Murray was now engaged in research in the libraries, developing his thesis, writing it, and preparing himself to defend it at some future date of his own convenience. Naturally he could attend any lectures at the University which he considered pertinent to his work, and he did attend them from time to time—usually those of illustrious guest speakers, like Cocteau, Camus, and Sartre, or Marcel Raymond, author of *From Baudelaire to Surrealism*. But for the most part, Murray devoted himself to less formal pursuits; he knew every Negro jazz musician in every club in Paris.

At night he made the rounds. If there was someone really great in town he would sit at the same bar all evening and listen to him; otherwise he made the rounds, one club after another, not drinking much, just listening to the music and talking to the musicians. Then, toward morning, he would go with them to eat—down the street to the Brasserie Civet or halfway across Paris to a place in Montmartre that served spareribs and barbecued chicken.

What was best though was to hang around the bar of his own

hotel, the Noir et Blanc, in the late afternoon during a rehearsal or a closed session. At these times everyone was very relaxed, telling funny stories, drinking Pernod, and even turning on a bit of hashish or marijuana, passing it around quite openly, commenting on its quality. Murray derived a security from these scenes—the hushed camaraderie and the inside jokes. Later, in the evening, when the place was jumping, Murray kept himself slightly apart from the rest of the crowd—the tourists, the students, the professional beats, and the French *de bonne famille*—who all came to listen to the great new music. And always during the evening there would be at least one incident, like the famous tenor-man's casually bumming a cigarette from him, which would prove Murray's intimacy with the group to those who observed. Old acquaintances from Yale, who happened in, found Murray changed; they detected in his attitude toward them, their plans, and their expressed or implied values a sort of bemused tolerance—as though he were in possession of a secret knowledge. And then there would be the inevitable occasion when he was required to introduce them to one of the musicians, and that obvious moment when the musician would look to Murray for his judgment of the stranger as in the question: "Well, man, who *is* this cat? Is he *with* it?" None of this lessened Murray's attractiveness, nor his mystery, no less to others, presumably, than to himself; but he was never too hard on his old friends—because he was swinging.

When the Negro pianist Buddy Talbott was hired, along with a French drummer and bass, to play the Noir et Blanc, he and his wife had been in Paris for only three days. It was their first time out of the States, and except for a few band jobs upstate, it was their first time out of New York City.

Toward the end of the evening, during a break, Murray went into the men's room. Buddy Talbott was there alone, in front of the mirror, straightening his tie. Their eyes fixed for an instant in the glass as Murray entered and walked over to the urinal; the disinfectant did not obscure a thin smell of hashish recently smoked in the room. Murray nodded his head in the direction of the band-stand beyond the wall. "Great sound you got there, man," he said, his voice flat, almost weary in its objectiveness. Buddy Talbott had a dark and delicate face which turned slowly, reluctantly it seemed, from the glass to Murray, smiling, and he spoke now in soft and precisely measured tones: "Glad you like it."

And, for the moment, no more was said, Murray knowing better than that.

Although Murray smoked hashish whenever it was offered, he seldom took the trouble to go over to the Arab quarter and buy any himself; but he always knew where to get the best. And the next evening, when Buddy Talbott came into the men's room, Murray was already there.

They exchanged nods, and Murray wordlessly handed him the smoking stick, scarcely looking at him as he did, walking past to the basin—as though to spare him witness to even the merest glimpse of hesitancy, of apprehension, calculation, and finally, of course, of perfect trust.

"I've got a box, man," Murray said after a minute, by which he meant record player, "and some new Monk—you know, if you ever want to fall by. . . ." He dried his hands carefully, looking at the towel. "Upstairs here," he said, "in number eight. My name is on the door—'Murray.' "

The other nodded, savoring the taste, holding it. "I'd like to very much," he said finally, and added with an unguarded smile, "*Murray.*" At which Murray smiled too, and touching his arm lightly said: "Later, man." And left.

The hash seemed to have a nice effect on Buddy's playing. Certainly it did on Murray's listening—every note and nuance came straight to him, through the clatter of service at the bar and the muttered talk nearby, as though he were wearing earphones wired to the piano. He heard subtleties he had missed before, intricate structures of sound, each supporting the next, first from one side, then from another, and all being skillfully laced together with a dreamlike fabric of comment and insinuation; the runs did not sound either vertical or horizontal, but circular ascensions, darting arabesques and figurines; and it was clear to Murray that the player was constructing something there on the stand . . . something splendid and grandiose, but perfectly scaled to fit inside this room, to sit, in fact, alongside the piano itself. It seemed, in the beginning, that what was being erected before him was a castle, a marvelous castle of sound . . . but then, with one dramatic minor—just as the master builder might at last reveal the nature of his edifice in adding a single stone—Murray saw it was not a castle being built, but a cathedral. "*Yeah, man,*" he said, nodding and smiling. A cathedral—and, at the same time, around it the builder was weaving a strange and beautiful tapestry, covering the entire structure. At first the image was too bizarre, but then Murray smiled again as he saw that the tapestry was, of course, being woven *inside* the cathedral, over its interior surface, only it was so rich and strong that it sometimes seemed to come right through the walls. And then Murray suddenly realized—and this was the greatest of all, because he was absolutely certain that only he and Buddy knew—that the fantastic tapestry was being woven, quite deliberately, face against the wall. And he laughed aloud at this, shaking his head, "*Yeah, man,*" the last magnificent irony, and Buddy looked up at the sound, and laughed too.

After the set, Buddy came over and asked Murray if he wanted a drink. "Let's take a table," he said. "My old lady's coming to catch the last set."

"Solid," said Murray, so soft and without effort that none would have heard.

They sat down at a table in the corner.

"Man, that sure is fine gage," Buddy said.

Murray shrugged.

"Glad you like it," he said then, a tone with an edge of mock haughtiness, just faintly mimicking that used by Buddy when they had met; and they both laughed, and Buddy signaled the waiter.

"I was wondering," said Buddy after the waiter had left, "if you could put me onto some of that."

Murray yawned. "Why don't you meet me tomorrow," he said quietly. "I could take you over to the café and, you know, introduce you to the guy."

Buddy nodded, and smiled. "Solid," he said.

Buddy's wife, Jackie, was a tall Negro girl, sort of lank, with great eyes, legs, and a lovely smile.

"What we'd like to do," she said, "is to make it here—you know, like *live* here—at least for a couple of years anyway."

"It's the place for living all right," said Murray.

Murray was helpful in much more than introducing them to a good hash connection. Right away he found them a better and cheaper room, and nearer the Noir et Blanc. He showed Jackie how to shop in the quarter, where to get the best croissants, and what was the cheap wine to buy. He taught them some French and introduced them to the good inexpensive restaurants. He took them to see *L'Âge d'Or* at the Cinémathèque, to the catacombs, to the rib joint in Montmartre, to hear Marcel Raymond speak at the Sorbonne, to the Flea Market, to the Musée Guimet, Musée de l'Homme, to the evening exhibitions at the Louvre. . . . Sometimes Murray would have a girl with him, sometimes not; or on some Sundays when the weather was fine he would get someone with a car, or borrow it himself, and they would all drive out to the Bois de Boulogne and have a picnic, or to Versailles at night. Then again, on certain nights early, or when Buddy wasn't playing, they might have dinner in Buddy and Jackie's room, listening to records, smoking a piece of hash now and then, eating the red beans and rice, the fish, ribs, and chicken that Jackie cooked. The most comfortable place in the small room was the bed, and after a while the three of them were usually lying or half reclining across it, except when one of them would get up to put on more records, get a drink, or go to the bathroom, everything very relaxed, not much talk, occasionally someone saying something funny or relating a strange thing they had seen or heard, and frequently, too, just dozing off.

Once Murray bought a pheasant, had it cooked, and brought it up to their room, along with a couple of bottles of chilled Lieb-fraumilch, some wild rice, asparagus, and strawberries and cream.

Jackie was quite excited, opening the packages. "You're too much, baby," she said, giving Murray a kiss on the cheek.

"What's the grand occasion, man?" asked Buddy, beaming at him.

Murray shrugged. "I guess we'll have to dream one up," he said.

"I guess we will," said Buddy smiling, and he started slicing up a piece of hash.

Afterward they lay across the bed, smoking and listening to music.

"It's funny, isn't it," said Murray, while they were listening to Billie, "that there aren't any great ofay singers."

The others seemed to consider it.

"Anita O'Day is all right," said Jackie.

"Yeah, but I mean you wouldn't compare her with Billie, would you," said Murray.

"Some of the French chicks swing," said Buddy absently, ". . . Piaf . . . and what's that other chick's name. . . ."

"Yeah, but I mean like that's something else, isn't it," said Murray.

Buddy shrugged, passing the cigarette, "Yeah, I guess so," he said, sounding half asleep; but his eyes were open, and for several minutes he lay simply staring at Murray with an expression of mild curiosity on his face.

"Murray," he asked finally, "did you want to learn piano . . . or what?" Then he laughed, as though he might not have meant it to sound exactly like that, and he got up to get some wine.

Jackie laughed too. "Maybe he just *likes* you, baby—ever think of that?"

"Yeah, that's right," said Buddy, making a joke of it now, pouring the wine, "that ought to be considered." He was still smiling, almost sheepishly. "Well, here's to friendship then," he said, taking a sip.

"You're making me cry," said Murray in his flat, weary voice, and they all laughed.

Then it was time for Buddy to go to the club.

"I'll make it over with you, man," said Murray, slowly raising himself up on the bed.

"Stick around," said Buddy, putting on his tie. "Nothing's happening there yet—you can come over later with Jackie."

"That seems like a good idea," said Jackie.

Murray sat there, staring at nothing.

"It's cool, man," said Buddy smiling and giving Murray an elaborate wink of conspiracy, "it's cool. I mean, you know—make it."

"Solid," said Murray, after a minute, and he lay back across the bed again.

"See you cats," said Buddy, opening the door to leave.

"Later," said Murray.

"Later, baby," said Jackie, getting up and going to the door and locking it. Then she went over to the basin and began brushing her teeth.

"That was a funny thing for him to say, wasn't it," said Murray after a minute, "I mean about did I want 'to learn piano, or *what?*'"

Jackie moved the brush in a slow, languorous motion, looking at Murray in the mirror. "Well, it's very simple really. . . . I mean, he *digs* you, you know—and I guess he would like to do something for you, that sort of thing." She rinsed her mouth and held the brush under the water. "I thought he made that part of it pretty clear," she said, then looking directly at him. She crossed over to the dressing table and stood in front of it, straightening her dress; it was a cream-colored jersey which clung without tightness to all of her. She stood in front of the glass, her feet slightly apart, and touched at her hair. He watched the back of her brown legs, the softly rounded calves, tracing them up past the cream-colored hem behind her knees into their full lean contours above—lines which were not merely suggested, but, because of the clinging jersey and the way she stood, convincingly apparent.

"That's a groovy thread," said Murray, sitting up and taking the glass of wine Buddy had left on the night table.

"Oh?" She looked down at the dress reflexively and again at the mirror. "Madame what's-her-name made it—you know, that seamstress you put me onto." She sat down on a chair by the mirror and carefully wiped the lipstick from her mouth with a Kleenex.

"Yeah, it's crazy," said Murray.

"Glad you like it, Murray." The phrase had become an occasional joke between the three of them.

"I was by the Soleil du Maroc this afternoon," he began then, taking a small packet out of his shirt pocket, unwrapping it as he leaned toward the light at the night table, "I just thought I would twist up a few to take to the club." He looked up at her and paused. "I mean, you know, if there's time."

Jackie's head was cocked to one side as she dabbed perfume behind an ear and watched Murray in the mirror. "Oh there's *time*, baby," she said with a smile, ". . . make no mistake about that."

When Murray had twisted one, he lit it and, after a couple of drags, sat it smoking on the tray, continuing to roll them carefully, placing them in a neat row on the night table.

Jackie finished at the mirror, put another record on, and came over to the bed. As she sat down, Murray passed the cigarette to her, and she lay back with it, head slightly raised on a pillow against the wall, listening to *Blue Monk*.

When Murray had rolled several, he put the packet of hash away and stashed the cigarettes in with his Gauloises. Then he leaned back, resting his head on Jackie's lap, or rather on what would have been her lap had she been sitting instead of half lying across the bed; she passed the cigarette to Murray.

"Has a good taste, hasn't it," said Murray.

Jackie smiled. "Yes, indeed," she said.

"Hadj says it's from the Middle Congo," said Murray with a laugh, " '*C'est du vrai congolais!* '" he went on, giving it the Arab's voice.

"That's just how it tastes," said Jackie.

With his face turned toward her, Murray's cheek pressed firmly against the softness of her stomach which just perceptibly rose and fell with breathing, and through the fine jersey he could feel the taut sheen of her pants beneath it, and the warmth. There was nothing lank about her now.

"Yeah," said Murray after a minute, "that's right, isn't it, that's just how it tastes."

They finished the cigarette, and for a while, even after the record had ended, they lay there in silence, Jackie idly curling a finger in Murray's hair. For a long time Murray didn't move.

"Well," he finally said instead, "I guess we'd better make it—over to the club, I mean."

Jackie looked at him for a minute, then gave a gentle tug on the lock of his hair, shrugged, and laughed softly.

"Anything you say, Murray."

That Sunday was a fine day, and Murray borrowed a car for them to go out to the Bois. Jackie had fried some chicken the night before and prepared a basket of food, but now she complained of a cold and decided not to go. She insisted though that Murray and Buddy go.

"It's a shame to waste the car and this great weather. You ought to make it."

So they went without her.

They drove up the Champs through a magnificent afternoon, the boulevard in full verdure and the great cafés sprawled in the sun like patches of huge flowers. Just past the Étoile they noticed a charcuterie which was open and they stopped and bought some more to put in the basket—céleri rémoulade, artichoke hearts, and cheese covered with grape seeds. At a café next door Murray was able to get a bottle of cognac.

At the Bois they drove around for a while, then parked the car and walked into the depth of the woods. They thought they might discover a new place—and they did, finally, a grove of poplars which led to the edge of a small pond; and there, where it met the pond and the wooded thicket to each side, it formed a picture-book alcove, all fern, pine and poplar. There was no one else to be seen on the pond, and they had passed no one in the grove. It was a pleasing discovery.

Together they carefully spread the checkered tablecloth the way

Jackie always did, and then laid out the food. Buddy had brought along a portable phonograph, which he opened up now while Murray uncorked the wine.

"What'll it be," Buddy asked with a laugh, after looking at the records for several minutes, "Bird or Bartók?"

"Bartók, man," said Murray, and added dreamily, "where do you go after Bird?"

"Crazy," said Buddy, and he put on *The Miraculous Mandarin*.

Murray lay propped on his elbow, and Buddy sat opposite, cross-legged, as they ate and drank in silence, hungry but with deliberation, sampling each dish, occasionally grunting an appreciative comment.

"Dig that bridge, man," said Buddy once, turning to the phonograph and moving the needle back a couple of grooves, "like that's what you might call an 'augmented *oh*-so-*slightly*.'" He laughed. "Cat's too much," he said, as he leaned forward to touch a piece of chicken to the mayonnaise.

Murray nodded. "Swings," he said.

They lay on the grass, smoking and drinking the cognac, closing their eyes or shading them against the slanting sun. They were closer together now, since once Buddy had gotten up to stretch and then, in giving Murray a cigarette, had sat down beside him to get a light.

After a while Buddy seemed to half doze off, and then he sleepily turned over on his stomach. As he did, his knee touched Murray's leg, and Murray moved lightly as if to break the contact—but then, as if wondering why he had reacted like that, let his leg ease back to where it had been, and almost at once dropped into a light sleep, his glass of cognac still in his hand, resting on his chest.

When Murray awoke, perhaps only seconds later, the pressure of Buddy's leg on his own was quite strong. Without looking at Buddy, he slowly sat up, raising his legs as he did, sitting now with knees under his folded arms. He looked at the glass of cognac still in his hand, and finished it off.

"That sort of thing," said Buddy quietly, "doesn't interest you either." It was not put as a question, but as a statement which required confirmation.

Murray turned, an expression of bland annoyance on his face, while Buddy lay there looking at him pretty much the same as always.

"No, man," said Murray, then almost apologetically: "I mean, like I don't put it down—but it's just not a scene I make. You know?"

Buddy dropped his eyes to a blade of grass he was toying with; he smiled. "Well, anyway," he said with a little laugh, "no offense."

Murray laughed, too. "None taken, man," he said seriously.

Murray had risen at his more or less usual hour, and the clock at Cluny was just striking eleven when he emerged from the hotel stairway, into the street and the summer morning. He blinked his eyes at the momentary brightness and paused to lean against the side of the building, gazing out into the pleasantly active boulevard. When the clock finished striking he pushed himself out from the wall and started towards the Royale, where he often met Buddy and Jackie for breakfast. About halfway along Boulevard Saint-Germain he turned in at a small café to get some cigarettes. Three or four people were coming out the door as Murray reached it, and he had to wait momentarily to let them pass. As he did he was surprised to notice, at a table near the side, Buddy and Jackie, eating breakfast. Buddy was wearing dark glasses, and Murray instinctively reached for his own as he came through the door, but discovered he had left them in his room. He raised his hand in a laconic greeting to them and paused at the bar to get the cigarettes. Buddy nodded, but Jackie had already gotten up from the table and was walking toward the girls' room. Murray sauntered over, smiling, and sat down.

"What are you doing here, man?" he asked. "I didn't know you ever came here."

Buddy shrugged. "Thought we'd give it a try," he said seriously examining a dab of butter on the end of his knife. Then he looked up at Murray and added with a laugh, "You know—new places, new faces."

Murray laughed too, and picked at a piece of an unfinished croissant. "That's pretty good," he said. "What's that other one? You know, the one about—oh yeah, 'Old friends are the best friends.' Ever hear that one?"

"I have heard that one," said Buddy nodding, "yes, I have heard that one." His smile was no longer a real one. "Listen, Murray," he said, wiping his hands and sitting back, putting his head to one side, "let me ask you something. Just what is it you want?"

Murray frowned down at where his own hands slowly dissected the piece of croissant as though he were shredding a paper napkin.

"What are you talking about, man?"

"You *don't* want to play music," Buddy began as though he were taking an inventory, "and you *don't* want . . . I mean just what have we *got* that interests you?"

Murray looked at him briefly, and then looked away in exasperation. He noticed that Jackie was talking to the patron who was standing near the door. "Well, what do *you* think, man?" he demanded, turning back to Buddy. "I dig the *scene,* that's all. I dig the *scene* and the *sounds.*"

Buddy stood up, putting some money on the table. He looked down at Murray, who sat there glowering, and shook his head. "You're too hip, baby. That's right. You're a *hippy.*" He laughed. "In fact, you're what we might call a kind of professional *nigger lover.*" He touched Murray's shoulder as he moved to leave. "And I'm not putting you down for it, understand, but, uh, like the man said, 'It's just not a scene I make.'" His dark face set for an instant beneath the smoky glasses and he spoke, urgent and imploring, in a flash of white teeth, almost a hiss, "I mean *not when I can help it,* Murray, *not when I can help it.*" And he left. And the waiter arrived, picking up the money.

"*Monsieur désire?*"

Still scowling, staring straight ahead, Murray half raised his hand as to dismiss the waiter, but then let it drop to the table. "*Café,*" he muttered.

"*Noir, monsieur?*" asked the waiter in a suggestively rising inflection.

Murray looked up abruptly at the man, but the waiter was oblivious, counting the money in his hand.

Murray sighed. "*Oui,*" he said softly, "*noir.*"

You
Gotta
Leave
Your Mark

IT WAS ONE OF THOSE HUGE, jagged emptinesses left wherever a building is improperly torn down in the tenement section of a city. Actually, it was New York; but seen out of context—say, in a cropped photograph—one might have said it was some place in Europe, destroyed by war: a part of London, or Hamburg, after a raid—except that there was nothing recent, or mysterious, about this rubble; it had settled, in impossibly uneven, hard-packed mounds, all molding and covered with soot. The children in the neighborhood called it "the lot."

Every conceivably usable thing had been wrenched out of the debris and dragged into the houses long ago, so the lot no longer held the remote chance of yielding treasure, except perhaps to the very, very young. Even the rotten pieces of lumber were gone, the two-by-fours that had stilted out so oddly, making strange inhuman shapes, or all too human shadows, to strike fear into young and old alike, passing the lot on summer nights, whenever gray clouds hazed the brightness of the moon. Now there were not even rusty nails to dare or dread at twilight, when the smallest played capture-the-flag, leaping the stagnant pools of oily water.

Out of expediency, the adults, too, when dealing with the children, called it "the lot." *Go get your brother, over at the lot, a* woman might be heard to say, or *Don't lie to me, I know you was at*

the lot, Mrs. Harley seen you there when she went to the store.
Among themselves, however, they pretended to be less familiar with
it, most often referring to it as "where the building used to be" or,
even more pretentiously, as "the excavation site": they also called it a
"shame" and a "menace." Then, at night, hidden from each other by
the darkness, they used it as a garbage dump.

It was strange, seeing children playing in the lot. It had the
spaciousness of a small park, but there was a certain bleak wildness
about the broken terrain, and the lighting was always bad: unreal,
like that on a print of underdeveloped film.

In the fall afternoon now, the sunlight filtered down across the lot
as though it were being strained through black gauze, making the
rust-brick building that formed the west wall of the lot loom up all
shadowed and dark, the color of bad blood. Near the ground,
scrawled across this wall in already graying white, was the single
word, "Panthers," and out about twenty feet, along the rise of a
refuse mound, sat the three boys, their backs to the wall.

The one who sat on the crest of the mound was named Vince.
Vince had the proverbial clean-cut intelligent young face of the
type often pictured on the backs of cereal boxes gleefully exclaiming, "Gosh, Mom," etc. He looked rather more wistful now though
than anything else; pensive, yet vague, as one engrossed in an
abstraction, a daydream. He held a large, heavy stick in his hand
which he swung in deliberate, measured blows against the upturned
side of a rust-eaten bucket half-buried in the debris. It made an
insistently harsh sound and sometimes a rasping tear.

The second boy, Ritchie, was hunched a few feet away, knees
drawn up beneath crossed arms on which he rested his chin,
watching the damage of the stick on the bucket with dull compre-
hension.

Slightly below them both, on the incline of rubble, the third boy,
Nick, lay sprawled on his side reading the comics of a tabloid daily
and absently picking his nose. The three boys were each fifteen
years old and looked quite a bit alike, except that the boy reading

the paper, Nick, was wearing a baseball cap and, in spite of it, gave the impression of probably not being as good at baseball as Vince and Ritchie were.

Near the sidewalk, two very small boys were playing. The older one had a little plastic airplane that he careened on an outstretched hand above his head and jiggled in simulated attack on the smaller boy. The other, a tiny child who could not have been over four, had a gigantic toy pistol, a great silvery six-shooter, which he pretended to fire at the plane. He was so small, and the toy gun so grotesquely large, that it was often necessary for him to use both hands to support it against the maneuvers of the plane. The boy with the plane droned out unceasingly the effects of the plane and its machine gun.

"Uh-uh-uh-uh-uh! Uh-uh-uh-uh-uh! Umm-rahhahh! Uh-uh-uh-uh-uh!"

"Kow! Kow! Kow!" the tiny boy would scream in reply, shaking himself and the great pistol.

Down this sidewalk, half a block in each direction, were the avenues where ten thousand buses, trucks and taxis were caught up in a writhing fantasy of noise and cross-purpose motion, the exposed segment of a tortured mechanical nerve, blindly, frantically threading the city. The sound seemed to funnel itself down the street from both ways and into this gap between the buildings, as into some huge amplifier, where, as a backdrop to the chorale of the two boys at war, the vicious timpano, and the quaking roar of the passing elevated, it made for a pure Bartókean nightmare of dissonance, while across the scene the dead light of afternoon seeped, in eerie, dismal shafts—winter light in a cathedral of dirty windows.

A blow from the stick rent the remaining length of the bucket, leaving now only the thick, turned rim which was already bent crescent shape. Vince strengthened his blows, his face visibly wracked with some nebulous, disturbing intensity, while Nick began to turn pages of the tabloid, wetting a thumb and forefinger for each.

"Hey, listenit this!"

He started reading aloud an account of how a woman had killed her husband with a meat hook. There was a suggestion of apology for the English language in the way Nick read. He faltered over certain words, not simply in ignorance as a seven-year-old might, but with a kind of embarrassment that such words should actually exist. Because of the noise, however, only a scattering of words were even audible.

" . . . scream . . . night . . . neighbor . . . the body . . . gruesome . . . punctured . . . the body . . . lacerations . . . police rushed . . . horrible . . . punctured . . . bloody . . . police said . . . crime . . . of passion . . ."

As his voice trailed off, bored with the account, or its ineffectualness on the others, a blow from the stick severed the last brittle strand of rim and the stick came to rest, as the boy sat, inert, staring at the completed work. After a moment he gave it another sharp blow, as for good measure, sighed, and dropped the stick, raising his face, still marked with some vague, ineffable anxiety.

"Hey, lookit!"

Nick started up on one knee.

"Lookit this!"

He struck the paper several times with the back of his hand.

"The 'Bandits' busted up the hunnert-an'-fort' last night and there's a *pitcher* of it! They left their mark and there's a *pitcher* of it!"

He hurried over as the two boys rose to meet him, crowding avidly, the nearest one, Ritchie, actually making a grab for the paper himself.

"Gimme that," yelled Nick angrily, warding him off, even gesturing a threat to destroy the paper rather than yield it.

"Let's lookit for Chrissake!" said Ritchie.

It was a close-up photograph of a schoolhouse window with all the panes broken except one—across which was written: "Bandits." It was obvious that the photograph had been heavily retouched to give the word glaring prominence.

"Okay, what's the other part say?" demanded Vince. "Jerk!"

Still keeping them at bay, Nick began to read aloud, with an awkward self-importance, painfully enunciating each word.

"'Public School one-hunnert-an'-four was entered late last night, according to authorities, by a teenage gang of vandals, known as The Bandits.'"

"Those *jerks!*" muttered Vince, stuffing his hands in his pockets and kicking at the torn bucket.

"'School Superintendent Adams said that while the damage has not yet been fully assessed it is expected to run close to a thousand dollars.'"

In his reading, Nick gave special emphasis to various words, including each mention of the rival gang, as though in the act of reading the item aloud, he alone could successfully identify himself with their exploits.

"'After breaking dozens of windows, desks, blackboards, and strewing ink and torn textbooks throughout the classrooms, the defiant youngsters left their gang signature, Bandits, in several places. See photo.'"

Ritchie made a gesture of contempt, but it poorly disguised the envy beneath it. "Let's have a lookit the pitcher again." And they all three huddled once more over the paper.

"'Bandits,'" said Nick, as though he were still the only one authorized to read whatever might come before them.

"Jerks," said Vince, spitting. "Couldn't they do any better than that?"

"You *kiddin'*?" said Nick, "they got the pitcher, din' they?" He looked down at the photograph again, to make sure of it.

"No, I ain't *kiddin'*," said Vince, seething, and he spat heavily on the page.

"Hey I din'finish with the paper yet, whatta you doin', I din'finish with it yet!"

"Yeah, well, ain't that too bad!"

They faced each other squarely for a moment, but the nameless, impersonal rage and hatred in Vince's face was so overpowering that Nick turned away, muttering something, and sat down again, crumpling the defiled page and throwing it aside.

Vince stood glaring after him, then he and Ritchie sat down too, together, some distance from Nick. For the next few minutes Nick turned the pages of the paper very self-consciously, feigning frowns of interest, expressions of amusement, finally even whistling a little, before he managed to speak again, as though nothing at all had happened:

"How come *we* din'get in the paper when we busted up the hunnert-an'-seven?" There was a slight whine in his voice.

Vince, who was still staring at him, merely spat, then looked away.

"Cause they din'know it was us did it!" said Ritchie. "Jerk!"

"You kiddin'? *Everybody* knew it was us did it."

"I mean the *papers* din'know!" Then, turning to Vince, he went on, "Jez, how dumb can a jerk get, huh?"

"You gotta leave your mark," said Vince tersely, as though he were talking to himself. "You gotta leave your mark next to somethin' *broke*—so they can take a pitcher of it."

Out along the sidewalk that bordered the front of the lot, where the two children played at their game of war, a little girl slowly passed, a cloth doll cradled to her chest. She was perhaps five years old and she walked with a vague sort of metronomic motion, putting one foot before the other, twisting her body in that direction with each step, and humming distractedly. Her passing struck the attention of the smaller boy, and he rushed out at once to confront her, lurching forward with the pistol in both hands at arm's length. "Kow!" he cried, then repeated the movement, point-blank, at the head of the cloth doll. "Kow!" With a haughty gesture of possessiveness, the little girl turned away, covering the doll's head with her hands, and hurried past. A few steps beyond, she resumed her dreamlike gait, while the little boy stood in the middle of the sidewalk looking after her, still aiming the pistol. "Kow! Kow!" he said softly, almost wearily.

That night, about three hours after supper, Vince and Ritchie were sitting on the curb opposite a small candy and cigar store, sitting just beyond the street lamp's circle of light.

"Naw, that's out," Vince was saying impatiently. "The *school* is kid stuff. It's gotta be somethin' . . . different, somethin' bigger than that. We can make them look *sick!*" He glanced menacingly toward the candy store as an old man came out and stacked some papers on the front stand. "And *I* know just what it is," he said softly.

"You mean old man Kessler?"

"And I know *just what it is.*"

"You mean bust up the—"

"Listen. Suppose old man Kessler din' come home tonight. Get it? His brother would call the cops, right? As soon as he din' show up, see, he'd call the cops."

"You mean *kidnap* 'im?"

"Naw, just so it would *look* that way. See? Then it'd get in the papers and they'd have to print it when they found him—that it was a gag . . . by the *Panthers.* But we'd say we din'do it, if they ask us, the police—like somebody else must of done it . . . and *left our mark.* See?"

"But *he'd* know we did it. He'd recognize us, he'd *tell* 'em we did it!"

"He won't know *nothin'!*"

Vince glanced around to see that they weren't being watched, then he leaned forward and pulled something from inside his jacket, allowing only a fraction of it to show.

"See this? Know what it is? Pilla'-case! Listen, I got it all figgered out. We wait in the doorway next to the store. Okay, when he locks up, he walks over to the car, right? Okay. Now *one* guy slips up behind him and puts the pilla'-case over his head—like that! Quick, you know? Then the other two grab'im—he don't see *none* of us; and we don't talk neither—durin' the whole time we don't talk."

"Yeah, then what?"

"Then we tie'im up and put'im in the car, and leave'im there. So when he don't show up, his brother phones the cops. Like he's *missin'*, see what I mean? And they put it in the paper: 'Old man Kessler missin'!' Jez, it's a riot! I tell you, it'll make those jerks look sick!"

Since the beginning of the talk, Ritchie's face had shown a

restrained and devious consternation. At this point, following a pause in the exchange, he seemed almost alarmed.

"How you gonna' keep'im from *yelling?*"

Vince threw another suspicious glance at the store, then he extracted the pillowcase entirely. It was folded and bulky. He put it on his lap and covertly raised the folded-over part of it. There were two rolled-up pieces of electric-light cord, a necktie and a wad of cotton the size of a man's fist.

"See this? Cotton. The guy that puts the pilla'-case over his head grabs his mouth, see? That's all he does. He puts the pilla'-case over his head and then holds his hand over his mouth—hard, you know? One arm around his head and the other hand over his mouth. He don't worry about the arms, 'cause the other two guys run up, quick, and grab his arms and tie'em behind'im. With this."

He gingerly indicated the tight twists of covered wire, then touched a finger to the necktie.

"The guy that's holdin' his mouth reaches up under the pilla'-case and puts the cotton in his mouth while the other two guys tie it, on the outside, across his mouth, you know—like this—it's open, see, with the cotton inside it, and the tie across it, *tight* see, it'll go around twice, pushin' the cotton down in his mouth so he don't yell. Then we put'im in the car and tie his feet."

Ritchie sat staring down at the paraphernalia, fascinated but ambivalent. Vince went on, hurriedly, as if only a certain urgency of voice were needed now to convince Ritchie.

"I got it all figgered out. Know where I got the pilla'-case? Outta the trash. No laundry mark, I tore it off it. They can't trace it—to *nobody*, see? The tie too. That's what gimme the idea—when I see the stuff in the trash."

So saying, Vince lapsed into a sort of silent reverence, perhaps pleasantly retracing the steps that had led to this moment of pure infallibility, while Ritchie continued to gaze down at the things, as though he, too, weren't already committed.

"We'd have to wear gloves," he said thoughtfully.

"Naw," said Vince, "just the one guy, the one that opens the car. The old man keeps all his keys together, you know? So when he locks up, he'll still have the keys in his hand on the way to the car. I mean we don't even have to look for the keys. And just the one guy'll touch the keys and the door."

Ritchie started to speak, as if to raise another objection, but then, as though having thought of something else, more important, said:

"Where'd we leave our mark?"

"I dunno," said Vince easily. "I haven't decided the best place for it yet."

Both boys looked up to see Nick approaching. He was munching an apple and still wearing his baseball cap. There was a suggestion of youth and naiveté in the way he walked slowly in order to finish all the apple before reaching them. When he arrived, Vince spoke to him before he had a chance to sit down:

"You got any gloves at home?"

"What kinda gloves?" asked Nick, still holding the apple, of which there was almost nothing left but the core.

"*Gloves,* jerk! Like you'd wear if you din'wantta leave your fingerprints someplace."

"Sure I got gloves at home."

"Okay, go get'em, and get one of your sister's lipsticks."

"What for?"

"*Get*'em! We'll tell you what for when you get back."

"Whatta you want the lipstick for?"

"Look, you want in on this or not?"

"Sure I want in on it."

"Well, get the *stuff* for Chrissake! We'll tell you when you get back."

"Okay, okay," said Nick, with enough inflection to suggest he was simply humoring their unreasonableness. He shrugged and started back down the sidewalk, walking slowly, still toying with the apple at his lips.

The two boys watched his departing figure in silence, until Ritchie nodded sagely and said:

"Lipstick's good to leave your mark on a car with."

Halfway down the block they could see Nick pause at the bottom of the steps where he lived and look up at the lighted windows above. Then he threw down the apple core which bounced off the curb and into the gutter—and in this movement there was something abrupt and decisive, somehow like the sudden dropping of a mask—and he bounded up the steps two at a time.

After the deed was done—and, surprisingly enough, it had come off almost exactly as planned—the three boys went down to Nick's and climbed the fire escape to sit outside his rooms and watch. It was a good vantage point, for from there not only could they see the shuttered front of the old man's store, but also the rear half of the automobile in which they had put him.

Because of the angle and the distance from where they were sitting, they could not actually read it; but they could see, in darkly iridescent traces, where the light of the arc lamp, falling in a yellow swatch across the back of the car, was caught up in the outline of their mark, "Panthers"—for, at the last minute, and all things considered, that was where they had decided to put the old man, in the trunk.

They watched for an hour, but no one passed, only some drunks stumbling along the opposite sidewalk. Then, at Vince's suggestion, they agreed to each go home and be in the presence of his family, so that they would all have an alibi, before meeting at the lot in the morning.

Morning.

Vince was still asleep. In a dim untidy boxlike room, containing a double bed and a dresser, with an empty baby crib standing in the one remaining corner, the only light was the gray-washed morning through a small window and it left the rumpled bedclothes and the sleeping boy's face discolored and wan. It was the room he shared with his older brother, Sid, and their infant sister.

Alone now, in his half-sleep Vince made vague efforts to cover his head with the pillow, but from somewhere voices rising in argument, the sputtering growl of a dozen radios and crash of pots and pans, the crying babies, the blare and screech and wrangle of the streets below—the sounds of the too-close, thin-walled, tenement day—had begun, and he awoke. He sat up and looked around anxiously, as though he had overslept. Then he got out of bed, wearing his undershorts, and quickly dressed. As he sat on the edge of the bed, bent forward in tying his shoes, he pushed open the door to the adjoining room where his father sat, eating breakfast and watching television.

A very large man, he sat squarely in the center of the divan, looking bloated in his tight trousers and fresh undershirt, his face rawly shaved and bleary-eyed from sleep, the hastily combed hair thinly criss-crossed on one side, as he leaned out over the low table, eternally in the attitude of eyes upraised to the set, mouth slightly agape, and fork poised with another bite of dripping egg.

This room was a slightly larger version of the other one, a box with two square holes punched in it for windows. It was the living room, but since the family took most of their meals there, in order to watch TV, it had an even more cluttered and abortive appearance than the big glazed seashell, leather- and glass-framed photographs, novelty plastic electric clock and additional, pathetic, bric-a-brackish attempts at mediocrity would have given it otherwise. Propped at one end of the divan was a year-old child who gazed at the TV screen with unrelenting saucer-eyed attention.

Half laughing, the father did not seem to notice when Vince entered the room, but he scowled when the boy passed between him and the set and even moved his head out to one side so as not to miss any more than necessary while a man on the screen wearing shell-rimmed glasses put a funny paper hat on a chimpanzee, for perhaps the thousandth time. The chimpanzee reached up and pulled off the hat, as he always did, and Vince's father resumed his show of amusement.

"That goddam monk!" he said, chuckling and averting his eyes long enough to slurp another bite of egg into his mouth.

Vince went in the kitchen. With a large oblong pot of water simmering on the two back burners of the midget stove, the kitchen was very much like a steam closet. His mother was there, wearing a satiny housecoat, her hair up in a kerchief.

"What'd he do?" she called over her shoulder to the man in the living room, then spoke quickly to Vince. "You lookin' for cereal, cereal's on the table."

She was a small, wasted woman whose rougeless face was stark and very tired. Her movements, however, were abrupt and nervous, and her voice was strident. She held a baby high on her chest, its head facing away over her shoulder.

"That goddam crazy *monk!*" came the father's voice as he laughed to himself again.

"What'd he do, huh?" she yelled in at him, her mouth anticipatorily forming a harsh, greedy smile of appreciation.

"Where's Sid?" asked Vince. "D'he go for a paper?"

"He went for milk, you'll have to wait on your cereal—bring your bowl and spoon, sugar and cereal's on the table."

Her manner of speech was extremely fast and wavering, as in a sort of restrained hysteria. When she left the kitchen, Vince followed her, taking a bowl and spoon from the wire dish rack.

"What'd he do, huh?" his mother demanded in the living room.

The father, however, was engrossed in some further development of the show. "Huh?"

"The *monkey,* what'd he do?"

The father took advantage of a station break to scoop some more egg into his mouth, at the same time chuckling to himself and shaking his head as if it were too complex or elusive a thing to reconstruct.

"Well, what'd he *do?*" his mother screamed.

"Aw, they put the hat on'im," said the father, deprecating the incident now with a shrug.

"Oh," said his mother, vaguely satisfied, then turned to Vince who was leaning against the divan. "Don't sit on that arm, you'll break it; what's the matter, why'n'cha put cereal in your bowl so's you'll be ready when your brother gets back with the milk? Go on now, I want you to help me today with the wash. Tell'im, Ed." She turned to the father who wiped his mouth and started talking at once to Vince: "Awright, yer gonna help yer mother today, y'unnerstan', yer gonna help—"

At this moment, the door opened and Sid came in carrying a

newspaper and a carton of milk in a sack. He placed them both on the table.

"They traded Heinke to the Giants," he said as he walked into the kitchen.

"What?" said the mother. "You lookin' for coffee, coffee's on the table."

The father grunted noncommittally, and Vince picked up the paper. "Free West Pledges Asian Defense," the banner read.

The father stood up, stretched himself grotesquely, as Vince started going through the paper, page by page. Nothing, nothing, nothing.

His mother was watching the father. "There's hot water on the stove," she said to him, "you had your shave already, don't take any more than you have to, I need it for the wash."

The father belched heavily, yawned, and started out of the room. "Who'd they get?" he said toward Sid in the kitchen.

At the lot Nick sat alone near the sidewalk, leaning against a refuse mound, munching a jelly roll as he slowly turned the pages of a fresh comic-book. Behind him, in the farthest reaches of the lot, the little boy with the giant pistol raced about in desperate, secret play.

At a near-by sound Nick raised his eyes momentarily, turning another page. Three boys were coming down the street past the lot. Their talk was loud and quarrelsome. They all seemed about Nick's age, but one of the boys was a head taller than the others. Nick looked at them briefly and then back down at his comic-book, finishing the jelly roll in two large bites. In another minute he was aware that the three boys had stopped talking and were standing on the curb watching him, but he didn't look up.

"Hey, kid," said the tall boy after glancing around the deserted block. Nick continued to stare at the comic-book, finally turning another page.

"Maybe he don't hear so good," said the tall boy, speaking to the others.

"Maybe he oughtta have his ears cleaned out a little," said the second boy.

They watched him silently, until Nick raised his eyes.

"You talkin' to me?" he asked.

"He wants to know if I'm talking to *him*," said the tall boy.

"He's nosey, ain't he?" said the third boy, making his voice mockingly shrill and effeminate.

"*C'mere,*" said the tall boy to Nick.

Nick slowly got up and walked toward them, folding the comic-book and stuffing it in his pocket.

"What's the matter?" he asked before he got there.

"*What's-the-matter,*" echoed the third boy in his taunting falsetto. "He wants to know what's-the-matter. Show'im what's-the-matter, Gino."

"Yeath, get Gino to show'im what's-the-matter," said the second boy.

Nick had stopped just out of arm's length. The tall boy raised a finger and motioned him forward as for something confidential, while the other two boys moved out on both sides of Nick, blocking his escape in either direction.

"What's that you stuck in your pocket?" asked the tall boy.

"What, this?" said Nick, taking out the comic-book and offering it to him. "Here, you can have it, I finished it awready."

"Oh, get that," said the third boy, "he finished it awready."

Nick glanced down the street toward where Vince and Ritchie lived. It was deserted, except for a man walking idly along in the distance.

"Expecting somebody?" asked the second boy.

Nick started to put the comic-book back in his pocket, having held it extended for some time.

"Gimme," said the tall boy, and Nick handed it over.

As the man approaching reached the spot where they were standing, the three boys fell silent, trying to assume casual attitudes while he passed. Nick, however, took advantage of the opportunity and tried to walk away. One of the boys grabbed his arm and the other two closed in, as the man, a few paces beyond, stopped, turned and slowly retraced his steps.

The three boys glared at the stranger with open hostility. He was a man of medium height and slight, wiry build, dapperly dressed and deeply tanned. Hatless, with a thick close-crop of silver-gray hair, he resembled one of those veteran movie actors who must keep trim and tanned to continue playing youthful, athletic roles. There was an extreme hardness about his eyes and mouth, however, and an unlit cigarette hung from his lips, so that perhaps more than an actor he looked like the romantic version of a highly successful criminal.

When he spoke to the boys, after a moment of silence, his voice was low and cold, with a slight, foreign accent.

"*Okay*," he said. "Beat it!"

The tall boy, half turning his head away, raised a hand derisively, muttering something like "Na-a-ah!" as though he couldn't be bothered even slapping the older man, whereupon an extraordinary thing happened: with an animal-quick movement, the man seized the tall boy's hand at the extended fingers, and in an abrupt, judo-like twist sent him writhing to his knees, at the same time slapping him across the face with such resounding force that he cringed like a wounded cat.

"I din' do nothin'!" he shrieked, "I din' do nothin'!" while the other two boys, frozen wide-eyed for a moment, broke and ran.

"That's my book he's got," said Nick piously, pointing at the comic-book that lay at the tall boy's feet.

"Why don't you give him back his book?" asked the man, twisting the arm so mercilessly the tall boy's free hand trembled as he handed the book up to Nick.

"Now, beat it," said the man, giving the arm a last vicious twist and poising his raised foot to show his willingness to kick out the tall boy's teeth if necessary. "*Fast*," he said softly, and the tall boy scrambled to his feet and fled, visibly shaking with sobs.

"Thanks," said Nick, very impressed, as the man lit his cigarette and glanced easily around the lot.

"You got nothing better to do?" said the man, referring with a nod to the comic-book in Nick's hand.

"Why, how'd you mean?" asked Nick, putting the book away, a little embarrassed.

The man shrugged and continued casually to survey the lot.

"Know where I could find the Panthers?" he asked after a pause.

Nick regarded him suspiciously.

"Why, what'd you want them for?"

"I thought I might put a little work their way," said the man.

"Yeah. What kinda work?"

"*Easy* work."

"I guess they'd wantta know what kinda work," said Nick.

The man smiled, as though Nick were too young to be trusted in these matters. "Well," he said, "I guess I'd wantta talk to *them* about that, wouldn't I?" He reached into his shirt pocket and lifted out the corner of a heavy fold of currency. "But it'd be *easy* work," he said.

"Well, you can keep talkin', mister," said Nick, "'cause you're talkin' to one of 'em right now, and the other two'll be here in a minute."

The man brightened slightly. "Oh," he said. "Well, that's great. Glad to know you."

He took Nick's hand in a firmly clasped handshake, at the same time raising his left in a signal toward one of the cars parked on the opposite side of the street a few doors away, and two other, more obvious plainclothes detectives got out and walked over to them.

"This is one of them," said the man. "Put him in the car and keep him quiet. The other two will be along. I'll give you a sign."

"Awright, eat'cher cereal now," Vince's mother was saying. "I wantta get started with my wash."

Vince was not listening, but having turned over the last page of the paper, he threw it aside so savagely that the movement startled and annoyed his mother, and she unleashed a torrent of sardonic bitterness against him.

"What's the matter with you? Somethin' in the paper you din' like? What's the matter, din' get your pitcher in the paper? What's the matter, din' get your name in the paper? What's the ma—"

"No!" shouted Vince, jumping to his feet. "No! No!"

His shouts set both babies crying, and his mother, enraged, began to hit at him wildly. At the same moment, he heard Ritchie calling his name from below and he made for the door.

"Where you think you're goin'?" his mother demanded, fiercely holding his arm. "You heard what your father told you! Ed! Ed!"

Vince shoved her aside and got out the door, but there was a look of apprehension on his face, as though he already knew that something was very seriously wrong.

On the stairs, leaning out over the stairwell, he could see Ritchie's face two flights below. Even at the distance it seemed livid and panicky.

They met on a dark landing halfway down the stairs.

"Vince," said Ritchie, breathlessly, "He's—he's *dead.*"

Vince was confused, not wanting to believe it. "What—how—how'd you know that?"

"At the store," said Ritchie, beginning to cry as he sensed Vince's helplessness. "They're all talkin' about it—they got a wreath up awready—they said he . . . *suffocated!*"

The voice of Vince's mother came down the stairwell, strident and loud.

"Vince! Vince!"

The two boys moved back against the dark wall, looking small and huddled now.

"What're we goin' to do, Vince?" asked Ritchie.

"C'mon," said Vince at last, hopelessly, "we . . . we gotta get over to the lot and see Nick."

At the lot the detective stood alone, smoking, looking down the street, waiting. It seemed very quiet.

Suddenly, rushing out from behind a heap of refuse, the little boy with the giant pistol was upon him.

"Kow! Kow! Kow!" he cried.

The detective was slightly taken aback, then he smiled wanly as the little boy seized his trouser leg and clung to it, holding the gun aloft in his outstretched hand.

"Kow. Kow."

They were standing like that, in that strange embrace, the detective looking down with a certain sadness in his eyes as he stroked the boy's head, and the tiny boy clinging to his leg, his face half hidden against it, voice muffled, wearily repeating, "Kow, kow, kow," when the little girl with the cloth doll appeared down the sidewalk near the lot. Slowly approaching, carrying her cloth doll on one arm, she raised her eyes and saw them, gave them a serious look, and turned away in a wide arc to pass, cradling the doll in both arms now, shielding it from their sight.

The Road
Out of
Axotle

THERE'S AN INTERESTING ROAD leading south out of Axotle, Mexico, that you might like to try sometime. It isn't on the Good Gulf Map, and it isn't on those issued by the Mexican Government. It is on one map—I wonder if you've seen it?—a map of very soft colors, scroll-edged, like some great exotic banknote; and the imprint of the publisher is in small black script along the lower left, "Ryder H. Raven and Son—San Jose, California." I came across it about a year ago.

The way it happened, I was with these two friends of mine in Mexico City—I say friends of mine though actually we'd met only a few days before, but anyway we were together this particular night, in their car—and the idea was to pick a town, such as the one we were in, and then to sort of drive away from it, in the opposite direction, so to speak. I knew what they had in mind, more or less, but it did seem that in being this strong on just-wanting-to-get-away-from, we might simply end up in the sea or desert. Then, too, at one point there was a kind of indecision as to the actual direction to take, like left or right—so I suggested that we look at a map. I knew there was a map in the car, because I had been with them earlier in the day when one of them, Emmanuel, bought a secondhand guidebook, of the kind that has folding maps in it.

"That is good, man," said the other one, who was driving, Pablo.

That was the way they talked, "That is good, man"; "This is bad, man." They were from Havana, and they spoke a fine, foppish sort of Spanish, but their English wasn't the greatest. Still, they insisted on speaking it, despite the fact that my own Spanish was good—in fact, the Mexican dialect part of it was so good that they preferred me to speak, whenever it was necessary, to the Mexicans—and it pleased their vanity to argue that, if *I* spoke, it was less obvious we were tourists.

Emmanuel got the guidebook from the glove compartment now and handed it to me in the backseat. We were at a corner southwest of the town, out beyond the stockyards and the slaughterhouse—at a crossroads. There was nothing happening here, only the yellow light from an arc lamp above, the yellow light that came dying down through the dead gauze of red dust which slowly rose and wound, or so it seemed, and bled around the car. That was the setting.

I had some trouble finding the right map and finally in seeing it, distracted, too, by the blast of California mambo from the radio; and it was then, while I was trying to hold the book up in a way to get more light, that something fell out of it.

"Let me see your lighter a minute, Pablo."

"What? What is?" He turned the radio down, just a bit. Sometimes he got quite excited if he heard his name.

What had fallen from the book was a map of Mexico, a map which had evidently been put there by the book's previous owner. One may say this because it was obvious the map was not a part of the guidebook; it was not of the same school of map making as were the maps in the guidebook. It was like something from another era, not handmade but somehow in that spirit: highly individual. It was large, but not as large as the ones given out by the gasoline stations —nor was it square; when opened, it was about eighteen by twenty-four inches, and was scaled 1:25.

The paper was extraordinarily thin—Bible paper, but much stronger, like rice paper or bamboo—and it was hazed with the slightest coloration of age which seemed to give a faint iridescence to those soft colors. They were Marie Laurencin colors, and it was like that as well, a map for a child, or a very nice woman.

"Where we are at this time?" asked Emmanuel, in a shout above the radio. Emmanuel was a year or two older than Pablo, and about one degree less self-centered.

I had looked at the map a few minutes without attempting the analogy, just tracing electric-blue rivers to cerulean seas, as they say, but I did know where we were, of course; and, almost at the same time, I saw where it might be interesting to go.

"Make a right," I said.

"A right, man," said Emmanuel. "Make a right." They had a habit of repeating and relaying things to each other for no apparent reason.

Pablo gave a sigh, as of pain, as though he had known all along that's how it would be, and he lurched the car around the corner, sliding it like a top over the soft red dust, and up went the radio.

I continued to look at the map. We were going due west, and the map showed that about twenty miles ahead, on this same road, was a little town called Axotle. The road ran through the town east-west and then joined a highway, and this seemed to be all there was to it. But holding the lighter quite close, I had seen another road, a narrow, winding road, as thin as the blood vein of an eye, leading south out of the town. It seemed to go for about twenty-five miles, and on it there were two other towns, Corpus Christi and San Luiz, and there the road stopped. A blood-vein, dead-end road, with a town at the end of it; that was the place to go all right.

Pablo drove like a madman, except that he was quite a good driver actually. He was supposed to be upset, though, about not having found the kind of car he wanted to drive in Mexico. His story—or rather, his-story-through-Emmanuel, since Pablo himself didn't do much talking—was that he had a Mercedes at home and had been looking for a certain kind of car to drive in Mexico, a Pegaso, perhaps, but had finally bought this car we were in now, a '55 Oldsmobile, which had three carburetors and was supposed to do 145 on a straightaway, though, of course, there weren't too many of those.

"Man, this old wagon," he kept saying, "I dunt dig it."

But he drove it like the veritable wind, making funny little comments to himself and frowning, while Emmanuel sat beside him, wagging his closed-eyes head, shaking his shoulders and drumming his fingers along with the radio, or else was all hunched over in twisting up sticks of tea and lighting them. Sometimes he would sing along with the radio, too; not overdoing it, just a couple of shouts or a grunt.

We pulled in then at a Gulf station for gas. We were about halfway to Axotle now, and I was looking at the map again, outside the car, standing under the light of the station, when it suddenly occurred to me to check with the more recent map of the guidebook to see if perhaps the town had been built up in the last few years; it would put me in an embarrassing position with my new friends if we drove to the end of the line, only to smash headlong into a hot-dog stand. So I got out the guidebook and found a map of the corresponding region—quite detailed it was—and that was when the initial crevice of mystery appeared, because on this map there was *no* road leading south out of Axotle; there was only the east-west road which joined the highway. No road south and neither of the towns. I got a map then from the service station. It was a regular road map about two feet square, and was supposed to show every town with a population of 250 or more . . . and the crevice became the proverbial fissure.

"This is bad, man," said Emmanuel, when I told him. Pablo didn't say anything, just stood there, scowling at the side of the car. Emmanuel and Pablo were both wearing dark prescription glasses, as they always did, even at night.

"No, man," I said, "this is *good*. They're ghost towns . . . you dig? That will be interesting for you."

Emmanuel shrugged. Pablo was still frowning at the car.

"Ghost towns," I said, getting into the backseat again. "Sure, that's very good."

Then, as we got under way, Emmanuel turned to sit half-facing me, his back against the door, and he began to warm toward the idea, or was perhaps beginning to understand it.

"Yeah, man, that is very *good*." He nodded seriously. "Ghost town. *Crazy*."

"It is very good, man," he told Pablo, while the radio wailed and the car whined and floated over the long black road.

"What is this, man," Pablo demanded then in his abrupt irate way, half-turning around to me, "this goat town?"

"Goat town! Goat town!" shouted Emmanuel, laughing. "That's too much, man!"

"Man, I dunt dig it!" said Pablo, but he was already lost again, guiding his big rocket to the moon. And I lay back on the seat and dozed off for a while.

When I woke up, it was as though I had been on the edge of waking for a long time; the car was pitching about oddly, and I had half-fallen from the seat. The radio was still blasting, but behind it now was the rasping drone of Pablo's cursing. And I lay there, listening to that sound; it was like a dispassionate chant, a steady and unlinked inventory of all the profane images in Spanish. I assumed we had gotten off the road, except we seemed to be going unduly fast for that. Then I saw that Emmanuel had his hands up to his mouth and was shaking with laughter, and I realized that this had been going on for some time, with him saying softly over and over, "Man, dig this . . . *road!* Dig this . . . *road!*"

So I raised up to have a look, and it was pretty incredible all right. It was more of a creek bed than a road, but occasionally there would be an open place to the side . . . a gaping, torn-off place that suggested we were on something like a Greek mountain pass. And then I saw as well, dishearteningly so, why we were going fast; it was because every now and then one of the side pockets stretched right up to the middle of the road, so that the back wheels would pull to that side, spinning a bit, as we passed over it. And, as we passed over it, you could see down . . . for quite a long way.

"What do you think it's like to the side?" I asked.

Emmanuel finally controlled his curious mirth long enough to turn around. "What do *I* think it's like?" he asked. "Man, it's *lions and tigers!* And . . . *big* . . . *pointy rocks!* Why? What do *you* think it's like?" And fairly shouting with laughter, he handed me another joint.

"*Goats,*" said Pablo with grotesque snicker. "There are the goats there."

"All right, man," I said, and lay back with a groan to express my disquiet.

Pablo snorted. "Man, I'm swingin'!" he said, reassuringly.

Emmanuel broke up completely now and laid his head down laughing. "Pablo's swingin'!" he cried. He could hardly speak. He had to hold onto the rocking dashboard to keep from falling to the floorboards. "Ma-a-an, Pablo is . . . too . . . much!"

It was too much all right. I lay there smoking, my thoughts as bleak as the black rolling top I stared at, though gradually I did discern, or so it seemed, a certain rhythm and control taking hold of the erratic pitching of the car, and the next time I sat up the road, too, seemed in fairly good shape.

The moon had come out and you would get glimpses now and then of things alongside—strange dwarf trees and great round rocks, with patches of misty landscape beyond. It was just about then that the headlight caught a road sign in the distance, a rickety post akimbo with a board nailed to it (or maybe tied with a strand of vine) across which was painted, crudely to be sure, *"Puente,"* which, in these circumstances, would mean toll bridge.

"Crazy road," I heard Pablo say.

There was a bend in it just after the sign, and the glow of a kerosene lamp ahead—which proved to be from the window of an old tin shack; and in front of the shack there was a barrier across the road: a large, fairly straight tree limb. Beyond it, vaguely seen, was the small, strange bridge.

When we had stopped by the shack, we could see that there was someone inside, sitting at a table; and, after waiting a minute while nothing happened, Pablo jerked his head around at me.

"You make it, man," he said, handing me his billfold, "I can't make these greaser."

"Very well," I said, "you rotten little Fascist spic." And as I got out of the car I heard him explaining it again to Emmanuel: "Man, I can't make these greaser."

Inside the shack, the lamp was full up; but, with the chimney as jagged and as black as a crater, I couldn't see too much of the room's appointments—only a shotgun leaning against the wall near the door, the barrel so worn and rust-scraped that it caught the yellow light in glints harder than brass. But I could see him all right—bigger than life, you might say, very fat, his sleeves twisted up, playing with cards. There was a bottle half filled with tequila on the table. I remember this because it occurred to me then, in a naïve, drug-crazed way, that we might have a pleasant exchange and finish off with a drink.

"Good evening," I said (with easy formality), then followed it up with something colloquial like, "what's the damage?"

He was squinting at me, and then beyond, to the car. And I recall first thinking that here was a man who had half lost his sight playing solitaire by a kerosene lamp; but he was something else as well, I realized, when I took it all in: he was a man with a *very* sinister look to him. He was smoking a homemade cigar, gnarled and knotted enough to have been comic, except that he kept baring his teeth around it, teeth which appeared to have been filed—and by humanity at large, one might presume, from the snarl with which he spoke, as he finally did:

"Where are you trying to go?"

"Corpus Christi," I said.

It occurred to me that it might be less involved, not to say cheaper, if I didn't divulge our full itinerary.

"Corpus Christi, eh?" He smiled, or it was something like a smile; then he got up, walked to the door, glanced at the car, spat out some of his cigar, and walked back to the table. "Five dollars a head," he said, sitting down again.

"Five dollars," I said, more in a thought aloud than a question, "Mexican dollars."

He made a sound, not unlike a laugh, and took up the cards again.

"You think you're Mexican?" he asked after a minute, without raising his head.

I had to consider it briefly. "Oh, I see—you mean, 'a-fool-and-his-money . . .' that sort of thing."

"You said it, my friend, I didn't."

"Yes. Well, you'll give me a receipt, of course."

"Receipt?" He laughed, spitting and wiping his mouth on his arm. "This isn't Monterrey, you know."

I hesitated, determined for the moment, in the responsibility to the rest of my party, not to be so misused; then I put my hands on the edge of the table and leaned forward a little. "I think you've probably picked the *wrong* crowd this time, Pancho," I said.

Whereas, actually, it was *I* who had picked the wrong party, for he laid his head back laughing with this—and an unpleasant laugh it was, as we know.

"Pancho," he said, getting up, "that's funny." Still laughing and wiping his hand across his mouth, his eyes half shut so that I couldn't quite see where he was looking, he walked around the table. "That's very funny," he said.

And you can appreciate how for a moment it was like a sequence in a film, where someone is supposed to be laughing or scratching his ear, and suddenly does something very aggressive to you—except that I stepped back a little then, and he walked on past me to the door . . . where it seemed my show of apprehension had given him not so much a fresh lease as a veritable deed on confidence.

"*You* don't need a receipt," he said, turning from the door, his eyes still two smoked slits, "you can trust me." Then he flicked his cigar with an air and gave his short, wild laugh, or cough, as it were. But when he faced the car again, he sobered quickly enough. And Emmanuel and Pablo were sitting there, peering out, frowning terribly.

"What have you got inside?" he asked, and his tone indicated this might be the first of several rare cards he intended.

Somehow I felt it would not do to involve my friends, so I started reaching for the money.

He kept a cold, smoky silence as he watched me count it out. Then he took it, leaning back in the smug, smiling, closed-eyes strain against cigar smoke and the effort of pressing the loot deep into his tight trousers.

"Yes," I said. "Well, thanks for everything."

He grunted, then stepped out and raised the barrier. I started to get into the car, but he said something and turned back into the shack, motioning me with him.

"Wait," he said, as a quick afterthought, and from one dark side of the room he came up holding a cigar box.

"You want to buy some good marijuana?"

"What?"

"Marijuana," he said, letting the word out again like a coil of wet rope, and proffering the lid-raised box for my inspection.

"Very good," he said, "the best."

I leaned forward for a look and a sniff. It didn't appear to be the greatest; in fact, it didn't appear to be Mexican—and it looked like it was about fifteen years old.

"What is it, a spice of some kind?"

"Very good," he said.

"How much?"

"How much will you give?"

I took a pinch and tasted it.

He nodded toward the car. "Perhaps your friends. . . . I'll make you a good price. You tell me your price, I'll make you a good price. Okay?"

I stared at the box for a minute, then made an eccentric grimace. "You don't mean . . . you don't mean marijuana . . . the loco weed? What, to smoke?" I shook my head vigorously, backing away. "No, thanks!" I said, while his face went even more sour than one might have expected.

"Come back when you grow up!" he snarled, shutting the box; and for the first time, as he turned into the shadow of the shack, he seemed slightly drunk.

The bridge itself was noteworthy. A bit longer than the car, but not a foot wider, it consisted of oil drums held together with barbed wire and covered with wooden planks, only the outer two of which seemed at all stationary. The device was secured at each bank by a rope attached to stakes driven into the ground.

We held back a few seconds before embarking, taking it all in. Then, as we crossed over, the whole thing sank about two feet, completely out of sight, swaying absurdly, as the black water rose up in swirls just above the running boards.

Nobody commented on the bridge; though once we were across, onto the road, and I was resting on the seat again, Emmanuel said:

"What happened back with the greaser, man?"

"Five dollars a head."

"That swine."

"That rotten greaser swine," said Pablo.

"You said it," I said, closing my eyes. I had not gotten to bed the night before; I was thinking, too, of a certain time-honored arrangement in Mexico whereby a cigar box full of marijuana is sold to a foreigner and then retrieved by the merchant at customs. I once heard that the amount of annual foreign revenue so gained in the consequent fines is second only to that from the tax on the shade-and-barrier seats at the bullfight. And I soon began to wonder, here on the soft-focus margin of sleep, how many, many times that particular box I just looked at had been sold. Ten? Twenty? How many miles? How many missions? Fifty missions to Laredo, and they would decorate the box and retire it. And smoke it. But, of course, it was no good. Why would they use anything good for a scheme like that? No, it would be like those bundles of newspaper money left for kidnapers; I suppose they send to New Jersey for it. Anyway, I decided not to mention the incident to my friends; it would only excite them unduly.

I must have been asleep when we reached Corpus Christi, because when I came up again to have a look, the car was already stopped. We were in the middle of the square, and Emmanuel was saying: "Man, dig this . . . *scene*. Dig this . . . *scene*," while Pablo was just sitting there, leaning forward over the wheel, his arms hanging to each side of it.

The town, if it may so be called, is simply this square of one-story frame buildings, fronted all around by a raised, wooden, sidewalk arcade. Besides the car we were in, there were two or three others parked in the square along with several small wagons that had mules or donkeys hitched to them.

"Now, this is your true Old West, Pablo," I began. "Notice the attempt at a rather formal—" But what *I* had failed to notice was that the shadowed arcades, all around the square, were lined with people. They were leaning against the storefronts, and lying on the wooden sidewalk, or sitting on the raised edge of it—not just grown people, but children as well; children, a number of whom were to be seen crawling about, in the manner of the very young indeed. This struck me as odd because it was now about two o'clock in the morning. But what was really more odd was the pure, unbroken torpor which seemed to overhang the crowd. For a large group of people—perhaps 200—their inactivity was marvelous to look upon, like an oil painting. It seemed that all of them were leaning, sitting, or lying down; and it was not apparent that they were even talking to each other. And here and there was someone with a guitar, his head down, as though playing for only himself to hear.

As I was speculating about the possible reasons for this, my attention was suddenly caught by something that was happening to a wall nearby, the side of one of the buildings—it seemed to be soundlessly crumbling, and I thought now I must be out of my skull entirely. But it was not crumbling, it was simply oozing and changing color all over, *green*, and shades of green, changing from one instant to the next, from bottle-dark to shimmering-Nile; and this, in a strange and undulating way. Had we been in Rockefeller Plaza or the Gilbert Hall of Science . . . but here there was no accounting for it. And while I was assuring myself that first-rate hallucinations are only doubted in retrospect . . . Emmanuel saw it too. I knew he had seen it because he quickly leaned forward and began changing the radio stations. Then he turned around with an odd look on his face.

"Man, what is that? On that wall."

"Well," I said, "it must be *oil* . . . or something like that."

"Oil? Man, that's not oil. What's happening? That wall is *alive*."

"Listen, let me get out of the car for a minute," I said, perhaps because of his tone. "I'm . . . curious, as a matter of fact, to see what it is myself."

As I got out of the car, I felt that if I took my eyes off the wall for a second, when I looked back it would have become just an ordinary wall—so I kept looking at it, and walked toward it then, very deliberately until I was there, leaning forward from two feet away to peer at it; and while I must have known before, it was not until my face was six inches from the wall that the field finally did narrow to the truth, a single moving inch: a green roach. For, true enough, that's how it was: alive—with a hundred thousand green-winged flying roaches, ever moving, back and forth, sideways and around, the wings in constant tremulous motion.

I looked around at the people then, sitting and leaning nearby. I started to say something—but I was distracted to see that they as well were covered with the roaches . . . not in quite the profusion of the wall, but only for the reason that from time to time they passed a hand in front of their faces, or shrugged. So I was not too surprised when I looked down at myself and saw that *I*, too, even as they and the immobile wall . . . and then I heard the sound, that which had been in the air all along—a heavy ceaseless whirring sound—and it was a sound which deepened intensely in the dark distance of the night above and around, and it seemed to say: "*You think there are quite a few of us down there—but if you only knew how many of us are out here!*"

I thought I understood why the people weren't talking: because the roaches would get in their mouths; or sleeping: because they would crawl up their noses. But I may have really felt that it was not so much because of this, but because of something else, past or impending.

I stuck my trousers into my socks, and my hands into my pockets, and started back to the car. I had heard about the green flying roaches, how they settle on a town like locusts, and now I felt a gleeful anticipation, like the first of a party to swim an icy stream—toward springing the phenomenon on Pablo and Emmanuel. I thought it might be good to pretend to have scarcely noticed: "What, those? Why, those are bugs, man. Didn't you ever see a bug before?"

When I got back to the car, however, I saw they had already surmised. Indeed, half the car was covered: the windshield wipers were sweeping, and inside, Pablo and Emmanuel were thumping wildly against the side-glass in trying to jar the creatures off.

"You finicky spics!" I shouted, snatching the door open and pretending to scoop and fan great armfuls in on them. Emmanuel jerked the door closed, and locked it; then he rolled the window a crack, and raised his mouth to it: "Man, what's happening?" he asked and quickly closed the glass.

I stood outside, gesticulating them out and pretending to shout some emergency information. Pablo had started the car, and was racing the engine, sitting all hunched over the wheel; I got a glimpse of his maniacal frown and it occurred to me that an experience like this might be enough to snap his brain.

After a second, Emmanuel rolled down the window just a bit again.

"Listen, man," he said, "we are going to drive over nearer to the bar, so we can make it into the bar—you know?"

I looked around the square. So they had already found the bar. None of the buildings had signs on them, but I suppose it wasn't too difficult to tell. I saw it then, too, on the side we had come in, and next to it, a café.

"Let's go to the café first," I said, "that would be much cooler."

Emmanuel nodded, and as I turned away, I knew he would be relaying it to Pablo: "The café first, man, that's much cooler."

We reached the door of the café at the same time, and went right in.

It was an oblong room, with a hard dirt floor and raw-wood walls; there were about ten tables, set two by two the length of the place—bare boards they were, nailed to four sticks, and accompanied by benches. We sat at the first one, near the door.

The place was not quite empty. There was a man, who was evidently the proprietor, sitting at a table at the end of the room, and a man who was evidently drunk, sitting at a table on the opposite side. The man who was drunk had his head down on the table, resting it there as in sleep; his head kept sliding off the table, causing him to shake and curse it, and then to replace it carefully, while the proprietor sat across the room, watching him. I construed the situation as this: that the proprietor was ready to close, and was waiting for the drunk to leave; this possibility seemed strengthened by the way he simply remained seated when we came in, staring at us until we ordered some coffee. When he had brought it, he went directly back to his table and sat down, there to resume watch on the drunk. There seemed to be a point of genuine interest for him in watching the drunk's head slide off the table. I noticed that it did, in fact, drop lower each time.

There were fewer roaches here, though still enough so that you might want to keep your hand over the coffee, or, in drinking it, hold it as though you were lighting a cigarette in the wind. Pablo didn't drink his coffee, however, and didn't bother to protect it, so that after a minute there were four roaches in it, thrashing about, not unlike tiny birds at bath. Whenever one of the roaches was scooped out to the rim of the cup, it would crawl along for an instant, fluttering like a thing possessed, and then jump back in. Pablo was poking about in the cup with a matchstick, and both he and Emmanuel regarded the roaches with manifest concern. Pretty soon they were talking about them as though they could distinguish one from another. "Dig this one, man, he's swinging!"

"Don't hold him under, man, he can't make it like that!"

For my own part, I was content to watch the drunk and the proprietor, and this was as well, for, very soon, there was a bit of action. The drunk straightened up and started looking around the room. When his eyes reached our party they stopped, and after a minute, he leaned toward us and vomited.

I turned to get the proprietor's reaction to this, he who was sitting, somewhat more stiffly in his chair now, still staring at the drunk, and frowning. Then he gave a short humorless laugh, and said in measured tones:

"Let's-see-you-do-that-again."

This caused the drunk to stop looking at us, and to turn around to the proprietor as though he hadn't seen him before; and after staring straight at him, he laid his head back down on the table.

The proprietor slapped the table and gave several short, barking laughs, then resumed his scrutinous vigil.

During this vignette, Pablo and Emmanuel had abandoned their cups, which, I saw now, were crowded with the drowned.

"Well, that seems to be that," I said, "shall we go to the bar?"

"Man, let's cut out of this place," said Emmanuel.

Pablo, with deeply furrowed brow, was staring at where the man had been sick. Finally he shook his shoulders violently.

"Man, I dunt dig . . . *vomit!*"

"Are you kidding?" I said, "I happen to know that you *do* dig good greaser vomit."

The remark amused Emmanuel. "Ha-ha-ha! Good greaser vomit! Pablo digs good greaser vomit! That's too much, man!"

"Listen," said Pablo, leaning forward in serious confidence, "let's go to the bar now, I think there are groovy chicks there."

Like the café, the bar was unpretentious; but, where the café had been sparse and fairly lighted, the bar was close and steeped in shadow—sinister enough, as dark places go, but there wasn't much happening, at least not to meet the eye. A few men at the tables, a few beat hustlers at the bar.

My friends, being at the head of our party now, chose a table in the very heart of things, and we ordered tequila.

Emmanuel nodded toward the bar, straightening his tie.

"See, man," he said, giving me a little nudge, "dig the chicks."

"Sure," I said, "you're swinging." Pablo kept involuntarily clearing his throat and making sporadic little adjustments to his person and attire, even touching his hair once or twice. But after a moment or two, this fidgeting turned into annoyance that the girls, though they had seen us come in, had not made a play; so very soon, he and Emmanuel got up and took their drinks to the bar.

The girls, there were four of them, appeared to be extremely beat—two, by way of example, not wearing shoes—and were each holding a glass, untouched it seemed, of dark brown drink.

It was interesting to see them and my friends at a distance, not hearing, only seeing the gestures of hands and mouth, the flash of teeth and the tilted glass—man at an ancient disadvantage.

Sipping my tequila, I began to pretend I had settled down around here—quite near the toll bridge, actually. And a few days after my arrival, there had been a nasty run-in with the fat road-block greaser, who, it developed, was loathed and feared throughout the region, and was known as "Pigman." I heard the hushed whispers of the gathering crowd:

"Good Lord! The stranger's smashed his face away!"

"Did you see *that*—a single blow from the stranger sent the Pigman reeling!"

"Smashed his face entirely away! Good Lord!" Etc., etc.

I was going along with variations on this, when Pablo and Emmanuel came back to the table, sullen now and unrequited.

"Man, those chicks are the *worst*," Emmanuel said, as they sat down, "let's cut out of this place."

Pablo was looking as though he might black out momentarily.

When I asked what had happened, it was to learn that the girls had said they weren't working tonight, that they *never* worked on Tuesday night (or whatever night it was—it wasn't Sunday) and to come back tomorrow.

I took another look at them, and whatever rationale was behind their refusal, they were evidently satisfied with it, though it was obvious they could have made their entire month off my madcap friends.

As we rose in leaving though, one of them raised her dark glass in a toast of promise, and tomorrow.

Now we were off for the second lost city: San Luiz. It would be ten or twelve miles along the road that had brought us, so we recrossed the square and drove out on the opposite side we had come in.

The road here was just two tracks across a flat, rock-strewn plain. In five minutes we were in wilderness again, and after ten miles or so, when we finally reached the place where the town was supposed to be, the road stopped dead, at an extraordinary wire fence—a fence about seventeen feet high and made of wire mesh the size of quarter-inch rope. We got out to have a look.

The fence was topped by four running strands of an odd-looking barbed wire, jutting outward, and along this, at intervals, was a large, white, professional sign which said in Spanish:

KEEP OUT

VERY HIGH VOLTAGE

DANGER OF DEATH

Beyond the fence, a trace of the old road's continuation was visible in our headlights for about fifty feet, before it disappeared into the night. On our side of the fence the road branched out left and right, and it ran alongside the fence in both directions for as far as one could see.

With the idea now of driving *around* the fence and picking up the road again, we got back into the car and took the right branch, following it until, shortly, at a ravine, it turned away from the fence and back toward the town. Retracing our route, we took the other branch of the road; again, after an eighth of a mile or so, the road turned away from the fence and back to the town, while the fence itself disappeared in the heavy growth.

Here it seemed to me that one might follow the fence on foot, and while I didn't think we could actually do it, having no flashlight, I was eager to try. So we left the car and walked alongside the fence, on a field of rock and stubble, but it was immediately so dense as to be almost impassable. The thicket grew right into the fence, and the fence had evidently been there for quite a while. Emmanuel soon turned back toward the car.

"It's a drag, man," he said.

Pablo, who had wandered off to the left, kept stopping and brushing at his clothes.

"Man, what is this? This is all scratch."

Finally he stopped completely and began striking matches; he seemed to be examining something in his hand. I beat my way through the brush to him.

"Man, this is bad," he said, "this is all scratch."

He was examining what appeared to be an invisible scratch on his hand.

"I couldn't see it," I said as the match died, "is it bleeding?"

"Bleeding?" He struck another match. "Man, is it *bleeding? Where?"*

We both peered at his hand.

"It looks all right," I said, "doesn't it?"

"Man, I dunt *dig* this place? What is this?"

I suggested that he go back to the car and I would try to follow the fence a little farther.

I had become obsessed by the mystery of it. What was it behind this fence, in the vast area where one town used to exist and no town was supposed to? The fabulous estate of a mad billionaire? The testing ground for some fantastic weapon? Why had not the sign proclaimed the source of its authority? Why had it not strengthened itself with "Private Property," or "Government Property"? No, here was a case of security so elaborate, so resolved upon, that even the power behind it would remain secret. Whatever it was—was so dreadful it was not supposed to exist.

Many are familiar with the story that infant-mortality (in childbirth) is not the figure it is represented to be—and that the discrepancy between the actual figure and the statistics are teratological cases—with the consequence that in every Christian country there is a monster-home, wholly secret, maintained by permanent appropriation, in the form of a "hidden-rider," self-perpetuating, and never revealed by the breakdown of any budget.

As I mused on this, moving cautiously along the edge of the black fence, and now at a considerable distance from the car, I stumbled against a rock and fell; I grabbed at the dry brush, but the terrain had changed, dropping away sharply from the fence, as did I with it now, about fifteen feet down into a small gully. Here there was even less light than above, and as I sat there in pitch blackness, momentarily rubbing my forehead, I had a sudden uneasiness of something very menacing nearby and moving closer. And, as suddenly, I knew what it was.

Wild dogs have existed in Mexico for so long that they are a breed apart; the dissimilarity between them and ordinary dogs is remarkable. Wild dogs do not bark; the sound they produce comes from the uppermost part of the throat—a frantic and sustained snarl, and the strangeness of it is accentuated by its being directed *down,* for the reason that they run with their heads very low, nose almost touching the ground. Even in a pack, with blood dripping hot from their muzzles, they keep their backs arched and their tails between their legs. Their resemblance, in many ways, is less to the dog than to the hyena; they do not spring—their instinct is to chase a thing, biting at it, until it falls to break a leg . . . whereupon they hit it like piranha fish, taking bites at random, not going for the throat, but flaying it alive. It is improbable that wild dogs will attack a person who holds his ground—at least, so I was told later—so that it was a rather serious mistake that I began to run.

Through the snarls, before they caught me, I could hear the teeth snapping, as though they were so possessed by rage as to bite even the air itself. I half stumbled and turned when the first one bit the back of my leg and clung to it, in a loathsome knot, like a tarantula; I kicked it away violently, but so much more in a fit of repulsion than in adroitness that I took a nifty pratfall, there to grope for a frantic second or two for a rock or stick of defense, before scrambling to my feet again while being bitten again on the same leg. Exactly how many there were I don't know—at least six. I was bitten two or three times more, on the legs, before I fell again; and the bites, having come at just the moment before I fell, gave me the strong impression that they were now *closing in.*

But abruptly the scene was flooded with white light and the scream of twisting mambo, as our car came lurching and crashing down the ravine, headlights bouncing; then it suddenly stalled.

For an instant the action became a frozen tableau, the dogs petrified in strange attitudes of attack, and myself crouching at bay—a tableau at which my friends in the car simply sat and stared.

"Man, what's he doing?" I imagined Emmanuel saying. "Dig those weird *dogs.*"

And by the interior light of the car I could see Pablo's expression of exasperated amazement.

I was on the verge of shouting urgent instructions about completing my rescue, when Pablo, apparently at the end of his tether, began honking the horn wildly and lunged the car forward with a terrible roar, lights flashing—and the dogs scattered into the night.

"Come, man," said Pablo, gesturing impatiently, "we cut out now."

There was no sign of life as we crossed the square at Corpus Christi, so we drove on to the outskirts of Mexico City where we managed to rouse a doctor. He gave me a shot of tetanus, a couple of sutures, and some morphia tablets—which I had to share with Pablo and Emmanuel, after the doctor indignantly refused to sell them a hundred goofballs. Pablo was more indignant about it than the doctor, and as we drove away, he leaned out the window and shook his fist at the dark building:

"Go to devil, you greaser quack!" This broke Emmanuel up, but we got home without further incident.

My friends left the pension a few days after that, on a Sunday. I came out to the car and we shook hands lightly.

"You ought to make it," Emmanuel said. He had a thin, unlit cigar in his mouth. "Swinging chicks in Guadalajara, man."

"Guadalajara? I thought you were going to Acapulco."

"No, man, I don't think we'll go there. I don't think anything's happening there. Why? *You* want to go to *Acapulco?*"

"No," I said.

"How about Guadalajara? Crazy town, man."

"No, thanks."

Emmanuel nodded.

"Okay, man," he said.

Pablo raced the engine and leaned over the wheel, turning his head toward me; he looked like a progressive young missionary in his white linen suit and dark glasses.

"Later, man," he said.

"Yeah, man," said Emmanuel, "later."

"Later," I said.

They took off with a roar. At the corner, a very old woman with a great black shawl over her head, started across the street without looking. Pablo didn't slow down or perceptibly alter his course, and as she passed in front of the car, it looked like he missed her by the length of a matchstick. She hardly seemed to notice it though, only slowly turned her head after them, but by then they were almost out of sight.

So that was that; and the point of it all is, they left me the map—that is, should anyone ever care to make it, I mean, down to the big fence on that road out of Axotle.

Apartment to Exchange

CHARACTERS:

FRANZ KAFKA: About 34, of medium height, slender build, and with a thin, haunted, extremely sensitive face; he is carefully dressed in the dark-suited style of a provincial bank clerk. There is an odd stiff meticulousness and deliberation in his behavior, which convey the heightened self-awareness he has of his every word and movement.

FRAU KAFKA, his mother: A high-strung, possessive woman of about 55—not *nervous* in the usual sense of being "fidgety," but seemingly in a state of constant impatience, bordering on exasperation and often plunging into it.

DOCTOR FREUD: About 60, a large and dynamic man with silver hair and a beard of professorial cut. He is also dressed in a dark suit; but, unlike Kafka, his clothes seem baggy and unkempt, as if such matters of appearance were of trivial concern. He is exceedingly self-assured, at times almost blustering, speech loud and jovial, movements *sweeping* in the grand manner—and while he occasionally lapses into momentary meditative silence (thoughtfully stroking his beard) there is a certain bright shrewdness which equally often lights his face . . . a curious sort of twinkling calculation, whenever he chances to overhear a telling remark.

Scene One

Early evening. We are in the apartment in Prague which Kafka shares with his mother. It is a small living-room in excruciatingly middle-class taste: divan and matching armchair, several hideous lamps, a mantle clock and family-portraits, two or three grotesque vases and plaster figures, a landscape painting, a large souvenir seashell, a radio, a row of books, etc. Near the wall, stage left, is a small writing-desk.

Despite the bric-a-brac, diligent housekeeping has given the room (in certain half-lights) the illusion of neatness and order, even, perhaps, of coziness.

As the curtain rises we see FRAU KAFKA seated in the armchair, center stage, staring straight ahead and drumming her fingers impatiently on the arm of the chair. After a second she glances at the mantel clock (it is six o'clock); she sighs elaborately, and at that moment there is a sound of the door, stage right, being unlocked. FRAU KAFKA folds her arms, stares at the door. FRANZ enters.

FRAU KAFKA: [*In a cheery sing-song voice, barely disguising the hysteria beneath it:*] Lay-ate, Franz! You are *lay-ate!*

FRANZ: [*Frowns, glances at his watch, checking it against the mantel clock, and speaks with maniacal calm:*] No, you're wrong there, Mother. I left the office at 5:35; it is two minutes after six now; the 27 minutes were spent in walking to and from each of the bus termini [*raises a finger, adds smugly as though playing his trump card*] and . . . *and* on the bus itself. [*Softens, reasonable.*] If by "*late*" however you mean in a *figurative* sense, it may well be that certain interpretations . . . *interpretations,* may I say which have—

FRAU KAFKA: [*Interrupts by seizing her head in both hands and screaming:*] Franz!

[*She gets up, walks quickly over to him, demands:*] Did you place the ad?

FRANZ: [*He has begun to remove his coat.*] Yes.

FRAU KAFKA: [*Impatiently.*] Well, let me *see* it!

FRANZ: [*His coat half off, down over his arms and binding them, he glances at the newspaper protruding from the coat's sidepocket, is momentarily undecided whether to finish removing his coat before giving her the paper, or to draw the coat back on, in order to free his arms, and give her the paper now; he makes one or two false starts in each direction, then steadies himself and speaks decisively.*] I'll just take off the coat first.

FRAU KAFKA: [*Angrily.*] Franz!

FRANZ: Oh well. [*He draws his coat back on, extracts the paper from the pocket, hands it to her, and continues lamely.*] I'll give you the paper first, and then I'll [*his voice trails away to become almost inaudible as he removes coat and turns his back to the audience in hanging it up*] . . . take . . . off . . . the . . . coat.

FRAU KAFKA: [*Crossing to her chair with the paper, she sits down and unfolds it.*] Where? Where *is* it?

FRANZ: Page five, column two, under the heading "Apartments to Exchange." [*He looks about the room, uncertain what to do next, glances at his watch, checks it against the mantel clock, then crosses to the writing-desk, stage left, sits down, cautiously withdraws a small notebook from his breast coat pocket, opens it, and studies the page.*]

FRAU KAFKA: [*Avidly scrutinizing a small section of the paper.*] Where *is* it, Franz? There's nothing *here*! Nothing!

FRANZ: [*Calmly.*] It is the one entry, on page five, column two, under . . . [*he pauses and speaks tentatively*] . . . no, *beneath* . . . yes, *beneath* the heading "Apartments to Exchange."

FRAU KAFKA: *Good God!*

FRANZ: [*Speechless, he merely frowns, staring at his mother.*]

FRAU KAFKA: [*Incredulous.*] This . . . *this* is the ad you put in?

FRANZ: Naturally I can only assume you are referring to the entry which I indicated earlier in the conversation; if this is so—

FRAU KAFKA: [*Quite beside herself.*] *This* is what you spent all day yesterday and half the night writing and rewriting?

FRANZ: [*With soft, dreamy pride.*] There was some rewriting, granted, but I *think* you'll find that the—

FRAU KAFKA: Why, it's senseless! Senseless and incomprehensible!

FRANZ: If by 'senseless' you mean—

FRAU KAFKA: Good Lord, Franz, you've written and rewritten all meaning out of the thing!

FRANZ: [*With a frown of patience.*] You're wrong on that count, Mother . . . unless by "meaning" you want to imply that the—

FRAU KAFKA: You say "tersely parallax!" Why in God's name did you have to say a thing like that? [*She begins to read from the ad slowly, in outraged astonishment.*] "I think it is fair to imply, and yet by using the word 'imply' I would not wish to suggest, or rather to limit *the* suggestion to that of mere *suggestion*, even though in the strict sense of the word it may well . . ." [*She breaks off the reading and strikes her head in anguish.*] Oh God! *More money down the drain!*

FRANZ: [*With great patience.*] I realize that you speak in a metaphorical sense when you—

[*There is a knock at the door.*]

FRAU KAFKA: Well, get the *door!* Just stand up, walk over, and open it!

FRANZ: [*Uncertain whether to put his notebook on the desk or in his pocket, he thumbs through it briefly, then decisively lays it aside, gets up, goes for the door; halfway there, he returns abruptly to the desk, picks up the notebook as though to pocket it, has second thoughts about this, lays it aside again and goes to the door. His mother has buried her face in her hands in anguished exasperation.* FRANZ *speaks briskly.*] Right! [*He opens the door.* DOCTOR FREUD *enters.*]

DOCTOR FREUD: [*Grandly.*] You are Herr *Kafka?*

FRANZ: [*Firmly, after having considered it for a second.*] Yes. Yes, that is true.

DOCTOR FREUD: Good! I am Doctor Freud—Doctor Sigmund Freud! Of Vienna! I have come about the advertisement in today's paper *An apartment to exchange!* [*He scrutinizes* FRANZ, *twinkling.*]

FRANZ: Please come in. [DOCTOR FREUD *sweeps into the room.*]

FRAU KAFKA: [*Demanding.*] What is it, Franz?

FRANZ: [*Rather smugly.*] Only what one might have expected—a *response* to the advertisement, which, if I may say so, would seem to bear out my— [*Realizes he has not introduced them.*] I beg your pardon. This is my mother, this is Doctor . . . Doctor . . . I'm afraid I didn't get—

DOCTOR FREUD: [*Adjusting his spectacles, he studies* FRANZ *interestedly.*] *Afraid,* Franz? *Why* are you afraid? [*He turns to* FRAU KAFKA.] Doctor Sigmund Freud, Madame. Of Vienna! [*He takes her hand and bows with Old World grace.*]

FRAU KAFKA: [*Charmed.*] Gay Vienna!

DOCTOR FREUD: [*With jovial mischief.*] Ah yes, *Gay Vienna!* Heh-heh-heh! Yes, yes, quite so! [*He rubs his hands, savoring the image, adjusts his spectacles once more, studying* FRAU KAFKA.] And you are the *mother!* Yes, of course!

FRANZ: [*Musing gravely.*] All the way fron Vienna, and so *soon.* Granted I had certain hopes for the advertisement, and yet I never dreamed . . .

DOCTOR FREUD: [*Shrewdly.*] Never *what,* Franz? Hmmm?

FRANZ: [*Slightly taken aback.*] No, of course I wouldn't have *dreamed* it, would I? [*He laughs nervously.*] The image was unfortunate, granted, and yet—

DOCTOR FREUD: [*Interrupting, briskly.*] Now as I interpret your advertisement—and may I say [*smiles mischievously*] that *interpretation* is, hee-hee, scarcely my weakest suit—as *I* interpret that advertisement, you wish to exchange *this* apartment for a *larger* one, hmm? [*He eyes* FRANZ *significantly.*] And preferably in the same part of the city? Is that correct?

FRANZ: [*With care.*] Yes, in essence, or rather in substance, I think it is fair to say—

FRAU KAFKA: [*Very strongly.*] That is *precisely* correct, Doctor!

DOCTOR FREUD: [*He nods darkly.*] I see. [*He continues to study both for a moment, then shrugs, as though somewhat let down that they have apparently failed to grasp certain hidden meanings at hand; he begins pacing about the room, looking it over.*] Very well then, let's have a *look* at this room. Hmmm, yes, very . . . *compact!* Very *orderly!* Good, I'm *looking* for an orderly place. I have quite a few ideas that need *putting in order,* yes indeed, *quite a few!*

FRAU KAFKA: [*Piously.*] You'll find it a *clean* house, Doctor. I somehow manage that [*gives* FRANZ *a sharp look*] in spite of everything.

DOCTOR FREUD: [*Nodding agreement as he continues to pace about.*] Clean, yes . . . and [*stops to face them both, raising a finger and arching his brows as though to call attention to something overlooked*] *and* COZY! Eh? heh heh. Hmmm. Yes, small, clean, and *warm!* [*He glances from one to the other, twinkling.*] And when the lights are *out*, hmmm? . . . Then it's *dark* as well. [*Casually, but with a knowing smile.*] Small, dark, and warm. [*Directly to* FRANZ] *Nice*, a room like that, eh Franz?

FRANZ: [*After a second.*] Without pretending that my own opinion is necessarily definitive, I *do* think, or rather *do* have reason to think—that is to say, to *believe* that such a room as you describe, *this* room, in fact, may—

DOCTOR FREUD: [*Having resumed his pacing about, he has reached the writing-desk where he now picks up the notebook* FRANZ *has left there and begins leafing through it avidly.* FRANZ *rushes over.*]

FRANZ: [*Desperately.*] Doctor Freud, I must *forbid* . . . [*He snatches at the notebook, which* FREUD *holds away at arm's length, and attempts to continue reading.* FRANZ *struggles with him, looks back over his shoulder, and shouts:*] Mother!

FRAU KAFKA: [*The two men are quite near to upsetting one of the lamps; she rushes toward them, screaming:*] The *lamp!* For God's sake, *watch out for the lamp!* [*With this outburst,* DOCTOR FREUD *relinquishes the notebook, adjusts his spectacles, and gazes interestedly at* FRANZ. FRANZ, *notebook in his hand, makes adjustments to his clothes; he seems somewhat sheepish at having displayed that much emotion and avoids the Doctor's eyes. During their silence—which is uneasy on Kafka's part, intently scrutinizing on Freud's—* FRAU KAFKA *rants about the lamp.*] Thank Heaven! One of my most cherished pieces. Twelve kroner it cost, in *der Schwindelstrasse!* [*Suddenly she turns to* DOCTOR FREUD.] Of course, Doctor, you realize that we would be taking *our things* [*she indicates the bric-a-brac in a gesture*] with us. *Objets d'art! This* collection, modest enough I suppose in some eyes, was begun . . . by *Papa*. [*She has crossed over to the mantel where she gazes reverently at one of the photographs. She turns back to* DOCTOR FREUD, *who, in his intent scrutiny of* FRANZ, *appears not to have heard anything she said.*] I say you *do* understand, don't you Doctor, that the *collection* does *not* go with the apartment?

DOCTOR FREUD: [*He looks at her dully, nods, turns back at once to* FRANZ. *There is a long pause, before he asks, narrowly, darkly:*] Why so secretive, Franz?

FRANZ: [*As though he has considered the possibility of this question, he shakes his head quickly in denial.*] I regret, Doctor, that I cannot accept such a usage of the term in the context you have given it—I say *"regret"* for this reason: namely that—

FRAU KAFKA: [*Interrupting irately.*] Franz is about half *off his rocker*, Doctor Freud, can't you tell that? [FRANZ *stares at his mother furiously, as though he may challenge something in the syntax of what she has said.* DOCTOR FREUD *expresses immediate interest and crosses over to where she is now seated in the armchair.*]

DOCTOR FREUD: Off his *rocker?* What do you mean by that?

FRAU KAFKA: Good God, don't you know what that means? [*She takes a finger and rotates it near her temple.*]

DOCTOR FREUD: [*Impatiently.*] Yes, yes, but why *rocker?* How curious that you should use that particular image. [*He begins to pace about, absently stroking his fly, musing half-aloud.*] Rocker, rocker, rocker . . . off his rocker. Hmmm. Rocks, rocking-chair, rocking-horse, rock-a-bye baby. [*He turns to* FRAU KAFKA.] Let me ask you this: did you ever, as a child, have a *horse?*

FRAU KAFKA: [*Irately.*] What on earth! Doctor, I think you are *forgetting* yourself. May I suggest that we return to the *purpose* of your visit?

FRANZ: I agree, Doctor. All this is well and good, and under other circumstances, I, for one, would welcome—

DOCTOR FREUD: Yes, yes, of course, you're quite right. Very well then, where were we? Ah yes, this *flat* [*He walks about, looking up and down.*] And all *this* [*he indicates the bric-a-brac*] is to be cleared out, right? Hmm. Yes, this will do quite nicely. Now get your coats, get your coats! [*He looks around the room, spots the coats hanging, quickly collects them, and helps* FRANZ *and his mother put them on.*] Good! Now then we'll just take a little walk, hee-hee, *over to my place* . . .

STAGE DARKENS AS THEY SLOWLY START FOR THE DOOR.

Scene Two

A dark stage. The sound of footsteps is heard on the stairs, off-stage-right, then the sound of the door opening. The lights come up, and we see DOCTOR FREUD, his hand on the light switch just inside the door; he enters, followed by FRANZ and FRAU KAFKA.

DOCTOR FREUD: [*Ushering them in, rubbing his hands together.*] Well, here we are! Here we are!

[*It is a huge loft-like room, bare of furniture except for a table, chair and a couple of mattresses; it is strewn with books, crumpled papers, and discarded food cans. Two trunks stand askew, lids up, near the wall, their contents sprawling out of them onto the floor. Against the wall, stage-left, is a small booth about four feet square. Near it, center-stage, is a hole in the floor about three feet square.*]

FRAU KAFKA: [*On appraising the scene.*] Good God! [FRANZ *looks about, frowning terribly.*]

DOCTOR FREUD: [*Walking quickly toward the booth.*] Have a look round, I won't be a minute. I just want to check on this . . . [*voice trails off as he reaches the booth, opens a peek-hole, peers in, extracts a notebook and makes a few hurried notations in it, then contemplates the notebook and what he has written.*] Hmm. Interesting I should say that. Curious, curious. [*Closes the notebook, then addresses the others:*] Well, what do you think of the place? Plenty of *freedom* here, eh Franz?

FRANZ: If by "freedom" you mean to convey the sense of—

FRAU KAFKA: [*Interrupting:*] But there are no . . . no *facilities* here, Doctor! Where is the *kitchen?* Where is the *bathroom?*

DOCTOR FREUD: [*Impatiently:*] Kitchen, kitchen, of course there is no kitchen. Beyond sustenance, food is merely an *escape,* surely you know that. As for waste-disposal, that goes *here.* [*Points to the hole in the floor.*]

FRAU KAFKA: [*Aghast, she comes over, peers into the hole, shudders, and nearly swoons.*] Franz! Take me home!

FRANZ: [*Trying to be reasonable:*] Now Mother, while our own values may not exactly coincide with, or rather, may not seem to exactly coincide with, values which we impute to, or at least—

DOCTOR FREUD: [*Firmly:*] Making a great to-do over waste-disposal is often where the trouble begins. Now take this case, for example [*indicates the booth*] . . . here is a young Samoan couple whom I've been observing . . .

FRAU KAFKA: [*Shocked:*] *A young couple?* What on earth! Do you mean to say there is someone *in* that thing? [*Walks toward the booth.*]

FRANZ: [*Following her:*] Mother!

DOCTOR FREUD: [*Shrewdly,*] You realize, of course, that they do *not* go with the flat.

FRAU KAFKA: [*Arrives at the booth, opens the peek-hole and peers in, is stunned by what she sees, reels backwards, shrieking:*] Franz! [*She tumbles into the waste-disposal hole.*]

FRANZ: *MOTHER!* [*He leaps in after her.*]

DOCTOR FREUD: [*He rushes across the room to fetch a rope and a flashlight, shouting:*] Hold on! Hold on! [*He hurries to the hole and peers in, kneels down, playing the flashlight about in the hole. His expression changes from alarm to fascination; he quickly lays the rope aside, takes out his notebook and begins making notations in it as he peers into the hole; he speaks with terse excitement.*] Yes, yes . . . that's it . . . excellent! . . . yes, yes, react! . . . *react!* . . . hee-hee . . . *REACT!*

STAGE DARKENS, LEAVING ONLY THE BEAM OF THE FLASHLIGHT
DARTING ABOUT IN THE CIRCUMFERENCE OF THE HOLE.

Love
Is
a Many Splendored

FIRST [SPLENDORED]: *A Call of Certain Import*

Scene: A winter evening of 1914 at Kafka's home in Prague, where he lived with his mother until the following year, when he reached the age of thirty-three.

FRANZ has just come in from his clerical job at the bank and is seated by a reading-lamp in the small living room. The evening paper is on his lap and, after looking thoughtfully at the floor for a moment or two, he begins slowly unfolding it—when the telephone rings. From the adjoining room, where she is arranging the table for dinner, HIS MOTHER quickly enters, wiping her hands and giving FRANZ a sharp accusative look, as she picks up the phone. FRANZ stops unfolding the paper and strikes an attentive attitude towards his mother at the phone.

HIS MOTHER: [*Frowning:*] Hello?
VOICE: Hello, is young Kafka there? Franz Kafka?
HIS MOTHER: *Franz?* Why . . . yes. Who is this calling?
VOICE: This is Sig.
HIS MOTHER: *Who?*
VOICE: *Sig.* I'm a friend of Franz.

HIS MOTHER: [*Rather annoyed:*] All right, you'll have to wait a minute. [*To* FRANZ, *with a pained smile:*] It's for you.

FRANZ: [*Raising his brows:*] Oh? [*He starts to refold the paper with care, then after a minute decisively lays it aside, gets up and crosses the room to where his mother stands holding the phone, one hand over the mouthpiece.*]

HIS MOTHER: [*As one not to be easily fooled:*] It's Sig.

FRANZ: [*In consternation:*] *Who* is it?

[HIS MOTHER *does not answer, but gives him a knowing look as she hands him the phone and leaves the room abruptly. She returns at once, however, and stands between the dining-room and the telephone, hands on hips, apparently waiting for* FRANZ *to finish the conversation.*]

FRANZ: [*Darkly intent at the phone:*] Hello.

VOICE: Hello, Franz? Is that you? Sig here. Eh?

FRANZ: Yes. Yes, this is Franz. Who is calling? I'm *afraid* I didn't . . .

VOICE: Oh, don't be *afraid*, Franz. Ha! It's *Sig*. You remember. Sig? Siggy. You know, *Vienna*. Sig. *Sigmund Freud*.

FRANZ: [*Astonished:*] Sigmund Freud? *Doctor Sigmund Freud?* [*Eagerly:*] Why, this is a . . . a . . .

VOICE: [*Jovially:*] Yes, it's Doctor Freud all right! Ho-ho! I was hoping we could get together, Franz. I've got some new ideas, you see—quite a lot of them actually, ha-ha . . . and, well, I'd like to *go over* a few things with you. What do you say to that, eh?

FRANZ: Well, I . . . Doctor Freud, I hardly know *what* to say. I mean, I never *dreamed* that I . . .

VOICE: [*Shrewdly:*] You never *what?*

FRANZ: No, no. I mean . . . well, naturally I wouldn't have *dreamed* it, would I? [*Laughs nervously:*] May I say I never dared to *hope*, or rather that I couldn't have *imagined* that my opinion . . . that is to say, that my . . .

VOICE: [*Impatiently:*] Now look here, Franz, I need your help and I need it badly! Now then, tell me this: Does *desire*—and, of course, I mean in the very strict sense of the word—does this so-called *desire* for ejaculation . . . eh? . . . desire-for-ejaculation *precede* state of erection? OR does state-of-erection precede this *desire?* Eh? Tell me *that*, Mister Franz Kafka! Eh? [*Laughs uncontrollably for a full minute: Ho-ho-ho! Ha-ha-ha! He-he-he! Etc.*] Franz! Hey, Franz! Still there? Eh? Well, it's merely a *joke*, Franz! *Merely another joke at your expense!* HAW! [*Hangs up.*]

FRANZ: Hello. Hello, hello. [*Jiggles the phone-hook:*] Hello, operator, we've been cut off. Hello, hello.

HIS MOTHER: [*Crossing to the phone and snatching for it, demanding crossly:*] What on earth is going on here?

FRANZ: [*Anxiously, backing away, clutching phone:*] It's Doctor Freud calling, Mother. We've been cut off. I'm trying to get the operator now. Hello, hello. [*Jiggles the hook wildly:*] Hello, operator, hello . . . *hello* . . . *hello* . . . *hello* . . .

SLOW CURTAIN

SECOND [SPLENDORED]: *An Orderly Retreat*

There is tiredness in a soldier's walk through nights of winter rain that holds off fear like a grotesque brother. Tonight how they move as each were apart, away, and alone—it is the incredible walk of the wooden doll, the heartbreaking walk of the huddled, shutting things out. Are they dead or alive?

Only Singer is smoking now. Beside him walks a man half-conscious, his feet too deep in the mud. He is bored, terrifically bored; the boredom has come all down into his chest and stomach, leaving his insides shot through like a torn sieve, threaded with morphine.

"Let's have some of that before you put it out, Singer."

Singer, withholding it, looks at him in concern. "Listen, Joe, you din't see Al back there, when was the last time you seen him?"

"I ain't seen him for chrissake, I told you, I ain't seen him since they come down off the road back there."

Singer passes the cigarette, heavily, as though it weighed more than a cocked rifle.

"What happen over past where you were at, Joe?"

What is talk but diluted hysteria? And how in his cupped hands now in the night rain the cigarette burns as a chemical light, soundless and without heat.

"Are you kiddin'?"

"I mean where them tanks come down off the road, how'd it look there where they were comin' down off the road?"

"Are you kiddin' for chrissake?"

"How'd it look when you seen it, Joe, it look like it was takin' everthing, didn't it, how'd it look when you seen it?"

The fear of the infantry stretches out through time into a single quivering wire of tedium—or it may shatter tiredness, hunger and cold, on one bleak afternoon when inside the head, somewhere just behind the eyes: *the world pops open.*

"Listen. You seen past the house from where you were at, din't you Joe? You seen along that ditch, din't you?"

"Are you goin' to start that again for chrissake?"

"I'm not goin' to start anything, you son of a bitch."

THIRD [SPLENDORED]: *A Bad Mother-hubber*

An extraordinary thing happened at City Clerk's Office the other day, where I went to get married.

The whole procedure, beginning with blood-tests, had come off quite casually. Granted, there had been certain delays—the usual thing, I suppose; but, in any case, the event I speak of occurred independently of the marriage, did occur, in fact, only just *after* the marriage, at the moment when the Clerk pronounced us "husband and wife." At that moment, my "wife" asked me what time it was, wanting, I suppose, to make some sentimental note of it—which didn't strike me as particularly objectionable, because it was in a more humorous than romantic spirit that she had asked—so I raised my arm, to uncover my wristwatch. In doing so, however, I upset a very large bucket of *paste* which had been sitting on a shelf at about head level just to my left. It fell on the Clerk, emptying all over the ceremonial robe he had donned before beginning the marriage. A paste, *this* muck had apparently once dried out because of the overheated office, and then had been remixed with too much water, so that now it was an incredible lumpy slop.

I was extremely embarrassed—and especially so, I believe, because I had made no previous attempt to be friendly with the man;

in fact, by having allowed my face to remain in repose, had appeared to ignore his one or two little overtures towards informality during the service. Moreover, I now realized I had no handkerchief to offer him, and I could not even bring myself to make the empty gesture of reaching for my pocket. Neither could I bear to imagine the sound of my voice saying, "I'm sorry," in the small room; that, too, would have been such a hollow gesture—such a *drop*, so to speak—for this man literally covered with a watery paste gone sour, a stinking muck.

My wife, appalled by my apparent indifference, sank into the nearest chair without a word, and remained there throughout the scene that followed. I at once became so absorbed in my new relationship with the Clerk that I forgot about her.

When I finally dared look at the man, I realized immediately that he was an eccentric. With his head bent down, brows furrowed, he kept clawing at the muck, muttering the while, and somewhat angrily—but *not at me*, and that was the queer thing about it. It was as if he had been standing alone on a street-corner, and a passing car had thrown mud, a lot of wet mud on him. He was raking off great globs of it and flinging them on the floor. From time to time he would stop and look down at himself in amazement, holding out his hands which were several inches thick with the muck. "How do you like *that?*" he would demand, "how do you like *that?*" Yet, he was not blaming *me*, that was clear enough; it was as though I had just arrived. But, even so, I could not meet his eyes: I was compelled to look past, over his shoulder. And it was then that I noticed the plaque on the wall directly behind him; it was a framed certificate, and I could make it out easily:

GERRARD DAVIS

NEGRO MINISTER AND NEGRO MAN

I forced myself to look directly at his face. With all that muck on his face, he was so *white*, or rather, so unlike anything I had ever seen before, that I asked at once:

"Are *you* Davis?"

He replied by immediately dropping his interest in the paste and robe and reproducing almost exactly the last lines of Michael Redgrave in the ventriloquist sequence of *Dead of Night;* and with precisely the same insane smile: *"I . . . I . . . I've . . . been . . . waiting . . . for you . . . Sylvester."* It took me thoroughly aback, but my previous humiliation had been so sharp that I was still on the offensive. *"Look,"* I said evenly, "that gag is old hat to me, Davis— *if,* in fact, you *are* Davis."

Now he regarded me narrowly and with exaggerated concern, like one of the old eccentric actors of the silent screen.

"What's the matter?" he demanded, in German [*Was ist los?*] I don't have much German actually, but I do know enough of it to recognize that he spoke the words in the harsh nasal twang of our own Texas and the Great Southwest. This was unmistakable, and yet the knowledge did not seem to give me any real advantage. Despite this I took him up abruptly, as though not to be put off: "I'll tell you this much, Davis—if you really *are a Negro,* or rather, if you are *Negro,* I'd ask you to fall by my pad, you know what I mean, like we could dig Bird and Orville and turn on a few joints of some great Panamanian green. Later, of course, you could cut out, or, like, split."

He looked past me and slowly around the room with intense apprehension, knitting his brows fiercely.

"Who dat who say 'NERO'?" he demanded.

Whether it was a slip of the tongue, or a deliberate distortion, I was not able to determine, because he suddenly began a song and dance. The dance was common enough, a simple two-step, but the song was remarkable: it began as a Benjamin Britten-Elizabethan type thing, of no particularly deep feeling, but with great surface complexity; and yet, at about the third bridge, it picked up the wailing funk of Ray Charles, blasting *"It's a Low-Down Liberal, Low-Down Liberal Shame."*

And then when the silence began to close in, somewhat like a shroud, he went *"Ooh-scubee-doo-bop"*—very softly, that's how hip he was.

Twirling
at
Ole Miss

IN AN AGE GONE STALE through the complex of bureaucratic interdependencies, with its tedious labyrinth of technical specializations, each contingent upon the next, and all aimed to converge into a single totality of meaning, it is a refreshing moment indeed when one comes across an area of human endeavor absolutely sufficient unto itself, pure and free, no strings attached—the cherished and almost forgotten *l'art pour l'art*. Such is the work being carried forward now at the Dixie National Baton Twirling Institute, down at the campus of Ole Miss—a visit to which is well worthwhile these days, if one can keep one's wits about.

In my case it was the first trip South in many years, and I was duly apprehensive. For one thing, the Institute is located just outside Oxford, Mississippi—and, by grotesque coincidence, Faulkner's funeral had been held only the day before my arrival, lending a grimly surreal aura to the nature of my assignment . . . namely, to get the story on the Baton Twirling Institute. Would reverting to the Texas twang and callousness of my youth suffice to see me through?

Arriving in Oxford then, on a hot midday in July, after the three-hour bus ride from Memphis, I stepped off in front of the Old Colonial Hotel and meandered across the sleepy square toward the only sign of life at hand—the proverbial row of shirt-sleeved men sitting on benches in front of the county courthouse, a sort of permanent jury.

"Howdy," I say, striking an easy stance, smiling friendly-like, "whar the school?"

The nearest regard me in narrow surmise: they are quick to spot the stranger here, but a bit slow to cotton. One turns to another.

"What's that he say, Ed?"

Big Ed shifts his wad, sluices a long spurt of juice into the dust, gazes at it reflectively before fixing me again with gun-blue-cold eyes.

"Reckon you mean, 'Whar the school *at?*', don't you, stranger?"

Next to the benches, and about three feet apart, are two public drinking fountains, and I notice that the one boldly marked "For Colored" is sitting squarely in the shadow cast by the justice symbol on the courthouse façade—to be entered later, of course, in my writer's notebook, under "Imagery, sociochiaroscurian, hack."

After getting directions (rather circuitous, I thought—being further put off by what I understood, though perhaps in error, as a fleeting reference to "the Till case") I decided to take a cab, having just seen one park on the opposite side of the square.

"Which is nearer," I asked the driver, "Faulkner's house or his grave?"

"Wal," he said without looking around, "now that would take a little studyin', if you were gonna hold a man to it, but offhand I'd say they were pretty damn near the same—about ten minutes from where we're sittin' and fifty cents each. They're in opposite directions."

I sensed the somehow questionable irony of going from either to the Baton Twirling Institute, and so decided to get over to the Institute first and get on with the coverage.

"By the way," I asked after we'd started, "where can a man get a drink of whiskey around here?" It had just occurred to me that Mississippi is a dry state.

"Place over on the county line," said the driver, "about eighteen miles; cost you four dollars for the trip, eight for the bottle."

"I see."

He half turned, giving me a curious look.

"Unless, of course, you'd like to try some 'nigger-pot.'"

"Nigger-pot? Great God yes, man," I said in wild misunderstanding, "let's move!"

It soon developed, of course, that what he was talking about was the unaged and uncolored corn whiskey privately made in the region, and also known as "white lightning." I started to demur, but as we were already in the middle of the colored section, thought best to go through with it. Why not begin the sojourn with a genuine Dixieland experience—the traditional jug of corn?

As it happened the distiller and his wife were in the fields when we reached the house, or hut as it were, where we were tended by a Negro boy of about nine.

"This here's a mighty fine batch," he said, digging around in a box of kindling wood and fetching out unlabeled pints of it.

The taxi driver, who had come inside with me, cocked his head to one side and gave a short laugh, as to show we were not so easily put upon.

"Why, boy," he said, "I wouldn't have thought you was a drinkin' man."

"Nosuh, I ain't no drinkin' man, but I sure know how it suppose to taste—that's 'cause times nobody here I have to *watch* it and I have to *taste* it too, see it workin' right. We liable lose the whole batch I don't know how it suppose to taste. You all taste it," he added, holding out one of the bottles and shaking it in my happy face. "You see if that ain't a fine batch!"

Well, it had a pretty good taste all right—a bit edgy perhaps, but plenty of warmth and body. And I did have to admire the pride the young fellow took in his craft. You don't see much of that these days—especially among nine-year-olds. So I bought a couple of bottles, and the driver bought one, and we were off at last for the Institute.

The Dixie National Baton Twirling Institute holds its classes in a huge, sloping, fairyland grove on the campus of Ole Miss, and it resembles something from another age. The classes had already begun when I stepped out of the cab, and the sylvan scene which stretched before me, of some seven-hundred girls, nymphs and nymphets all, cavorting with their staffs in scanty attire beneath the broadleaf elms, was a sight to spin the senses and quicken the blood. Could I but have donned satyr's garb and rushed savagely among them! But no, there was this job o'work to get on with—dry, factual reportage—mere donkey work, in fact. I decided the correct procedure was to first get some background material, and to this end I sought out Don Sartell, "Mister Baton" himself, Director of the Institute. Mr. Sartell is a handsome and personable young man from north of the Mason-Dixon line, acutely attuned to the needs of the young, and, needless to say, extremely dexterous *avec les doigts*. (By way of demonstrating the latter he once mastered a year's typing course in a quick six days—or it may have been six hours, though I do recall that it was an impressive and well-documented achievement.)

"Baton twirling," he tells me straight off, "is the second largest girl's youth movement in America—the first, of course, being the Girl Scouts." (Veteran legman, I check this out later. Correct.) "The popularity of baton twirling," he explains, "has a threefold justification: (1) it is a sport which can be practiced alone; (2) it does not, unlike other solo sports (sailing, skiing, shooting, etc.), require expensive equipment; and (3) it does not, again like the aforementioned, require travel, but, on the contrary, may be practiced in one's own living room or backyard."

"Right," I say. "So far, so good, Mister Baton—but what about the intrinsics? I mean, just what is the point of it all?"

"The point, aside from the simple satisfaction of mastering a complex and highly evolved skill, is the development of self-confidence, poise, ambidexterity, disciplined coordination, etcetera."

I asked if he would like a drink of nigger-pot. He declined graciously: he does not drink or smoke. My place, I decided, is in the grove, with the groovy girls—so, limbering up my six-hundred-page, eight-dollar copy of *Who's Who in Baton Twirling*, I take my leave of the excellent fellow and steal toward the sylvan scene below, ready for anything.

The development of American baton twirling closely parallels the history of emancipation of our women. A larger version of this same baton (metal with a knob on the end) was first used, of course, to direct military marching bands, or, prior to that, drum corps—the baton being manipulated in a fairly straightforward, dum-de-dum, up-and-down manner. The idea of *twirling* it—and finally even *flinging* it—is, obviously, a delightfully girlish notion.

Among those most keenly interested in mastering the skill today are drum majorettes from the high schools and colleges of the South and Midwest, all of which have these big swinging bands and corps of majorettes competing during the half at football games. In the South, on the higher-educational level, almost as much expense and training goes into these groups as into the football team itself, and, to persons of promise and accomplishment in the field, similar scholarships are available. Girls who aspire to become majorettes—and it is generally considered the smartest status a girl can achieve on the Southern campus—come to the Institute for preschool training. Or, if she is already a majorette, she comes to sharpen her technique. Many schools send a girl, or a small contingent of them, to the Institute to pick up the latest routines so that they can come back and teach the rest of the corps what they have learned. Still others are training to be professionals and teachers of baton twirling. Most of these girls come every year—I talked to one from Honey Pass, Arkansas, a real cutie pie, who had been there for eight consecutive years, from the time she was nine. When I asked if she would like a drink of pot, she replied pertly: "*N* . . . *O* . . . spells 'No'!" Such girls are usually championship material, shooting for the Nationals.

Competitions to determine one's degree of excellence are held regularly under the auspices of the National Baton Twirling Association, and are of the following myriad categories: *Advanced Solo;*

*Intermediate Solo; Beginners Solo; Strutting Routine; Beginners
Strutting Routine; Military Marching; Flag; Two-Baton; Fire Baton;
Duet; Trio; Team; Corps; Boys; Out-of-State;* and others. Each
division is further divided into age groups: 0–6, 7–8, 9–10, 11–12,
13–14, 15–16, 17 and over. The winner in each category receives a
trophy, and the first five runners-up receive medals. This makes for
quite a bit of hardware riding on one session, so that a person in the
baton-twirling game does not go too long without at least token
recognition—and the general run of *Who's Who* entries ("eight
trophies, seventy-three medals") would make someone like Audie
Murphy appear rudely neglected.

The rules of competition, however, are fairly exacting. Each
contestant appears singly before a Judge and Scorekeeper, and
while the Judge observes and relays the grading to the Scorekeeper,
the girl goes through her routine for a closely specified time. In
Advanced Solo, for example, the routine must have a duration of
not less than two minutes and twenty seconds, and not more than
two and thirty. She is scored on general qualities relating to her
degree of accomplishment—including *showmanship, speed,* and
drops, the latter, of course, counting against her, though not so
much as one might suppose. Entrance fees average about two
dollars for each contestant. Some girls use their allowance to pay it.

In the Institute's grove—not unlike the fabled Arcadia—the
groups are ranged among the trees in various states of learning and
scanty attire. The largest, most central and liveliest of these groups
is the one devoted to the mastery of Strutting. Practice and instruction in Strutting are executed to records played over a public-
address system at an unusually loud volume—a sort of upbeat rock
and roll with boogie-woogie overtones. *Dixie, The Stripper,* and
Potato Peel were the three records in greatest use for this class—
played first at half speed, to learn the motions, then blasted at full
tempo. Strutting is, of course, one of the most fantastic body-
movement phenomena one is likely to see anywhere. The deliberate
narcissistic intensity it requires must exceed even that of the Spanish flamenco dancer. High-style (or "all-out") Strutting is to be seen
mainly in the South, and what it resembles more than anything else

is a very contemporary burlesque-house number—with the grinds in and the bumps out. It is the sort of dance one associates with jaded and sequin-covered washed-out blondes in their very late thirties—but Ole Miss, as is perhaps well known, is in "the heartland of beautiful girls," having produced two Miss Americas and any number of runners-up, and to watch a hundred of their nymphets practice the Strut, in bathing suits, short shorts, and other such skimp, is a visual treat which cuts anything the Twist may offer the viewer.

The instructor of the Strut stands on a slightly raised platform facing her class, flanked by her two assistants. She wears dark glasses, tight rolled shorts, and looks to be about 34–22–34. She's a swinger from Pensacola, Florida, a former National Senior Champion and Miss Majorette of America, now turned pro. When not at the Dixie Institute at the University of Mississippi, or a similar establishment, she gives private lessons at her own studio, for six dollars an hour, and drives a Cadillac convertible.

As for other, more academic, aspects of baton twirling, an exhibition was given the first evening by members of the cadre—all champions, and highly skilled indeed.

Instruction in speed and manipulation is a long and nerve-racking process. There is something quite insane about the amount of sheer effort and perseverance which seems to go into achieving even a nominal degree of real excellence—and practice of four hours a day is not uncommon. In the existentialist sense, it might well be considered as the final epitome of the absurd—I mean, people starving in India and that sort of thing, and then others spending four hours a day skillfully flinging a metal stick about. *Ça alors!* In any case it has evolved now into a highly developed art and a tightly organized movement—though by no means one which has reached full flower. For one thing, a nomenclature—that hallmark of an art's maturity—has not yet been wholly formalized. Theoretically, at least, there should be a limit to the number of possible manipulations, each of which could legitimately be held as distinct from all others—that is to say, a repertory which would remain standard and unchanged for a period of time. The art of baton twirling has not yet reached that stage, however, and innovations arise with such frequency that there does not exist at present any single manual, or similarly doctrinaire work, on the subject. Doubtless this is due in large part to the comparative newness of the art as a large and intensely active pastime—the Dixie National Baton Twirling Institute, for example, having been founded as recently as 1951. The continuing evolution of the art as a whole is reflected in the names of the various manipulations. Alongside the commonplace (or classic) designations, such as *arabesque, tour-jeté, cradle,* etc., are those of more exotic or contemporary flavor: *bat, walk-over, pretzel,* and the like . . . and all, old or new, requiring countless hours of practice.

During the twirling exhibition I fell into conversation with a couple of graduate law students, and afterward went along with them to the campus coffee shop, the "Rebel Devil"—nearly all shops there have the word "Rebel" in them—and we had an interesting talk. Ole Miss prides itself, among other things, on having the only law school in the state which is accredited by the American Bar Association—so that these two graduate law students were not without some claim to representing a certain level of relative advancement in the community of scholars. They were clean-cut young men in their mid-twenties, dressed in summer suits of tasteful cut. In answer to a question of mine, we talked about Constitutional Law for ten minutes before I realized they were talking about *State* Constitutional Law. When it became apparent what I was driving at, however, they were quick to face the issue squarely.

"*We* nevuh had no Negra problem heah," said one of them, shaking his head sadly. He was a serious young man wearing glasses and the mien of a Harvard divinity student. "Theah just *weren't* no problem—wasn't till these *agi-ta-tors* came down heah started all this problem business."

They were particularly disturbed about the possible "trouble, an' I mean *real* trouble" which would be occasioned by the attempted registration of a Negro student [James Meredith] which was threatening to take place quite soon, during that very summer session, in fact. As it happened, the authorities managed to delay it; I did, however, get a preview of things to come.

"Why they'll find *dope* in his room the first night he's heah," the other student said, "dope, a gun, something—*anything*, just plant it in theah an' *find* it! And out he'll go!"

They assured me that they themselves were well above this sort of thing, and were, in fact, speaking as mature and nonviolent persons.

"But now these heah young *unduh*graduates, they're hotheaded. Why, do you know how *they* feel? What *they* say?"

Then to the tune of *John Brown's Body*, the two graduate law students begin to sing, almost simultaneously: *"Oh we'll bury all the niggers in the Mississippi mud . . .",* singing it rather loudly it seemed to me—I mean if they were just documenting a point in a private conversation—or perhaps they were momentarily carried away, so to speak. In any event, and despite a terrific effort at steely Zen detachment, the incident left me somewhat depressed, so I retired early, to my cozy room in the Alumni House, where I sipped the white corn and watched television. But I was not destined to escape so easily, for suddenly who should appear on the screen but old Governor Faubus himself—in a gubernatorial campaign rant—with about six cross-purpose facial ticks going strong, and he compulsively gulping water after every pause, hacking, spitting, and in general looking as mad as a hatter. At first I actually mistook it for a rather tasteless and heavy-handed *parody* of the governor. It could not, I thought, really be Faubus, because why would the network carry an Arkansas primary campaign speech in Mississippi? Surely not just for laughs. Later I learned that while there is such a thing in television as a *nation*wide hookup for covering events of national importance, there is also such a thing as a *South*wide hookup.

The Institute's mimeographed schedule, of which I had received a copy, read for the next day as follows:

7:30	Up and at 'em
8–9	Breakfast—University Cafeteria
9–9:30	Assembly, Limber up, Review—Grove
9:30–10:45	Class No. 4
10:45–11:30	Relax—Make Notes
11:30–12:45	Class No. 5
1–2:30	Lunch—University Cafeteria
2:30–4	Class No. 6
4–5:30	Swim Hour
6:30–7:30	Supper—University Cafeteria
7:30	Dance—Tennis Court
11	Room Check
11:30	Lights Out (NO EXCEPTIONS)

The *"Up and at 'em"* seemed spirited enough, as did the "NO EXCEPTIONS" being in heavy capitals; but the rest somehow offered little promise, so, after a morning cup of coffee, I walked over to the library, just to see if they really had any books there—other than books on Constitutional Law, that is. Indeed they did, and quite a modern and comfortable structure it was, too, air-conditioned (as was, incidentally, my room at the Alumni House) and well-lighted throughout. After looking around for a bit, I carefully opened a mint first-edition copy of *Light in August,* and found "nigger-lover" scrawled across the title page. I decided I must be having a run of bad luck, as a few minutes later, I suffered still another minor trauma on the steps of the library. It was one of those incredible bits of irony which sometimes do occur in life, but are never suitable for fiction—for I had completely put the title-page incident out of my mind and was sitting on the steps of the library, having a smoke, when this very amiable gentleman of middle age paused in passing to remark on the weather (102°) and to inquire in an oblique and courteous way as to the nature of my visit. An immaculate, pink-faced man, with pince-nez spectacles attached by a silver loop to his lapel, nails buffed to a gleam, he carried a smart leather briefcase and a couple of English-literature textbooks which he rested momentarily on the balustrade as he continued to smile down on me with what seemed to be extraordinary happiness.

"My, but it's a mighty warm day, an' that's no lie," he said, withdrawing a dazzling white-linen handkerchief and touching it carefully to his brow, ". . . an' I expect you all from up Nawth," he added with a twinkle, "find it especially so!" Then he quite abruptly began to talk of the "natural tolerance" of the people of Mississippi, speaking in joyfully objective tones, as though it were, even to him, an unfailing source of mystery and delight.

"Don't mind nobody's business but yoah own!" he said, beaming and nodding his head—and it occurred to me this might be some kind of really weirdly obscured threat, the way he was smiling; but no, evidently he was just remarkably good-natured. " 'Live an' let live!' That's how the people of Mississippi feel—always have! Why, look at William Faulkner, with all his notions, an' him livin' right ovah heah in Oxford all the time an' nobody botherin' him—just let him go his own way—why we even let him teach heah at the University one yeah! That's right! I know it! Live an' let live—you can't beat it! I'll see you now, you heah?" And his face still a glittering mask of joviality, he half raised his hand in good-by and hurried on. Who was this strange, happy educator? Was it he who had defaced the title page? His idea of tolerance and his general hilarity gave one pause. I headed back to the grove, hoping to recover some equilibrium. There, things seemed to be proceeding pretty much as ever.

"Do you find that your costume is an advantage in your work?" I asked the first seventeen-year-old Georgia Peach I came across, she wearing something like a handkerchief-size Confederate flag.

"Yessuh, I *do*," she agreed, with friendly emphasis, tucking her little blouse in a bit more snugly all around, and continuing to speak in that oddly rising inflection peculiar to girls of the South, making parts of a reply sound like a question: "Why, back home near Macon . . . Macon, Georgia? At Robert E. Lee High? . . . we've got these outfits with *tassels!* And a little red-and-gold skirt? . . . that, you know, sort of *flares out?* Well, now they're awful pretty, and of course they're *short* and everything, but I declare those tassels and that little skirt get in my way!"

The rest of the day passed without untoward incident, with my observing the Strut platform for a while, then withdrawing to rest up for the Dance, and perhaps catch Faub on the tube again.

The Dance was held on a boarded-over outdoor tennis court, and was a swinging affair. The popular style of dancing in the white South is always in advance of that in the rest of white America; and, at any given moment, it most nearly resembles that which is occurring at the same time in Harlem, which is invariably the forerunner of whatever is to become the national style. I mused on this, standing there near the court foul line, and (in view of the day's events) pursued it to an interesting generalization: perhaps *all* the remaining virtues, or let us say, positive traits, of the white Southerner—folk song, poetic speech, and the occasional warmth and simplicity of human relationships—would seem rather obviously to derive from the colored culture there. Due to my magazine assignment, I could not reveal my findings over the public-address system at the dance—and, in fact, thought best to put them from my mind entirely, and get on with the coverage—and, to that end, had a few dances and further questioned the girls. Their view of the world was quite extraordinary. For most, New York was like another country—queer, remote, and of small import in their grand scheme of things. Several girls spoke spiritedly of wanting to "get into television," but it always developed that they were talking about programs produced in Memphis. Memphis, in fact, was definitely the mecca, yardstick and *summum bonum*. As the evening wore on, I found it increasingly difficult, despite the abundance of cutie pieness at hand, to string along with these values, and so finally decided to wrap it up. It should be noted too, that girls at the Dixie National are under extremely close surveillance both in the grove and out.

The following day I made one last tour, this time noting in particular the instruction methods for advanced twirling techniques: 1-, 2-, 3-*finger rolls, wrist roll, waist roll, neck roll,* etc. A pretty girl of about twelve was tossing a baton sixty feet straight up, a silver whir in the Mississippi sunlight, and she beneath it spinning like an ice skater, and catching it behind her back, not having moved an inch. She said she had practiced it an hour a day for six years. Her hope was to become "the best there is at the high toss and spin"—and she was now up to seven complete turns before making the catch. Was there a limit to the height and number of spins one could attain? No, she guessed not.

After lunch I packed, bid adieu to the Dixie National and boarded the bus for Memphis. As we crossed the Oxford square and passed the courthouse, I saw the fountain was still shaded, although it was now a couple of hours later than the time I had passed it before. Perhaps it is always shaded—cool and inviting, it could make a person thirsty just to see it.

Recruiting
for
the Big Parade

ONE NIGHT NOT LONG AGO I was sitting around the White Horse Tavern, in New York City's colorful Greenwich Village, having a quick game of chess with a self-styled internationally famous blitz-chess champ. Six snappy ones and I pretty well had the game sewed up, when the champ suddenly said: "Say, see that guy at the bar—he was in the Cuban fiasco."

"Cut the diversionary crap, Champ," I countered, not bothering to look around, tapping the board of play instead, "and face up to the power." I had slapped the old de Sade double cul-de-sac on his Lady—and, as Bill Seward says, that's a rumble nobody can cool.

"No, man," insisted the champ in petulance, "I'm not kidding—just ask him and see."

Well, to make a short preface even terse (the champ, by the way interfered with the pieces when I did look around, and so eked out another shoddy win), I investigated further to find that it was, in fact, true: this man *had* participated in the Cuban fiasco, of April 17, 1961, right up to the eleventh-hour moment of the fiasco proper, "Bad Day at the Pig Bay." His story was so interesting that my immediate hope was to share it with whatever sort of sensitive readership I could muster, and to that end I invited him over to my place for some drinks and a couple of hours tape-recording of his curious tale. Here then is the story of Boris Grgurevich, thirty-three, born and raised in New York City; it is a verbatim transcript of the recorded interview; and what is even more weird, it's *true:*

Well, now let me ask you this, how did you get involved in this Cuban fiasco?

It was *cold,* man . . . you know, like January. You remember that big snowstorm? When they pulled all the cars off the street? Yeah, well that was it. . . . *Cold.* And this friend of mine, Ramón, comes by. I know him ten, fifteen years, but you know, haven't seen him for a while, so there's a big bla-bla hello scene . . . and he was running from something, I mean that was pretty obvious, but he was always very high-strung, moving around a lot—Miami, L.A., Mexico—and right away he says, "Man, let's go to *Miami,* where it's *WARM.*" And he had this *car,* and well, I mean it wasn't difficult him talking me into going, because of the weather and all. So that was the first thing—we went down to Miami.

Had he mentioned anything about Cuba before you left for Miami?

No, man, he didn't say anything about *Cuba*—or maybe he *did* mention it, you know, fleetingly . . . like "bla-bla-bla the Cuban situation," or some crap like that, but we were just going to *Miami.* I mean he probably *did* mention it, because he was *born* in Cuba, you dig, and speaks Spanish and so on—but Castro was all right with me . . . I mean he had that *beard,* you know, and he seemed pretty interesting. No, we didn't talk about that, we get down to Miami, and we have three great days at the track, and then we have four terrible ones—we were reduced to moving in with Jimmy Drew, a guy I know there. And so Ramón's taking me around—I mean, he knows Miami, see, and there's a *liquor* store in the neighborhood and he introduces me to this guy owns the liquor store—nice guy to know, owns a liquor store, and we get very friendly, you know, and he's giving us bottles of *rum.* Well, he's *Cuban,* dig, and he and Ramón start yakking it up about *Cuba* and "bla-bla Castro" and so on, and now he's talking about the *"inva-sion"* and how he's going to get back what they *took* from him and all that jive. And naturally I'm *agreeing* with him—well I mean he keeps laying this *rum* on us, about three bottles a day . . . but he's, well he was obviously full of crap, a kind of middle-aged hustler businessman . . . and all these cats hanging around the liquor store all looked like *hoods*, but sort of *failing*, you know? Anyway, we were meeting all these hood-faces hanging around this liquor store, mostly Cubans, or born in Cuba, and one of them took us to this . . . well, they had this recruiting station, you know, where they're all signing up for the *invasion*, and Ramón, well he's getting more and more excited about this—he's a *salesman* actually, I mean that's what he does, you know, in real life, sell things, and so he's selling himself on this idea, invading Cuba . . . and of course he was selling me on it too.

Well, now this recruiting—this station—was this being done quite openly?

Openly? Well, man, it was open twenty-four hours a day. You know, like in the middle of town.

This was about the time Cuba raised this question in the U.N. and the U.S. delegation so emphatically denied it. If recruitment was being done as openly as you suggest, how could they deny it?

Well, use your bean, man—what are they supposed to do, *admit* it?

All right, now let me ask you this, what was Ramón's idea exactly—I mean, if the invasion was successful, did he think he would get something out of it?

Well, Ramón's what you might call an *essentialist*—and he just more or less figures that the man with the gun is, you know, *the man with the gun.*

And how did you feel about it?

The money was the thing that interested me—I mean we'd had these four very bad days at the track, and I had no *money*. Well, they were offering two-fifty a month and, you know, room and board, and . . . let's see, what else . . . yeah, *a trip to Guatemala.* But I guess the main thing was these cats at the recruiting station, giving this big spiel about "bla-bla-bla the American Government, the C.I.A., the U.S. Army," and so on. I mean the picture *they* were painting had *battleships* in it, Dad—you know, rockets against pitchforks. Well man, I mean how could we lose? Cuba versus America—are you kidding?

So it was pretty obvious even then that it was an American project?

Well *of course*, man—that was the whole pitch. You don't think they could have got these guys in there any other way, do you? I mean most of *these* guys were just sort of tired, middle-aged businessmen, or young hustlers . . . *they* weren't going to do anything, anybody could see that. It was like they were recruiting for the *parade*, you know, to march through Havana—and these guys were joining up to be *in* the parade, that's all. I mean there was a *slight* pretense at a front—the *Juan Paula Company*, that's the way the checks were paid, from the *Juan Paula Company*—and then there were some of these C.I.A. faces running around, trying to make a cloak-and-dagger scene out of it, but that was just sort of a *game* with them. I mean everybody in Miami knew about the recruiting.

Did you meet other Americans who wanted to go?

Well, they didn't want Americans, you see, they wanted *Cubans*—for the big parade, dig? So you had to be Cuban, or if you were American, like Ramón, you had to be born in Cuba. But yeah, there were some other Americans down there, trying to get in—guys from the South mostly, these real . . . you know, anything-is-better-than-home types. Most of them had been in the Army or something like that. But they didn't want them—they wanted Cubans.

So how did you get in?

Well, man, I mean they didn't make an *issue* of it or anything like that, not as far as *I* was concerned, because we had gotten sort of friendly with them, these C.I.A. cats . . . and they weren't bad guys really—I mean they thought *they* were doing the right thing and they thought *we* were doing the right thing, so we had a pretty good relationship with them. They were nice guys actually—just sort of goofy.

Where did you see the first C.I.A. person? At the recruiting station?

That's right, they would fool around this recruiting station . . . but they were sort of flunky types. The first, what you might call "higher-echelon" C.I.A. face, was this guy directing the loading, you know, when we left for the airport. Young, dapper, sort of prematurely gray, crew-cut, very square, would-be hip-looking cat. I guess he was a faggot actually.

How did you get to the airport?

Well, one night about a week after we signed up and had finished taking these physicals they said, "Okay, this is it"—you know, very dramatic—and they picked us up, there were about ninety of us altogether, in these trucks . . . sort of like moving vans, and, well, went to the airport.

Was this the Miami International Airport?

No man, it was some kind of abandoned *military* airport. Took us about an hour to get there—then we were inside this huge hangar, and that's where they issued the uniforms. Khaki uniforms, shoes, and all that jazz. Then we get on the plane . . . C-47 . . . with the windows taped up, you know, no light, very cloak-and-dagger. And the trip . . . well, we took off that night and landed the next morning. Guatemala. And it was *hot*, man . . . wow, was it *hot*. Cats falling out all over the place—I mean, *these* guys were in no shape to start with, and then this *heat*. Well, there were these trucks there to pick us up—sort of red, commercial-type trucks, like farm trucks, you know, big open trucks. And they took us from the airstrip to the camp—that was outside Retalhuleu, the airstrip—and it takes about an hour and a half to get to Trax, the camp, the last half hour very *steep,* like straight up a mountain. First we pass a Guatemalan outpost, then a Cuban one. And it's all *lava*—the campsite was all lava . . . cut right out of the side of this mountain about 8,000 feet up. It was laid out in three levels, you dig, like huge terraces. The first level had the firing range, parade ground, the second had the barracks, mess hall, and so on, and then at the top was where the C.I.A. lived—separate, with their own mess hall, movie, and all that. Anyway it's all lava . . . like crushed coral, you know, crunch, crunch, crunch, everywhere you step. And it was supposed to be a secret camp, but of course everyone knew about it—I mean there were fifteen hundred guys up there eventually, blasting away all day—rifles, machine guns, mortars. And it was written up in all the newspapers and magazines—including *Bohemia Libre*. Know that one? It's the big anti-Communist magazine there.

Was this formerly a Guatemalan army camp?

No, man, this was formerly *nothing*. They were still working on it when I got there—I mean the camp was built for this, you know, this particular project, and they were still working on it.

Well, had you gotten to know any of the other men yet? What were they like?

You mean the guys on the plane? Well, let's see, there was this guy, Martinez . . . he was about fifty-two or -three, had been in the Batista army, a clerk—beautiful handwriting . . . well, you know the type, man, a *clerk*. And he was there because that was all he knew—the army and how to write. I mean that was the whole story with him. And then you get someone else, like this kid Raúl— young country boy, thinks his old man has been beat for a couple of *cows* or something. Very sincere cat. Well, you know, man, there were all kinds, like any army. Mostly pretty simple cats though— well, you know, like any army.

Can you describe the camp more fully?

It was the usual scene, man—a *camp*. A military *camp*. The barracks . . . well, a couple of them were quonset huts, but most of them were just ordinary wooden barracks—hold about seventy guys, something like that. Mess hall, orderly room, quartermaster, motor pool, and so on . . . like an ordinary American Army camp . . . a little shabbier maybe, you know, more makeshift.

How was the food?

Well, that was a pretty funny scene all right—that whole mess-hall scene. They had these three American cooks, you dig, and a lot of Guatemalans to do KP—with a couple of translators, you know, so the cooks could tell the Guatemalans what to do—and the food was okay, sort of typical American fare, but the Cubans didn't particularly dig it. I mean they like different things, you know—black beans, rice, pork, they eat a lot of pork. Anyway, sometimes they wouldn't eat in the mess hall—they would cop a *pig* somewhere, you know, off a farmer, somebody like that . . . trade him a gun for it, anything—I mean, there were, you know, quite a few little black-market operations going on. So they would have the pig . . . a live, squealing *pig*, man, and they'd butcher it right outside the barracks and build a big fire and cook it. They'd have a ball—a kind of little *fiesta*, you know, singing and dancing, lushing it up, cooking this pig. It was a crazy scene.

Did you start your training right away?

Yeah, you started off as a group. . . . They would keep all the guys who arrived together as a group, right through Basic Training —you know, marching, calisthenics, rifle range, and so on. And then they would train you for some specialty—like mortar, machine gun, or something. But we didn't get started until the next day. I mean there was a little confusion when we arrived, because there had just been a take-over the night before—a Batista coup—and the San Román boys had taken over. These were two brothers, Pepe and Roberto San Román—they were very tight with the Americans. See, the Americans never knew what was happening—I mean, they lived apart, ate apart, none of them spoke Spanish, and they never had any idea what was going on in camp—so if some guy came to them and said "bla-bla-bla Communist plot" or some crap like that, why they had to *believe* him—they really had no choice, they always had to take the word of the guy who was telling them. So they'd say: "Okay, *you* take over—get those Commies outta there!"

Had there actually been a plot?

No, man, this was just *politicking*. There was a lot of maneuvering going on, you dig—I mean, these guys were sort of divvying up the spoils, you know, even before they got there. That's how sure of themselves they were. And so the San Román brothers finally came out on top. Short-lived though it proved to be.

Anyway they had these three cats in the can—not the regular stockade, but a tin-roof shack built just to hold these guys. They were the ones who had taken all the weight in the coup—you know, supposed to be Communist spies. It was like that shack in *The Bridge on the River Kwai*, and those cats were in there for *three months,* man. Nobody was allowed near them except whoever was guarding the shack—and the guy who brought their chow . . . and, that's right, there were a couple of G-2 faces would question them sometimes. But they never cracked—I saw them the day they came out—they were strong cats, man.

Do you suppose they were Communist spies?

Well, I think they were just strong, dangerous cats, man—who, you know, disagreed with the Batista clique. So when they pulled off this coup, these guys caught all the heat.

So the San Román brothers became . . . what, the commandants of the camp?

Well, Frank Bender, the C.I.A. guy, was in charge of the operation—I mean he was in charge of the *whole* thing, you dig, but Pepe San Román was *nominally* the camp commander, from the, you know, Cuban point of view—and Roberto, his brother, he was in charge of the heavy-weapons company, the four-point-two mortars . . . that was the most important company in the outfit.

What were the American instructors like?

Well, they were all specialists—you know, *instructors,* mostly from the Army: World War II, Korean War, or young cats from, I don't know, *Ohio* or some weird place like that. There were about thirty-five or forty of them. And it was just a gig for them. They were getting seven-fifty, and they were usually pretty conscientious about whatever it was they were teaching—they didn't have any particular interest in the political side of it. They were sort of typical Army faces—but *specialists,* you know, pretty humorless cats, except for the guy training the paratroopers, and he was about half off his nut. And some of them, being from the South and all, were very color conscious—they didn't really *like* the Cubans, you know, because they were different. And of course they were very down on any kind of *mixture,* and the Cubans . . . well, my company commander, for example, was a mulatto—big six-foot-two cat, very temperamental, would shout himself hoarse, that kind of guy, you know? A very uneven cat—one day he would be great, outgoing, very friendly, and the next a mean mother. Anyway the fact that these guys didn't really dig the Cubans, and were down on color, and couldn't speak Spanish—it gave, well, a kind of comic-opera quality to the thing in front.

Would you talk to them about what was going on?

Well, you know, they don't crack—I mean you ask them a direct question and they fade you right out. But, of course, in most cases they didn't know what was going on themselves. Like we used to buzz these instructors—you know, "When are we leaving bla-bla-bla?" but they just "Man, we don't know, we're waiting for orders," that kind of thing.

I don't understand why they couldn't get C.I.A. people who spoke Spanish.

Well, man, I'm inclined to believe that they'd rather *not* have guys who speak the language—I really think their fear is that deep . . . you know? I mean they figure that if these cats get to *talking* to these people they might be in some way *corrupted* by them, you dig. Like they don't trust their own boys, that's what it amounts to. And you can see their point in a way—because there was really nothing holding these cats together . . . they were all there for different reasons, mostly *personal* reasons—and of course because they thought they were going to *win*, that was the main thing. But there was no single idea behind it—you know, the sort of sense of purpose you need to pull off something like that. There were too many guys just looking out for number one—you know, *collectors* . . . they collected things. When it came time to ship out for the invasion, some of those guys had so much *stuff*, man—stuff they had copped . . . transistor radios, binoculars, anything they could cop. They would be carrying an extra pack full of this crap—I'm surprised they could even get off the landing craft with all that weight. They thought they were going on a picnic. Not all of them naturally—I mean there were some sensitive faces there too—sort of fatalistic cats, like this kid Juan on the mortars . . . he used to say: "Land on Monday, get captured on Tuesday, and shot on Wednesday." Very sensitive, sort of morbid type. So it was like that, all fragmented. A lot of different factions and ideas. But the real nucleus of the outfit, the heavy-weapons company, was very strong —they knew their jobs, and they were ready to fight. Well, they were just *wasted*, guys like that. And then there was a huge bunch of goof-offs—cats who had never done *anything*, and weren't going to start now. A lot of them stayed in the guardhouse, you know, like *permanently*—and they had it pretty good . . . they would let them out for chow, they'd get to go to the head of the line, that sort of thing. Some of them were very popular with the men, like clowns. They let all of them out just before the invasion, and a lot of them were made sergeants and so on.

What were the weapons you trained with?

Well, we started with the carbine and the M-1, then the M-3—that's the one that replaced the Thompson, you know, looks like a grease gun? And the Army .45, of course. And then the bazooka, machine gun, and mortar—finally the heavy mortars. That was the largest thing they had . . . these four-point-two mortars. And the Cubans dug that part of it—you know, the shooting. Especially the mortars—they were really *good* with the mortars. Primitive cats, you know, very good with their hands . . . and they'd do great things with the mortars, like dead reckoning, very unorthodox, and it would wig these C.I.A. faces, because they were all specialists—you know, they had learned by the numbers, and that's how they were trying to teach it—and one of these cats, like a young farm boy, would step up and just estimate the distance and drop it right in the top of a barrel about seventy-five yards away . . . and it would flip the instructor. "Tell him that's not the right way to do it," he'd say to the interpreter.

Were all the weapons American?

Everything was American, man. Blankets . . . well, you know, *everything*.

What else do you recall about the training?

The training was a big drag, except on the firing range, that was pretty interesting. Very corny lectures and training films . . . well, there were a couple of paratrooper films that weren't bad. And we had this group, you know, which was *training* to be paratroops, and they were a gas . . . about a hundred and twenty guys, they were being trained by this guy from California, very funny cat, like something out of a movie, about forty years old, very *tough*—you know the type, fires a 30-caliber machine gun from the hip. And this was the toughest training on the base. But it was a big joke—I mean *this* cat and his paratroopers, it was like Ali Baba and his hundred and twenty thieves. They would go through the most outlandish things you can imagine in order to cop a pig or something off another company—like one guy pretending he's hanging himself, you know, to attract attention, while the other cats cop the pig. They were a wild bunch of studs, man—the paratroopers.

Did you have any tanks there?

No, the tanks never came to the camp—they were put directly on the ship. The tank crews arrived along toward the end, but they had already been trained—in New Orleans I believe.

What did you train for after you finished Basic?

Well, Ramón and I decided that *telegraphy* might be a good thing—I mean they wanted some guys to train for it, so five of us went into that. But it wasn't as easy as it sounded—you know, da-da-dit all day long in a box about the size of a phone booth. Very hot, man, and *coffee flies* . . . terrible, you have to hit them mop-mop-mop and nothing happens. Extremely difficult to kill. The telegraphy hut was right next to the *church*, you dig—it was just a shack, but there were these *priests* . . . not Cuban, *Spanish* . . . Spanish priests, man—they had imported these cats, and *they* were *something*. Very pretentious, very contemptuous of the Cubans—spoke Spanish with a lisp, you know? And one of these cats was too much—weird face, had a weird turn of mind . . . he had been there when they were building the camp, and a guy had been killed . . . fell from a cliff where they were working. And this priest . . . well, we'd step outside the hut, for a smoke, and he would engage us in conversation, like "Why don't you come to church and bla-bla-bla?"—so we'd talk to him and he'd tell about this guy falling over the cliff, but in extreme detail, man . . . how they found the body, how there were traces of where he had clutched at the grass trying to keep from going over the edge, and so on. Very morbid cat.

When did you learn that you weren't going to take part in the invasion itself?

Not until the very last minute. We had *no idea* we weren't going, and it was a big drag man—I mean we'd been there *three months*, dig, and we wanted to *go*. We bugged the hell out of the Americans, Ramón and I, trying to get on that ship—but they wouldn't crack. "There's nothing we can do, your names weren't on the list," was all they would say. There were fourteen of us who didn't go— Ramón, myself, Molinet, who was the quartermaster, the guy in charge of the motor pool, one of the priests, two guys who were clerks, and about seven guys who were on weapons. We were all sore as hell about it—because of course we were sure we were going to win . . . but it wasn't just that—I mean we'd been through a lot together during those three months, and we wanted to go with them.

What do you suppose the reason was?

Well, it wasn't *coincidence*, I'm pretty sure of that. One story was that we were supposed to become cadre—you know, and help train the next group. Like replacing part of the C.I.A., you dig. I don't believe it was because Ramón and I were American, because there was one other American there, a translator for the cooks, and he went.

And when did you learn the outcome of the invasion?

Well, we set up this shortwave radio, with a huge antenna, and listened—tuned in directly to Cuba. And at first it sounded like it was a success . . . so there was a big celebration got started—then after a while Castro came on, announcing how he wiped us out. And that brought everyone down, you know, very hard.

I simply can't understand how they could make such a mess of it.

Well, man, it was one of those things. They *wanted* to do it, but they wanted to do it without really *doing* it—you know, like a broad. So that was that . . . and the camp became a terrible drag after that, and of course everyone wanted to *leave*—you know, back to civilization. But these recruits kept arriving from Miami, about two hundred of them during the next couple of weeks—and this brought on the weirdest scenes of the whole time there . . . because these cats were *bugged*, man. I mean it was obviously a dead issue, and these guys wanted to go back to Miami. But the Americans were still trying to keep up some kind of training routine—you know, "Keep 'em busy, good for morale," the old Army crap. But these guys' attitude was "Okay, we lost, so let's get the hell out of here." And they didn't want to do *anything*. They had a meeting and sent a delegation up to see the Americans and told them they didn't want to drill or anything, they wanted to go back to the States. Well, that wigged the Americans—they thought it was "Communist agitation." See, they were still waiting for orders from Washington about what the hell they were supposed to do next. Anyway, the same day one of the toughest of these cats draws guard duty, and when the guy wakes him, he says, "If you wake me up again I'll blow your head off"—you know, *that* kind of reaction. Well, this guy goes back to the orderly room and tells Martinez Arbona, the guy who was acting camp commander, and Martinez Arbona comes down to the barracks and says, "This is insubordination, bla-bla-bla," and the other guy starts to beat him up. So Martinez cuts out, up the hill, tells the Americans—and this *really* flips them. Now it's a "Communist *mutiny*," you dig, "they're beating up the C.O.!" and so they're scared out of their wits. "We've gotta get those guns away from them!" But they had no idea how to go about it, so they were wigging completely. Well, *we* all knew they weren't Communists—I mean they just wanted to get the hell *out* of there. We told the C.I.A. cats, "Man, all you have to do is tell them to *turn in the guns and they can go home.*" But they kept trying to figure out some tricky muscle way of doing it—and God knows what would have happened if we hadn't gone down and told them if they would turn in the guns they could go home. And of course that's what they did. But the Americans never did really believe it—they were very suspicious of them . . . kept them completely separated from the rest of us. And when we got to the airstrip, they sent them right out . . . you know, like thank God they're gone!

So everybody went back to Miami?

Yeah, we get back to Miami, go to the recruiting station—that's where they'd been sending our checks, dig—pick those up, and go our separate ways. Very sad scene at the recruiting place because they've got the lists of guys that got wiped or captured, and relatives and so on are falling by to look at the lists. And we talked to a couple of guys who got away—swam out and got picked up by boats.

What did they have to say about the invasion?

What did they say? "We got wiped, man . . . *wiped.*"

I
Am
Mike Hammer

ONE SPRING EVENING ten years or so ago I found myself
sharing a large table, outside the Café Flore, with several people
who had just attended the premiere of Serge Lifar's ballet, *Lucifer*.
One of the persons at the table was Jean-Paul Sartre, and another
was a young American cutie-pie, who was getting far more
attention than she deserved. The darling girl, emboldened perhaps no less by Pernod than by the saucy pertness of her cash-
mered bosom—which not even the great philosopher could have
failed to discern—had the audacity to ask: "Monsieur Sartre,
have *you* ever considered writing a ballet?" Out of politeness, no
doubt, he replied with a smile and a simple *"Non."* And that might
well have been that—except for a fantasy which appealed to me
later, in the secrecy of my private night. I think it was the very
blandness of his reply that prompted it; in any case, I imagined that
Sartre had, in fact, gone mad, had written a ballet—and then,
despite his lack of formal training, his unwieldy girth, and the wise
counsel of friends notwithstanding, he had *insisted* on dancing the
leading role himself. The idea of Sartre—heavy glasses, as stout as a
giant turnip-man in close-fitting ballet garb—gravely dancing to
rather common schmaltzy music, or whirling dervishlike to some
kind of weird electronics, was irresistible. I pursued this fantasy
down many avenues: First, the incredible frown of consternation on

the faces of those receiving invitations to the premiere of this ballet "To be Danced by the Author Himself!" Then in the dress circle, his distinguished colleagues from the great universities, muttering, *"Mais c'est un vrai scandale!"* And finally the intermission; what would they say—Camus, Cocteau, Malraux—something like *"Il ne danse pas mal, Jean-Paul . . ."*? Fantastic. And yet the cold reality is that Sartre *was*, in fact, in a position to do precisely that. No impresario in Paris would have refused; had they even hesitated he could have hired the theatre and staged the thing himself to an S.R.O. house. All that was necessary for him to have done this was that he go slightly off his rocker—but, of course, this never occurred.

Well, this old fantasy—which over the years an increasing number of skeptics and unimaginative sorts had pooh-poohed as being "farfetched"—received a tremendous boost in vividness the other day when I learned that Mickey Spillane had decided that he himself would play the role of Mike Hammer in the film version of his novel, *The Girl Hunters*.

Mickey Spillane's literary status has never been fully defined in America. Hard-core quality-Lit. buffs, however, will recall how he smashed into international prominence, in 1947, by concluding his first novel, *I, The Jury*, in a manner which made Malaparte, Céline and the other high priests of the *roman noir* look like a bunch of pansies:

> The roar of the .45 shook the room, Charlotte staggered back a step. Her eyes were a symphony of incredulity, an unbelieving witness to truth. Slowly, she looked down at the ugly swelling in her naked belly where the bullet went in. A thin trickle of blood welled out. . . . Her eyes had pain in them now, the pain preceding death. Pain and unbelief.
>
> How could you? she gasped.
>
> I only had a moment before talking to a corpse, but I got it in.
>
> It was easy, I said.

This confused girl, to make matters even more delightfully *noir*, was a psychiatrist.

Since then Spillane has written eight additional novels which in turn have compiled as yummy a set of statistics as have yet been garnered in the belles-lettres game. They have sold more than seventy-four million copies. In terms of foreign translations, this body of work is now seeded fifth in world literature, topped only by Lenin, Tolstoy, Gorki, and Jules Verne. He is the only contemporary whose work figures among the best sellers of all time. According to Alice Payne Hackett's informative volume, *Sixty Years of Best Sellers*, of the ten best-selling fiction titles in the history of writing, *seven* are by Mickey Spillane (and it only remains to be added, in all fairness, that when Miss Hackett's book was published, in 1956, Mr. Spillane had then *written* only seven).

The denouement of a Spillane story is always softly understated, but not so the middle distance. Here's an engaging high point from *The Girl Hunters:*

> My hand smashed into bone and flesh and with the meaty impact I could smell the blood and hear the gagging intake of his breath. He grabbed, his arms like great claws. He just held on and I knew if I couldn't break him loose he could kill me. He figured I'd start the knee coming up and turned to block it with a half-turn. But I did something worse, I grabbed him with my hands, squeezed and twisted and his scream was like a woman's, so high-pitched as almost to be noiseless, and in his frenzy of pain he shoved me so violently I lost that fanatical hold of what manhood I had left him, and with some blind hate driving him he came at me as I stumbled over something and fell on me like a wild beast, his teeth tearing at me, his hands searching and ripping, and I felt the shock of incredible pain and ribs break under his pounding and I couldn't get him off no matter what I did, and he was holding me down and butting me with his head while he kept up that whistlelike screaming. . . .

"Will you be able to re-create the exact mechanics of that fight scene in the movie?" I asked the Mick when I visited him on the set.

"Well, some of that scene will simply have to be *indicated*," he replied with simple candor.

The Girl Hunters, like *I, The Jury,* is a story of personal vendetta and eye-for-eye (or maybe even two-for-one) justice. Due to a miscalculation, which Mike himself feels responsible for, his beautiful assistant Velda (more friend then employee) has been killed, or so it is presumed, and Mike hits the road with good old-fashioned plasma-and-pulp vengeance in mind.

The film is being made on the MGM lot at Elstree Studios just outside London. It's a Robert Fellows wide-screen production, directed by Roy Rowland, and features, besides the author, Lloyd Nolan, Shirley Eaton and Scott Peters. One of the more unusual aspects of the book is that (like *Fail-Safe*) it also includes a real-life person as one of the major characters—in this case none other than Hy Gardner.

"I think it's a nice touch," said Mickey. "And Hy is going to play himself in the movie."

Spillane's literary conceptions have received strong endorsement from unexpectedly intellectual quarters—most notably from grand Ayn Rand, author of *Atlas Shrugged,* and the founder of the objectivist philosophy.

"Spillane," she says, "is the only writer today whose hero is a white knight and whose enemies represent evil." He is alone, she contends, in having accepted the responsibility of taking a forthright moral position. Mickey himself speaks less abstractly about it. "I've been in the business for twenty-five years. I moved out of pulps because there was more money in the novel field."

For someone like myself, with a Café Flore and White Horse Tavern orientation—where the whole point was not to write a book but to talk one—speaking with Spillane in regard to the Lit. Game was refreshment itself.

"Mick," I said, "the issue of the magazine I'm preparing this for is entirely devoted—except for ads and the like, natch—to the American Literary Scene."

After a terrific guffaw, and a slow, rather deliberate and somehow menacing cracking of knuckles, the Mick said, "Yeah, I've seen those articles—they never mention me; all they talk about are the Losers."

"The Losers?"

"The guys who didn't make it—the guys nobody ever heard of."

"Why would they talk about them?"

"Because they can be condescending about the Losers. You know, they can afford to say something *nice* about them. You see, these articles are usually written *by* Losers—frustrated writers. And these writers resent success. So naturally they never have anything good to say about the Winners."

"Is it hard to be a Winner?"

"No, anybody can be a Winner—all you have to do is make sure you're not a Loser."

"What brought about your decision to portray Mike Hammer yourself?"

"Well, everyone was making a mess of it; they were all missing the point. You see, Mike is a genuinely dedicated person. He's also a *real* person—I mean he's not suppose to be like an actor. You know, a lot of people *believe* in Mike Hammer—they write letters to him, asking his advice about certain things, giving him tips and so on. And it's even stronger than that. For example, I was autographing my last book in a big bookstore down in Puerto Rico, and they ran out of the Spanish edition. So these people started buying the *English* edition—they couldn't *read* it in English, you understand, but they wanted to have the new one with them anyway. It seemed to make them feel more secure to have it with them, even though they couldn't read it."

"I suppose you have certain theories now about acting. What do you think of The Method?"

"Pretending to be a *tree* and so on? No, that doesn't interest me. I have no interest in acting as such. Besides, this is not really an *acting* job."

Before I could get a clarification of this last remark, he was called back to the set, and I took the opportunity to corner the luscious Miss Eaton. She was lolling on the sidelines in a black bikini, a veritable darling, adding a provocative touch of vermilion to her toenails.

"What do perfect young darlings like yourself find attractive about a man like Hammer, if I may ask?"

I detected a slight and exciting flush of ambivalence as she lowered her smoldering gaze.

"Well," she said softly, "if you like tigers . . ." then confided with a disquieting twinkle, "and what girl doesn't—at least in her dark wild dreams? Hmm?"

"Are you kidding?" I asked, but her half-closed eyes and cryptic smile told me no more.

Miss Eaton is a professional and accomplished performer, as are, of course, Lloyd Nolan and the rest of the cast (except perhaps Hy Gardner). Could Mickey hold his own in this crowd? I sought out Mr. Robert Fellows, amiable producer of the film and seasoned vet of Hollywood flicker productions since the heyday of de Mille.

"Now see here," I said, "Spillane admits to no training as an actor—how will he cope?"

Mr. Fellows handed me a British press release, headed *Spillane an Actor?* which quoted Mickey as saying among other things: "I will tell you this much, I *am* Mike Hammer!"

"He *is* Mike Hammer? Is he serious?"

"Mike Hammer is Mickey's alter ego," Mr. Fellows explained quietly, "as you'll find out quickly enough if you ever get drunk with him. Not that I would advise that," he added with an ominous chuckle.

"You mean he starts kicking people's teeth out?"

"No, no," said Mr. Fellows with a frown of distaste, ". . . at least not unduly."

Actually Mickey Spillane seems to be a rather warm and likable person—relaxed, unselfish, with a genuine naturalness that impresses everyone who meets him. Like his manner, his opinions are strong and somewhat direct.

"Thomas Wolfe was a lousy writer," he said. "He didn't know what he was doing."

"How about Hemingway?"

"I'll tell you something about Hemingway—he knocked me out of *Life* magazine once. I was set for a spread in *Life* and Hemingway had those plane crashes and it knocked me out of the issue."

"Well, what about his work?"

"No, his work was too morbid for me."

"How about Cain, Chandler, and Dashiell Hammett?"

"Well, Chandler was all right except that he could never come to a conclusion. But these guys are all in the past. You see, in this business you've got to progress, you've got to keep ahead—or else you just stay behind, being imitated."

"Do you like anyone's work in particular?"

"Most writers don't seem to know what they're doing—they can't come to a conclusion. But I do like Fredric Brown and John D. Macdonald; they're good—they have a point of view and they follow it."

Mickey Spillane's books are now required reading in the writing courses of six different universities.

"How do you feel about literary criticism of your books?"

"The public is the only critic. And the only *literature* is what the public reads. The first printing of my last book was more than two million copies—that's the kind of opinion that interests me."

Then the Mick was called to the set again, back to the turbulent embrace of Miss Eaton. So I decided to walk over and see for myself how things were going. There beneath lights and camera lay a lavish patio pool, framed in the swank courtyard of a Westport-type mansion. The blonde Miss Eaton was reclining on a chaise lounge—black bikini, vermilion nails—a perfect vibrant darling as she stretched lithely forward to lay a persuasive hand on Mickey's sleeve.

"I think I could like you, Mike . . ." she said in a voice both husky and tremulous, "quite a lot."

Mickey shook his head, unsmiling.

"I'm trouble, baby," he said earnestly.

And I must say the Mick looked pretty good in there. Exactly the way Tiger Mike would have handled it, I thought.

The filming of *The Girl Hunters* represents the first time, of course, that a protagonist has been portrayed by its author on the silver screen. If Spillane's undertaking is a successful one, and it appears quite possible, will it not definitely signal a new trend in creative fiction? Many writers are, in fact, already regarding this as a unique and long-awaited opportunity for having their way not merely with the run-of-the-mill starlets but with their *ideal woman*, the girl of their dreams, the marvelous heroine of their own creation. Does it not follow that our literary chaps, with their voraciously inquiring minds, their insatiate quest to get to the bottom of things, will start writing in outlandishly heroic sex scenes, with an eye to ultimate personal realization? It must also be remembered that your writer is notoriously more virile, more sexually interesting, and unscrupulous than is your effete or coldly professional actor. Also generally better-looking. This is known fact. I say we may anticipate some almost incredible developments on the shooting set. An irate and astonished director shouting, "Cut! Cut!" is apt to have precious little effect on chaps like Mailer and Kerouac once they are swinging.

But what about the broader implications? Is it not just remotely possible that here we have stumbled onto the key to obtaining certain highly sought and hitherto unavailable film rights—Holden Caulfield's, for example? Has anyone sounded J.D. about this? But, of course, the real coup will be when some enterprising producer signs up grand old Henry Miller—providing, natch, that Hank is given free rein, and the books are done *right*, without your usual cinematic compromise.

The Butcher

THEY STOOD ALONE NOW, in the street outside the cinema, hesitant, as though they expected him there.

"*Eh alors?*" said Monsieur Beauvais raising his hands to draw the scarf closer. He shrugged. "I knew that it would be difficult."

"We can spare ourselves looking," she began, touching his arm, "just as I told you, you see. We will find him at home."

"Oh yes," he agreed shaking his head a little, "yes, yes," and they began to walk.

Old Beauvais' son was just back from the fighting, and now he had gone out of the cinema and left them, during the newsreel.

Certainly. And yet (it had to be considered) what had there been? Pictures of soldiers and trucks moving past, some explosions in the distance. What was it, artillery shock? Nerves? Weren't his nerves alright? Oh yes. Surely. But he had gone to a café no doubt, to get a drink, a girl. Perhaps even to get really drunk. So they said, so they said.

"Perhaps he had seen it before," she said, not wholly serious. She was old too of course, as old as he, but never so old as the way they walked now, slowly, together in the market street, in the late afternoon.

"Seen it before?" said he, "how could he have seen it before? They don't show the newsreels to soldiers."

"No, naturally not. But in some other place. On the boat, or in a town. There are towns there of course. And don't forget, we've seen that reel before. It may be two or three weeks old."

"Of course," said Beauvais, "and there's the point. It may well have been an action he participated in, and seeing it again just now would have reminded him, could have brought up some certain memory."

"No, he isn't like that," she said, "I'm sure of it. I don't know how they can stand it of course, any of it, but he has never been that way, never. You know he isn't nervous now, you've watched him. I was so thankful when I saw that his nerves weren't affected. He's never been nervous, I've always been thankful for it."

"Oh yes," Beauvais went on quietly, "I've seen it before. There are things a man hides. It was the same with my brother when he came home in '18. Any talk of it made him sick at his stomach."

"Yes, a very different case," she said, stopping in front of a cart of green vegetables, "he was always finicky, and his nerves were bad, even as a child."

Beauvais shook his head. "It isn't so much a question of that," he said.

"I want to get a nice cauliflower," she said, "some nice *boules-de-neige,* you know how he liked cauliflower with melted cheese and a good dressing."

"Yes, of course," he replied, not caring about that now.

Where they stopped again for the cheese, there was a crowd, and Beauvais stood outside the open door, while of his wife everyone asked about the boy, back from the war.

"We are all thankful," they said, "that his wound was not a more serious one."

"No, not serious," said Madame Beauvais, "he must still have his cane of course, but not so serious that they can't take him away again."

"Yes, that is always the worst. But then perhaps it will be over soon."

"They are too young now," said an old woman seriously, "too young for that."

"Yes, perhaps it will all be over soon."

"Yes, oh yes, let us certainly hope so."

Beauvais hardly listened. Not serious? But would he be there?

He was there of course, sitting in the dreary little front room, reading the paper.

"You need not spoil your eyes," said his mother switching on the lamp, "we have the lights here at five in the winter, just as always."

No one spoke of his having left the cinema so abruptly, though once or twice he seemed on the verge of trying to explain, or at least to lie about why it had happened. But they were careful not to press him, so nothing about it was said.

After dinner, he and his father went to a bar down the street. It was a workingman's bar, friends of his father from the *abattoir* were there, mostly strong men and above middle age like M. Beauvais himself, their wives, and with some their children.

"The 'postman's walk' is it?" they said to Beauvais, after they had praised and welcomed the son and stood the two a drink, "what my wife says is if we can't get out of the city, then we're not taking your two weeks until they give us the weather along with it. A holiday's no better than its sunshine she says. And that's how it is with the women, can't wait to get off more clothes, though precious little they've got on as it is. But then it's different with you of course, you've your boy back from the war and in your place there's no doubt I'd do exactly the same. Here let's have another."

Before the evening was out they were both a little drunk but they enjoyed it. Once the boy nearly got into a fight with another young man at the bar. A young punk really, who kept talking very loud though about nothing in particular, until, when one of the older men there with his wife told him to quiet down, the young punk said something really insulting. So the man who was there with his wife started for him, but was held back. And while the younger man stood there ranting still, Beauvais' son took it up against him, he who turned then on both father and son, and actually got in one wild swing before someone managed to grab him—

and Beauvais' son too, who had suddenly made for him, holding his cane like a club. It was over so quickly that hardly anyone noticed, and by the time Beauvais and his son left, feeling very good, the whole crowded bar was singing together.

"I've been thinking," said the boy the next day, "you might want to take a trip somewhere. After all, there's no sense in wasting the vacation here in the city on my account."

His father shook his head. "No, you've your friends to see here. And besides, I'm only taking a week now. We can have a week later, when it's warmer."

The young man shrugged. "My friends," he said, as though this were no reason at all now. Beauvais said nothing, but nodded his head in evident understanding.

After lunch, the boy went out. He wasn't back until late.

"Do you remember," he asked his father at dinner, "the summer I worked in the *abattoir*, there was someone else there in our section about my own age, a son of one of the cutters, I don't remember his name now."

"About your age," repeated the old man, trying to remember, "not Fouché's boy? old Fouché, the head cutter."

"Perhaps," said Beauvais' son, "but it doesn't matter. I was only wondering."

Afterwards, Beauvais went to the bar alone.

"No, he's tired tonight," he said to the *patron*, "he wanted to stay in and read."

"He seems alright," said the *patron*.

"Oh yes. Yes, he's alright."

When Beauvais got home, he found the boy still sitting in the front room. There was a magazine torn into pieces around his feet. Apparently he had just done it.

"Sorry," he said, "it's these picture magazines. I can't stomach them. To see the photographs one would think there was no war at all."

Beauvais sat down heavily. He felt he'd had too much to drink at the bar. He nodded. "Yes, it must be strange to you, that what has been your life for the past year seems to occupy such little, or such misdirected concern of those who forced it on you."

The boy bent down and got one of the torn pages off the floor. "Look at this," he said, bringing it over. He fitted the pieces together under the lamp at his father's chair.

Old Beauvais looked closely. What was it? A torn page, several blurred pictures, convoys in the rain, men picking their way over a town's rubble, artillery explosions at a distance.

"That isn't war," said the young man.

Beauvais nodded. "No," he said, "of course not."

That night the boy had a terrible dream; he woke them up screaming. The father went to him. The boy was alright at once, as soon as he was fully awake, and he apologized.

"You saw the newsreel," he said, "you were there. You know what a farce it was."

Beauvais touched the boy's hand, his warm moist brow. "Yes," he said softly, "yes, yes."

After lunch the next day they were in the dreary little front room and the boy began to talk, sitting on the divan—not smoking—simply sitting there alone with his father beside him in the dull light, the boy sitting out on the edge of the divan, letting his hands clasp and unclasp in telling his secret, with only the rise and fall of his voice to violate the deadly monotony of the afternoon.

"In the first attack, the first *bayonet* attack, I held back, and in the second as well. No one noticed of course. There were plenty of others, falling down as if they were shot. It didn't matter. But the next day, the very next morning, there was a terrible fight and they overran our position. We knew it would happen. I knew it. But no one could get out, the officers were everywhere. *We had to fix bayonets*.

"I couldn't get the bayonet on at first. My hands were trembling. You see, I didn't want to cut them. Shoot at them, yes, but I couldn't cut them open—in training they tell you to stick the bayonet in, as hard as you can, and twist up—I didn't want to be cut open, you understand, to die cut open. I wanted to surrender, to huddle on the ground and cry.

"When the shelling stopped they started coming of course, across

the field, not close at first but small, like crabs at an impossible
distance and as though they were running sideways not knowing
where we were. But they came on, falling, always, falling and
getting up, until they were falling closer and closer. Everyone was
firing now. I had begun to fire without knowing it. A second before
the shelling stopped I had no control over myself, I only knew that
when it stopped and they started across the field I would scream
and run. But now I was shooting. They came. Falling. Falling and
getting up. *How many had to fall before they stopped coming?* Then
the first wave did stop. When they fell, they didn't get up. And the
wave after that, and after that. But each fell a little closer until they
were not waves falling but faces. It was absurd, the way we went
on firing from the hole, lying there, aiming the rifle, just as though
they were still two hundred yards away when now they were trying
to throw grenades as they fell. And then falling too close to throw
them, and finally not falling at all, when the face I was shooting at
didn't stop coming.

"I couldn't think about it, there was no time at all. I only raised the
bayonet to keep him from coming down on me, just as with a
stick you might try to fend off a falling bird. But I lunged it. I
lunged it, twisting it up from his stomach.

"He was a huge man, I had to go back under his weight, holding
the bayonet in his stomach. And the way he was, looking angry and
surprised, not wanting to admit that it was there, pressing me back
like he were a bull. Then I lunged it again, twisting it up and out,
and it sawed straight up his stomach, parting the cloth with it and
cutting his belt in two so that his pants fell open. And standing there,
still looking surprised, and ridiculous now, we both looked down
at his stomach, how it was hanging wide open, though only for an
instant, then everything went down with his blood and the screaming. I can tell you it happened in an instant. Then the blood was
everywhere of course. It was over me, all around me. I was standing
straight up. I should have been killed then, standing up in the hole.
But I knew at once, the way the firing was going, that we were
falling back, and I got out of the hole and began to run.

"That night I couldn't sleep for thinking about it. I went over it again, every move, a thousand times. I put the bayonet in—slowly this time, to see exactly what happened. It was terrible. When I closed my eyes, it was there. All night I had chills and fever, once I even began to cry, but I always came back to it. There was something there, something—and I knew of course, even then I knew, but I pushed it back.

"I began to remember the instant of pressure against the bayonet before it went into his stomach, how for just an instant the stomach had resisted it. I went over it on a screen, in slow motion, thought of it diagramed on paper, as in the hygiene folders: a blue arrow here, red dots there, a segmented line. It was something fantastic, the bayonet and the stomach. Unreal, and for a while it was unbelievable. But most of all, while it was unreal it was terrible. And that was why of course.

"Nothing happened for a week. But I thought about it. The inside of the stomach, delicate and precise, even subtle. And then the bayonet was there, unexpected, so inexplicably there, and what it *did* when it moved through the stomach was so unreal that it couldn't have happened. Then it did happen again. And it was the same thing, exactly the same thing, except that I knew then, just as I had almost known before, that it was *real*. And that was it. Once it was real, it wasn't terrible, you see. No, it wasn't terrible. I tried to keep it terrible, as a priest does things, because I was afraid, and I *am* afraid. But it was real, can you understand that? Once it was not a dream or an abstraction it couldn't be terrible. I tried of course, I tried. The others did it, it didn't bother them. I said, 'It isn't a stomach, what it is, is destroying an enemy. It's terrible of course, but it's no more than that. It's no more than terrible.' Because if one could keep it there, not let it out, it would be alright. I was afraid, you see, not afraid of being a coward, I was a coward of course. But afraid of losing my mind. Once I tried to talk to someone about it. He said I had too much imagination. 'But it's real,' I said, 'it really happens doesn't it?' 'Don't think about it so much,' he said.

"He was killed two days later. He was almost deaf from concussion and he couldn't hear the shells coming in. I yelled to him—he was standing up in his hole when the first shell came—and I yelled. He couldn't hear me of course, he was half deaf from concussion. It hit ten feet in front of him. It exploded in his face.

"I crawled over to see. I knew he was dead, but I went over. 'See if you can help him,' I said, '*see.*' I knew he was dead of course.

"There was plenty of time. It was getting dark, no one else was around. There was plenty of time to see his face. It was inside out. I knew it was his face because of the way the feet were turned. Absurd isn't it? More as though his neck were very long like a dressed fowl, without a head. But I wasn't sick. In fact, it didn't bother me. It was understandable: industrial accident, railway disaster. Hospitals must get them every day. It was even abstract and believable. What it really was, was impersonal. The way you drop in the mortar shell and close your ears and perhaps your eyes too. Or throw the grenade and hide on the ground. Never look. Throw as well as you can, nothing more. Don't look. Keep your head down. You'll find them in the holes. But they may have been dead for a week, even the ones still moving. A terrible thing of course, still nothing to do with you, finding them like that, the face inside out, like a chicken's neck.

"But it was more than that. Because I never enjoyed shooting anyone. I only shot *at* them. Even when I could see I might have hit, it was still only shooting *at* them. Nothing ever happened. You shot, and if you could see anything, you either hit or missed. But I never cared about that because nothing ever really happened. I wasn't simply a killer, you see, I was something else, a butcher.

"After that, I used to lie in the hole, not firing anymore, just waiting, praying they would come. In the attack, I was always in the first wave. I won't try to tell you what it was like then, killing them with the bayonet. It was like something, anything that had suddenly stopped being terrible. Yes, it was the opposite of terrible, but it was stronger. Because when it was terrible, I had to quiet it, hold it back. Now I gave over to it. Not at first, I was too afraid, but finally I gave over to it completely. I had to, you see, since it was real. You can understand that, that it was really happening, a fantastic and incredible thing was happening. Before the attack I strained like a leashed dog, do you know what that means? to kill violently? To butcher something and know what you're doing while you're doing it? It's unreal isn't it. Yes, of course. A kind of insane drunkenness. It was unreal to me too. But I couldn't keep it that way, unreal and terrible. I thought I would go mad before the attack, my whole head throbbed, my hands shaking with impatience. To butcher them, cut them open. Not just the stomach, but the throat and the face, to crush in the face with the rifle butt. It was real, you understand, real, and I was doing it.

"But you can't see it can you? No, you won't see it. I know that. You see something else, like fear and death, or courage, or something you can see on paper. But you *could* see if you only listened, if you really got the meaning there, behind the words, the feeling: not just to 'take life' but really to take an alive thing in your hand and cut it in half. It's behind the words, you see, the thing I'm talking about, the real thing, is behind the words.

"I'll tell you this: I didn't need the bayonet. I used it, why shouldn't I? There was no secret about what it was for. The others knew. But they were fools, they didn't believe it, even after it happened. *They didn't know what they were doing.* Of course I used it. I would have torn a face apart with my mouth. But I used the bayonet. We all had them, since training, everyone knew about it. I had mine, and that's how I killed them. And nothing else mattered. Nothing. Of course I had to get there. I had to get there without being killed. But that was only annoying, tantalizing sometimes. There was no danger. I shut that out completely so as not to spoil it. And I was careful, you see, but I was also fast. I had to get there, but I had to get there quickly.

"One morning there were two attacks on a hill outside S. and I was decorated for leading a charge while wounded. I didn't know, you understand. I was shot in both legs. After it was over, I saw I was wounded and I couldn't stand up. During the attack I had been running. The surgeon said it was impossible. Later I even showed him the citation. He never believed it of course."

And he was done. The boy finished as simply and quietly as he had begun, having only once or twice shown any emotion about what he was saying. Now he sat back with his chin on his chest, his eyes soft, offlooking down across the floor, not in wanting or even anticipation of anything from his father beside him.

And Beauvais felt no need to speak, felt nothing for the moment. Then, 'Of course,' he said to himself, 'the boy's getting it off his chest.'

Beauvais returned to his job the next day, to one of the large *abattoirs* on the edge of the city where he worked as a cutter.

He had to get there early, for the whole day's work of the *abattoir* began in his section. So when he stepped off the bus, the morning still hung gray and wet around the open square where only the yellow arc lamps shone.

Flat, black, far back off one side of the open square sat the *abattoir*, so great and dismal, an uncertain form in the half night when Beauvais crossed the square.

White lights burned through the mist from the Café du Sang des Bêtes on the corner, and Beauvais went inside. A dozen or so workers were standing around having a glass of coffee at the bar, or a hot wine.

"*Tiens!*" someone cried.

"Here he is now."

They greeted Beauvais noisily, moved toward him, old Fouché waving a newspaper.

It was a local morning paper, and on the fourth page they had found a little item about Beauvais' son, saying that he had been repatriated and was convalescing. It gave Beauvais' name and address, and said that the boy had been decorated for bravery, and the item ended quoting the following citation, furnished by the War Minister's Office, which old Fouché now read aloud for what must have been the sixth time that morning:

" 'During the action of the morning of the 19th, Private Gerard Beauvais distinguished himself and his unit by pressing forward in attack, under heavy fire, despite severe leg wounds, leading a courageous and successful bayonet charge on a vital enemy gun emplacement, and personally destroying three of its crew in the subsequent action.

" 'Apart from individual merit, such a display of ardent will and valor by a private soldier serves to inspire fellow troops to acts above and beyond the call of duty, and stands in the finest tradition of the Service.' "

"*Voilà un homme!*" said someone warmly.

"He's his father's son," they all agreed.

Fouché cut out the item with his pocket knife and gave it to Beauvais. They all stayed at the café a little longer than usual. Most of those who were drinking hot wine had a second glass.

The men left the café and crossed the square in a loose body, but by the time they were halfway down the broad approach to the *abattoir*, they had fallen apart into talking about war, football, and the price of food, mostly meat.

Beauvais walked with old Fouché the head cutter and two men from waste disposal. Ahead now, they could see them moving, far back along the great dismal side of the building where already the boxcars sat, in unloading.

"Back not a moment too soon," said Fouché, "sixteen carloads from the north this morning."

In the dank vastness of the *abattoir*, under the gray vaulted skylight, the men crisscrossed to their departments, parting with a wave of the hand or an obscene jest.

At the lockers Beauvais hung up his coat and jacket, put on the great leather apron and his high rubber boots.

On the way to the racks he stopped at the sharpener's corner.

"I've been saving it for you," said the sharpener, who had been drinking hot wine at the café, and now passed over to Beauvais a thin curved blade, so whet that its edge died away in a sheen of light.

"Give me a keen edge," said Beauvais, "they say we'll have our hands full this morning."

"Try it," said the other, baring the black curls of his forearm.

Swiftly, Beauvais' hand swept the edge down and back, and across the forearm the hairs fell cleanly away in a narrow swath.

"Haven't lost the touch I see," said the sharpner.

"Nor you," said Beauvais, "it's a needle and a razor."

In the cutter's section it was a great morning for Beauvais. Everyone stopped round to welcome him back, asking about his son, wanting to see the clipping.

Finally he stuck the clipping on the high end of his cutting rack so he wouldn't spoil it, getting it in and out of his pocket with wet hands.

White steam rose thick from the rack, the sloshing floor, and the heavy soaked apron. Beauvais worked steadily. And while his eyes may have shone with their joy, his hands were none the slower for it and held the deftness of twenty years experience.

"Here now," cried old Fouché in a bluff humor from the next rack, "we're not at the beach today. There's work here." He nudged one of the handlers standing alongside, "Never send a cutter on vacation to the Riviera," he said coarsely. "Martinis give an unsteady hand and the sunshine weakens their eye." They all laughed, Beauvais the heartiest. He was the best among them.

The handlers rolled them in on a wide flat cart, the bleating sheep, struggling a little under the thongs.

Lying on the rack, stomach up, they were perfectly still, the heads hanging over backwards, stretching the throat up in a gentle white arch.

Beauvais passed down the line, taking them one at a time, quickly, silently, the left hand firm on the lower jaw stretching the throat a little more, arching it up just so, and the right hand slipping in the long blade below the ear, deep into the throat, bringing it around in a swift clean slice to the other ear. He cut the throat as smooth and quick as a surgeon would lance a tiny boil, laying the whole of it open with such speed and grace that for one gaping instant there was no wetness, only the great hollow redness of the wound, and scarcely had the hot steaming blood surged up and over his apron when the blade was sliding like a razor in cream cheese thru the white throat of the next. And the crimson heads dropped limp as he went, left hanging by the threads of a muscle as so many broken flowers while the racked bodies rocked in the convulsion of trying to expel all their blood in one big spurt.

By the time Beauvais reached the end of the rack, his feet were sloshing above the ankles in blood, the hot, rarefied pungence of it rising with its steam to cloud over the whole rack and dim the eyes of the men in the cutting section.

Then they were done, till the steam died away. And Beauvais looked over to where two or three of the others paused against the wall by Fouché's rack for a cigarette.

"Swim on over," called Fouché, "he's just back from Monte Carlo," he said, nudging someone beside him in the same old joke.

Between them, out from the racks the concrete floor sloped down to a great red flooded gutter trough. Beauvais started across, slipping a little, stepping out so as not to slosh it, slowly, deep on his boots, the smell of it coming up on the steam.

He stamped his dripping feet when he was across, kicked them against the wall, leaving a splotch of red and dark splatters.

Fouché reached out, touched his arm lightly, proferred a cigarette. *"Bienvenue,"* he said to Beauvais, and there was an odd warmth in his voice.

Beauvais stood with them, but closer to the wall, the blood tide lapping at his boots.

"I haven't noticed Louis around," he said carefully, leaning back, "and the boys from disposal. They seem late in getting around with the brooms this morning."

The
Automatic Gate

"IT IS FANTASTIC," said Monsieur Pommard from his chair at the ticket gate. He hesitated, cigarette paper at his lips, wishing certainly, to augment this. "It is truly fantastic," he said, and switched his tongue back and forth over the gummed edge, moving his head as he did so, a little unnecessarily. "Do you know that I am actually sick?" and he touched, on his jacket, an old brass button where his heart might have been.

A taller man, in like uniform, stood sullenly, watched the outgoing train, only thinking under the passing rush of noise that *it was really too bright here*, that, in fact, he could see the dirt in the pores on the back of his hand. His eyes traced the track, low set between sweeps of clean concrete, all cast a sterile rose green from the overhung fluorescence. One could change at Etoile, he thought, and seeing how the few people on this platform stood so well dressed, oddly at leisure for the hour—and all, or as it seemed, so near to where the first-class carriage would stop, thought again, it would take longer certainly, but one could change at Etoile.

And he saw then that the *portillon automatique* to their left, the electro-pneumatic gate which admitted or shut out transferring passengers automatically, was so freshly painted it looked wet.

"I said to my wife," M. Pommard went on, " 'in the first place, if she is not French, why should she prepare a French dish?' Tell me that." And this time, he offered it up with his eyes and in such complete faith that the other man, even he, must come back quickly, and be there, so as not to spoil it entirely.

"Probably she wished to make a good impression," he replied, thinking, there it is then, the needle is threaded again.

"Certainly," said M. Pommard, his gratitude too tacit now, even to be assumed, "her intentions were well, I'm sure of that, but all the same! And consider this: my cousin, a man of affairs, a very important business in Lyon. It is not as though he gets to Paris every day, on the contrary. A well established man you understand, I'm sure he was sick, I'm sure of that."

The other nodded, only taking it up conversationally, "Yes, those things happen." And even now they were cleaning the tiles here. These lights, like an American toilet, he thought.

"But can you imagine it," M. Pommard pressed, impatient perhaps with the other man's youth, his brief service with the Company, "a *fondue* made with Camembert? And with all the mold no doubt!"

"Yes, it could be dangerous, a thing like that." A most important station, they said, not large but exclusive. The rich and the poor; he hated most especially, he believed, the very rich.

"There you are then," said M. Pommard and seemed on the verge of standing, "realize this: a child at the table, my daughter, less than six, a baby really. For myself it makes no difference, on the contrary, I have a strong constitution. During the war, as a soldier," and he touched absently, not as he had his heart, a bit of red on black lapel, "we ate everything." And as he opened his gate and began to punch the tickets, he told, aside the line of incoming passengers, how once he had eaten of a putrified horse, or some such, an uncooked chicken perhaps. As he did this, laughing to himself sometimes, he handled the tickets expertly, not too fast, but very careful, often holding them to the light, just to see perhaps if they had not been twice punched already, and once, when a well dressed woman stopped to ask about some train connection or other, he directed her with firmness and authority.

Here the younger man watched, trying to be apart, disdainful even, but was, in fact, only a little embarrassed. His uniform was shabby, and there was some dirt on the back of his hand.

"You will change at Odeon for the direction of St. Cloud," M. Pommard was saying, when there was a commotion behind the *portillon automatique* on their left, some running on steps, and this heavy steel door, just closing as the lights of the train appeared at the far end of the platform, was caught and held back by a man on the other side who wedged his body into the narrowing opening and squeezed thru.

M. Pommard had already closed his own gate, and he came to his feet at once, "*Attention!*" he cried, "*Vous vous trompez, Monsieur! Attention!*" and he hurried after the man who ran now, as without noticing him, toward the waiting train.

He came back, shaking his head from side to side, a little out of breath. He had worked in the Metro for twenty-five years, he was an old man now.

"The pig," he muttered, stopping to examine the automatic gate. He was obviously upset.

"I shouldn't worry," said the other, thinking certainly he must catch the next train himself.

"The dirty pig," said old Pommard, his voice quite unsteady.

"Yes, it is scarcely worth it," the other went on, "Oh I know the type certainly. My God, at Clignancourt! But I never bother, tell me, why should we on our salary?"

"Yes, but all the same," said M. Pommard, taking his chair, "it sickens me. Besides, we have our orders, isn't that so?"

"Listen," M. Pommard was saying to the Clignancourt gatekeeper the next evening, "you understand, I know this man. Certainly. It is not the first time for him, far from it, he has rushed the automatic gate before, running ahead on the steps no doubt, and then just squeezing thru as it shuts. Wednesday night it happened, I'm sure it was the same man, again last night as you saw for yourself, and then tonight."

"Tonight? It happened again tonight?" the other replied as incredulous, thinking he must not miss two or three trains home again tonight listening to the old man's stories.

"Certainly. What did you expect," said M. Pommard making a

sweet-bitter face, "that he would allow the gate to shut properly, when he's in a hurry?"

"In a hurry, eh? So much the worse for him then!" said the other laughing in a patronizing sort of way.

M. Pommard did not laugh. "It will not happen again," he said in a challenge to the younger gatekeeper, "make no mistake about that."

"Yes. Well of course you could report him to the Company, or to the police for that matter," answered the other without any sincerity at all.

"To the *Company?*" said the old man, a little astonished probably. "What would you have me do then, go to the Company and say, 'Here now, I am no longer able to keep my gates'?" At this he drew himself straighter in the chair, "After twenty-five years service, August eighth, and nine as keeper of this gate, you will have to find a new man! A younger man no doubt." He looked down the empty platform, where now the *portillon automatique*, like his own gate beside him, stood open wide. "What you may not understand," he went on, shaking a finger without any real malice, "that in a matter of this kind, *I* am the Company." There he stopped full, hesitating, as at some kind of distance. "After all," he began finally, but his voice caught up so that he stopped again, and looking about him, made a small gesture with his hands, "after all, these are my gates," and when he raised his eyes, for the young man, seeing the dead dry waste of the old man's face, it was terrible, the tears there.

The old fool, he said to himself, surprised almost at saying it. "I shouldn't worry," he said aloud, and for all his hypocrisy, placed a hand on the other's shoulder.

"It will not happen again," said M. Pommard, shaking himself and standing. He walked toward the automatic gate, "Shall I tell you why? Because I served three years as apprentice mechanic with the Company, and two years following as full mechanic. In those days," he stopped before the automatic gate and faced the other gatekeeper, "there were no shortcuts in the Service. One began at the bottom." He paused as if this point should be allowed to stand alone for a moment, or as if perhaps, he had forgotten the larger point altogether. "Consequently," he went on then, "I am able to adjust this automatic gate myself, that is, to regulate the pressure so that it will function properly as intended. Notice this," he continued, leaning over to touch the pressure apparatus at the bottom of the gate, "by turning this valve, the closing pressure is increased; by turning the other, it is decreased. Now you see I have increased the closing pressure."

He looked at the other man who nodded then as if he had followed it closely. "There you are then," said M. Pommard wiping his hands, "not a complicated thing certainly, but a matter of knowing how," he shrugged, "of experience, as they say." And his voice at once became lighter, as they walked back to the chair, a hand on the other's shoulder, he was almost jovial, wanting to be told again which the younger's station was, and how long he had been there.

A useless old man, thought the other, feeling quite suddenly very violent, as he felt also the weight of the knife in his pocket.

On the following night the Clignancourt gatekeeper and old Pommard had been talking for only a moment when an incident, something like those of the previous evenings, occurred. From where they were standing, it was difficult to know exactly what happened when the man entered the automatic gate as it was shutting.

This metal door, standing open to admit the *correspondance* passengers, had, as the lights of the train appeared at the far end of the platform, begun closing inward as usual, very steadily, and when the opening was less than a foot wide, the man had stepped sideways between the door and the iron sill, and very quickly thru and onto the platform. Evidently the man had been running, to reach the door as it closed, but whether he actually retarded its closing, one could not say. Certainly it had touched him, and for the briefest instant he stood, his chest against the door's edge, his back against the sill, yet the door continued to close, or so it seemed, steadily.

As before, it happened so quickly that M. Pommard must have been taken by surprise. He broke off in the middle what he was saying to the other gatekeeper, "*Attention!*" he shouted, "*vous vous trompez là! Attention!"* and he went after the man, calling out, running, hopping in wrath, across the platform to the very door of the carriage.

When he came back he was evidently quite shaken. He looked once defensively at the other gatekeeper, "What would you have me do then, hold up the train?" and here he began something about Schedules, forgetting for the moment how much the other knew, by heart as well.

"Yes, he is a pig, that one," mused the Clignancourt gatekeeper as he stared after the passing train, "how well I know the type! A rich pig," and, remembering vaguely, wondered once if it was really the same man. This one went into first-class. Naturally, he thought, fat rich pig.

"He's an anarchist," said the old man gravely.

"Anarchist?" echoed the other, really surprised.

"Certainly. What did you expect? He has no respect, no respect for the regulations. He squeezes his way thru the *portillon automatique*, while it is closing, do you understand? But then, of course, you saw it yourself."

"Yes, I know," said the other, coming back, "that happens. At Clignancourt they are like cattle. When they see the automatic gate closing, sometimes they run and hold it back by force. Twice they've broken it this year. The people are crazy," just as one day, he thought, they will break these city gates again. And, as for the fat pigs then! He picked at his nose and spat, almost in the same motion.

"Broken! There you are then," said the old man with a shrug. He turned back to the automatic gate, made some more adjustments there. "Now a team of oxen could not hold back that gate," he said flatly.

"So much the better," said the young man, thinking of other things no doubt.

There were only a few people on the platform the next evening when M. Pommard closed his gate as the lights of the 11:03 for the Porte de Versailles appeared at the far end.

In the *correspondance* passage now, was the Clignancourt gate-keeper himself, late from some violent political meeting. He was just coming down the last flight, even as the lights of the 11:03 were closing inward, caught up and twisting on the cold gloss of the automatic gate. Then he was thinking how, in seeing him, the useless old gatekeeper here would raise two fingers to his cap, would slowly, dutifully get to his feet and come over, *noblesse oblige*.

Thinking this, he thrust one hand, as automatically as the closing gate before him, deep in his pocket and rushed absently ahead, reached the gate and stepped thru freely, onto the platform.

M. Pommard was sitting easily, and in fact, as anticipated by the other, had just raised two fingers to his cap in greeting, but as their eyes met, holding for one instant the fearful contempt between them, there was some commotion from behind, in the automatic gate. And there, for this same sharp instant, on a young lady's face was a look of astonishment, child at a magic show, blotted over now by the rush of blood from her nose and mouth.

They both turned at the noise, and M. Pommard nearly bowled the young man over, rushing past, shaking his head, crying aloud through the screams, *"Attention! Vous vous trompez! Attention!"*

But then a crowd was already gathering, closing in boldly, as even now under no apprehension themselves, yet making it more difficult, to be sure, for old Pommard, with his halting push and pummel, to get through to the trouble there in the automatic gate.

A Change
of
Style

AT FIVE O'CLOCK the afternoon sun wanes aslant the smart low-roofed shops of Westwood, hangs heavy over corners like a loose saffron shawl, flooding office and showroom with folds of yellow light, turning the cream-walled cubicles of the Mayfair Coiffeur to a golden rose.

Seated before the mirror in one of the cubicles, hat and purse on her lap as she pays another last tribute to her own new, fascinating image, Grace Owen feels a sudden, novel affinity for sunlight. She remembers now what it does for blondes, how it darts and shimmers through the strange, beautiful hair lying half-hidden in it, glinting out from deep, opaque recesses.

She takes the hat from her lap, tries it at a tentative angle. Amazing. Who would have guessed that blonde hair could make such a difference—all the difference in the world. What will Ralph say? Ralph had always wanted a blonde and now he would have one. Perhaps it is true, after all, that men do prefer blondes!

For an instant her eye leaves the hat and falls on the chromed bell of the hair dryer. How harshly bright the silvery metal is in the light of the sun! There's really no comparison between gold and silver. Gold has softness. Grace feels a small, unaccountable shudder at the sun's sharp glare on the chrome and, again, at the faint resurgence of the odor that has filled the cubicle all afternoon:

peroxide, by now dried away, almost to memory. She realizes it is getting late.

At the door of the beauty shop Mrs. Owen says good-afternoon to the receptionist and, in the street, immediately feels a growing excitement.

The quick-march tempo of early-evening traffic has not yet set in: the sidewalks are still in possession of the casual shopper, the woman in slacks, the young couple leaving the matinee; and, in the street, lazy convertibles pull out slowly from the Xanado Drive-In. Only near the supermarket, where housewives, harried and off schedule, fumble in their bags to tip the boys who carry the sacks to the car, is there any other apparent tension in the afternoon.

Grace walks quickly. As her eyes catch at her passing reflection in store fronts, the rest of her fights to appear unconcerned. Five doors beyond the beauty salon, she pauses at a furniture-shop window. But the expanse of plate glass recasts the studied blonde image as Grace recalls from somewhere a tall girl, rising in the surf like an ivory statue, striding up a blazing beach and dropping to one knee to pull off her bathing cap and shake her head. The bronzed face was tilted back and the golden hair fell in a lustrous sweep across her shoulders as the sun glinted through the whole honeyed sheen in a thousand tiny spangles.

Waiting for the changing light, she risks a touch at her hair, and at once senses the eyes of the couple beside her, the quick, lynx-look of the woman, the unmistakable scrutiny of the man. Grace turns her head away casually, drawing in her trim-girdled tummy a bit more. The light changes and she starts across, feeling the loose, clean toss of her hair as she steps from the curb.

Halfway across, looking toward the tightening stream of cars, she draws herself up sharply, catching her breath in a gasp. But Harry was looking past her, toward the drugstore. Had he already seen her and deliberately looked away? She continues briskly ahead, remembering the new suit and her hair. He hadn't recognized her, of course. Before she reaches the opposite curb she is certain of it, and she has an impulse to stop and turn around. Not that it isn't all over between them; of course it is. Still, how would he look if

he saw her now? What would he say? Slowed almost to a stand-
still, Grace vaguely considers it, examining her hands, the two rings
she has worn for seven years, the bright-colored nails. Anyway, it
is certainly not the right moment; she must get home before Ralph.
So she hurries on, feeling some accomplishment in what she has
done, telling herself that Ralph had never guessed about Harry.
How could he?

Grace reaches her car and searches through her purse for the keys
before finding them in the ignition. She smiles, a little scornfully,
thinking of Ralph's own carelessness about leaving the keys in the
car and how she has scolded him for it. How, in fact, their relationship has gradually been reduced to almost just that, her complaints
and his acquiescences, the perfunctory kisses as he leaves for the
office, and the circle of friends they see mechanically. But sitting
here, her fingers on the keys, she suddenly has a glimpse of Ralph
as she had seen him that first time long ago, on a shaded terrace,
bending politely toward the seated hostess, lean and tanned, with
something of the serious little boy in his smile. She remembers, too,
the same smile in other shaded places: the beach at Acapulco, a
cottage in Havana during the idyllic month they spent without
clocks or newspapers. And Grace Owen finds herself in love with
her husband all over again. It isn't too late to make up for the nag-
ging, the perfunctory kisses. At least she is sure of Ralph, and that
is the main thing. She looks at herself in the car mirror. No, it isn't
too late at all.

She starts the car, backing out slowly into the growing traffic,
ready to turn in the direction of home, away from the shopping
center and the beauty salon. But then, on an impulse, she decides
to turn the other way and pass by the drugstore.

She sees Harry's parked car, empty, and feels relieved, telling
herself again that it is all over, and that this, too, she will make
up to Ralph.

Circling the block and pulling back into the stream of cars going
away from the shopping village, she drives faster, picturing to herself the scene at home when Ralph comes in from the office. "Hello,
darling," he'll say, and then, in little-boy astonishment, "Why,

darling, you're absolutely beautiful!" And he'll take her in his arms and kiss her in a way she's almost forgotten—in a way, too, she knows he can kiss no one else.

Ralph isn't home when Grace reaches the house. For a while she sits in the living room, looking out over the lawn and front walk. Now she stands before the long glass, touching her hair and the jacket of her new gabardine suit; coral, she decides, is an attractive color for blondes.

She begins to pace the floor, wondering what she will say when Ralph comes in. No, she won't say anything. But he—what will he say? What if he doesn't notice at all? But, of course, he will notice it. She will be sitting under the light. He will notice immediately that her hair is a different color, a rich golden blonde.

Outside, the sunlight is fading. Standing in the center of the room now, she hears his footstep on the walk and, as her heart begins to beat faster, there is a sudden stab of doubt. Has it been a mistake? She crosses to the mirror. No, it's all right. It's perfect. She sits down on the sofa, and then moves to a chair near the window, where the light is stronger. There's still time to put on the overhead light, but no, that will be too obvious. This is it, by the window, in the dusk. She half-forms the words, *Hello, darling,* and they dissolve in her throat. She tries to think of the tall girl standing in the surf, but can only think of Ralph's expression, and she begins to blush. His feet are now on the steps, now on the porch. Grace feels the hot flush of her cheeks, and she lowers her head and covers her face with her hands. She hears the door swing open behind her, his footsteps on the threshold, and then the abrupt stop. She thrills to the sharp catch of his breath, the husky, unfamiliar panic—and something more—just before he says:

"For Christ's fucking sake, Elaine, I told you never to come here!"

The Face
of
the Arena

NOW, IT MAY HAVE BEEN THE HEAT—for certain August afternoons in Barcelona blaze with a strange and terrible light—or, it may have been that people were feeling fed up, in some serious way they didn't yet understand; but today, waiting for the fourth bull, the filled Arena rose up and around like the inside of a great cauldron, the living walls a huge, tortured mosaic that wavered in the black-lined heat, as though the whole thing were slowly coming to a boil.

Below, at the base of a shadow stretching halfway across the ring like a giant's pointed hand, the veteran capeman, Rafael Marulanda, leaned heavily against the barrier, looking into the crowd, a deep, dark emptiness in his eyes, feeling nothing. He had felt nothing towards the crowd for a long time, only the hollow certainty that he himself went unnoticed.

He knew that the bull would be bad, and the matador, too, full of false grimaces, like an Italian wrestler. But for Marulanda the knowledge was only vague, and deep; it was no longer bitter, nor even alive. One would have said that he was very, very tired.

The truth was that today was a sort of anniversary for him. Twenty years ago he had made his début as a novillero. In fact he had made two débuts. On the first occasion, he had been unable to kill his bull, and had given such a poor performance otherwise that he was knocked down with cushions and bottles, and could not finish on the program. In his second, and last fight—which had taken place in this very Arena—he had been gored in the back while climbing the barrier. Since then he had worked, for twenty years, as a capeman, an assistant to the matadors.

He did not even hear the *clarine* sounding the entrance this time, only the noise of the crowd as the bull came out—the great whispery gasp of the crowd, as always, in astonishment, and he was dully reminded of his work to be done. He was the first, as it happened, for the huge bull, after an instant's incredulity past the trap, moved rapidly forward across the ring in a big, swaying trot, his head high, nostrils searching the wind, and then broke towards Marulanda's cape that was swinging out over the safety-break in the barrier. He watched the bull without focusing his eyes and, as he withdrew the cape, he saw the bull rage past, a heavy unevenness on the dancing light.

Very often lately Marulanda did not bother to fix things with his eyes; and now, as the bull ravaged by, and on toward the next cape, Marulanda stepped into the Arena, and he stepped against the flank of Machito's horse, the first picador horse, which at that moment, was blindly, laboriously clanking past. The fat, shapeless Machito, all thick-neck and sour-faced, was perched on the horse like a huge egg. "What's the matter?" he cried, pointing a stirrup at Marulanda, a stirrup thickened with spangles of copper and brass. "Drunk, is he?" and his laugh was a raucous chain of coughs. But, of the whole funereal entourage of red-shirted peones trudging with the horse, only one turned his head and shrugged.

The others were looking at the magnificent bull.

Motionless now, on the far side of the Arena, in the full brilliance of the sun, he was as a great hewn thing, a wedge of solid black, looking heavy as wet marble with his monstrous hump of back a sheen through the glassy heat.

For the next five minutes Marulanda did his work by reflex, not thinking in helping to place the bull for the picador, making wide, circling passes, and then stepping back until he was needed.

The fourth time he took the bull however, something came alive inside him, and with a sudden steely tenderness and the leaning poise of a ballerina, he executed an intricate three-chicuelina faena that culminated in facing the bull squarely before the picador, drawing a savagely sharp burst of applause from the crowd, and causing a matador leaning against the barrier to frown oddly and mutter an aside to an attendant at his elbow.

He scarcely saw the bull after that, but looked past him, sometimes into the crowd, seeing the bull as a dark image that flowed across the screen of his mind, coaxed and avoided, impersonally.

Then he was not needed with the second picador, and he stood against the barrier, holding his cape folded to his chest, the way a girl will stand with her schoolbooks. From here he saw them place the bull once more, a haze of lines and points, tracing an old, monotonous pattern—so that on the instant of the bull's last charge, he could not have noticed how high above the satin black rock of shoulders spread the great horns, feathering out all golden, to points of brilliance in the sun.

Then Machito was down, squirming and scrambling with one leg under the horse, while the over-anxious bull rooted the ground in blind ferocity before him and the crowd jeered and whistled and stamped their feet, perhaps because Machito was in no real danger and had piced the bull badly.

They say, or did say, that Marulanda was a typical failure—through ineptitude and cowardice. This no longer disturbed him, though it used to disturb him: how it *was* strange, in fact, that he should have been a bullfighter at all, or rather, that he should have wanted it so badly. And he must have wanted it very badly, for beyond a certain point in his youth, after he had told his father, it was simply taken for granted; and all later memory turned round his father's proud sacrifices, and the make-believe Arena, the little wooden bull, playing endless hours with the stick and cape, taking the charge with classic grace, as his friend José rushed crouching behind a wooden stool. And he had given José the torero smile, the sneer of complicity and disdain, while his father and old Gonzales, or some other friend brought along from the fields to see, looked on, unspeaking, exchanging nudges and soft, knowing smiles, and occasionally raised a glass of the cheap red wine with grand dignity: *"al torero."*

Now the banderilleros had begun, and the first pair were placed, exciting a great, meaningless response from the crowd, and it was then that Marulanda, waiting his turn, really *saw* the bull—at an instant when the first pair were placed, and the bull rose, almost as in slow-motion, hooking the empty air, then left, at the level of the man's throat, determinedly, without heat, as though it were a question of form alone—and for Marulanda, at that instant, something like a dry flame crossed his wrist. He walked half the length of the Arena then, back to the safety-break, from where he would make his approach, without bothering to watch the second pair.

Just as he reached the break in the barrier, however, a remarkable thing happened: a child, of perhaps five or six, rushed out, laughing and shouting, into the Arena. He came out the side of the break Marulanda was standing by, so that Marulanda actually had to step aside to let him pass.

The child had entered the Arena at the worst possible moment, for the bull, having just received the second pair of banderillas, was running completely unattended and, though on the opposite side of the Arena, had turned almost at once, and was now moving straight for the child, like a gigantic toy on a string.

Stepping aside, Marulanda had thought of nothing, but as he felt the child brush past him and beyond on the tremendous roar of the Arena, it came to him as a dream of something that had happened long ago, and for an instant he thought he saw his dead father's face in the crowd on the far side of the Arena. But the image passed with confused abruptness, leaving only the fact of the child in the Arena. And it was an awesome sight—the child and the bull, moving head-on from opposite sides of the Arena. Still, it may have been only an illusion that the bull was charging the child, that being directly opposite, and at such a distance, the bull could not have seen the child, or, even so, that he was distracted, by a chance shadow, or movement, for he suddenly veered off the line that would have brought them together and plunged towards the nearest group of men and capes—so that it was over as quickly as it had begun–though by chance, to be sure, because: in the Arena, near the bull, there was no-one who had seen the child come in; and now they were suddenly so lost, ranged around the bull in a new man-oeuvre, that they failed to notice when Marulanda overtook the child and gathered him up, almost exactly in the centre of the Arena. Then they *did* notice; and they all turned to watch. And while it is not an uncommon sight–spectators rushing into the Arena, children, zealous young men flourishing their coats–it is a sight that always brings an instant of doubt, and the immobility of disbelief; so that for seconds on end, the men simply stood watching Marulanda gather the child, writhing and flailing now, and start back toward the barrier. And in those seconds the inevitable thing happened: the bull, no longer ambivalent as to which moving thing to destroy, broke toward the one line of motion in the Arena; and he broke so quickly that he was beyond the cage of men and capes before it could move again. Marulanda saw it, just as it happened, and while he ran now as fast as he could, the sharpest reality was not of the bull, but of the fantastic roar of the Arena. This finite realization came in a moment of panic, and in that moment he may have for-gotten about the child, for at a point, perhaps ten feet from the barrier, when he knew the bull was upon him, he turned to face it, or avoid it, still holding the child before him, almost it appeared now, as a shield. The terrible impact was simultaneous to his turning, and while it left Marulanda, stunned, on the ground, it bore the child from him, and away.

The spectacle had an extraordinary effect on the Arena. It was as though all the people and radios of the world were screaming into a volcano. It reached a high, splitting noise, and sustained, seeming to threaten the very walls of the Arena, while on the ground, far along the barrier, the bull nudged and worried the limp body of the child, and the gathering spectators, matadors, and assistants surged wildly around the bull, at frantic cross-purposes, in trying to manoeuvre him away.

Marulanda could not get up. He seemed buried under the noise of the screams. Suddenly, a bottle struck his leg, and another hit the ground near his head, throwing up dirt; then one bottle hit another one and broke as though they had exploded. At this point, the sound seemed to go abruptly beyond endurance, beyond hearing; and he thought his eardrums would burst as he slowly got to his feet, because in the Arena now there was absolute silence.

Not daring to think, he started walking towards the break in the barrier, where two policemen were standing. Just before he reached it, a well-dressed man in the second row, directly in front of him, slowly got up, and carefully raising his arm, threw a bottle as hard as he could. It struck Marulanda squarely in the chest and he crumpled to the ground, as the roar of the Arena fell on him again like an avalanche. Everything fled upward past his eyes: the huddled policemen, guns drawn, nervously backing away, towards the exits—and beyond, the face of the Arena, a livid white, all the small faces fused by the heat into a single screaming mask.

They were all screaming that he must fight the bull.

Lying on the floor of the Arena, hearing only their screams—

"MARULANDA! !"

—he began to cry, quietly, not with pain or remorse, but like a child, or a puppy, incredulous, whimpering a weird gratitude.

The Moon-shot Scandal

A SIGNIFICANT DIFFERENCE between Soviet and American space efforts has been the constant spotlight of public attention focused on the latter, while our antagonist's program has been carried forward in relative secrecy. This has presented tremendous disadvantages, especially in its psychological effect on the national-mind, and it harbors a dangerous potential indeed. If, for example, in climax to the usual fanfare and nationally televised countdown, the spacecraft simply explodes, veers out crazily into the crowd, or burrows deep into the earth at the foot of the launching-pad, it can be fairly embarrassing to all concerned. On the other hand, it is generally presumed, because of this apparent and completely above-board policy, that *everything* which occurs in regard to these American spaceshots is immediately known by the entire public. Yet can anyone really be naive enough to believe that in matters so extraordinarily important an attitude of such simple-minded candor could obtain? Surely not. And the facts behind the initial moon-shot, of August 17, 1961, make it a classic case in point, now that the true story may at last be told.

Readers will recall that the spacecraft, after a dramatic countdown, blazed up from its pad on full camera; the camera followed its ascent briefly, then cut to the tracking-station where a graph described the arc of its ill-fated flight. In due time it became evident that the rocket was seriously off course, and in the end it was announced quite simply that the craft had "missed the moon" by about two-hundred thousand miles—by a wider mark, in fact, than the distance of the shot itself. What was *not* announced—either before, during, or after the shot—was that the craft was *manned by five astronauts*. Hoping for a total *coup*, the Space Authority—highest echelon of the Agency—had arranged for a fully crewed flight, one which if successful (and there was considerable reason to believe that it would be) would then be dramatically announced to an astonished world: "Americans on the Moon!" Whereas, if not successful, it would merely remain undisclosed that the craft had been manned. The crew, of course, was composed of carefully screened volunteers who had no dependents, or living relatives.

So, in one room of the tracking-station—a room which was *not* being televised—communications were maintained throughout this historic interlude. Fragmented transcripts, in the form of both video and acoustic tapes, as well as personal accounts of those present, have now enabled us to piece together the story—the *story*, namely, of how the moon-bound spaceship, "Cutie-Pie II," was caused to career off into outer space, beyond the moon itself, when some kind of "*insane faggot hassle*," as it has since been described, developed aboard the craft during early flight stage.

According to available information, Lt. Col. P. D. Slattery, a "retired" British colonial officer, co-captained the flight in hand with Major Ralph L. Doll (better known to his friends, it was later learned, as "Baby" Doll); the balance of the crew consisted of Capt. J. Walker, Lt. Fred Hanson, and Cpl. "Felix" Mendelssohn. (There is certain evidence suggesting that Cpl. Mendelssohn may have, in actual fact, been a woman.) The initial phase of the existing transcript is comprised entirely of routine operational data and reports of instrument readings. It was near the end of Stage One, however, when the craft was some 68,000 miles from earth, and still holding true course, that the first untoward incident occurred; this was in the form of an exchange between Lt. Hanson and Maj. Doll, which resounded over the tracking-station inter-com, as clear as a bell on a winter's morn:

Lt. Hanson: "Will you *stop* it! Just *stop* it!"

Maj. Doll: "Stop *what?* I was only calibrating my altimeter—for heaven's sake, Freddie!"

Lt. Hanson: "I'm not *talking* about that and you know it! I'm talking about your infernal *camping!* Now just stop it! Right now!"

The astonishment this caused at tracking-station H.Q. could hardly be exaggerated. Head-phones were adjusted, frequencies were checked; the voice of a Lt. General spoke tersely: "Cutie-Pie II—give us your reading—over."

"Reading thpeeding," was Cpl. Mendelssohn's slyly lisped reply, followed by a cunning snicker. At this point a scene of fantastic bedlam broke loose on the video inter-com. Col. Slattery raged out from his forward quarters, like the protagonist of *Psycho*—in outlandish feminine attire of the nineties, replete with a dozen petticoats and high-button shoes. He pranced with wild imperiousness about the control room, interfering with all operational activity, and then spun into a provocative and feverish combination of tarantella and can-can at the navigation panel, saucily flicking at the controls there, cleverly integrating these movements into the tempo of his dervish, amidst peals of laughter and shrieks of delight and petulant annoyance.

"Mary, you silly old fraud," someone cried gaily, "this *isn't* Pirandello!"

It was then that the video system of the inter-com blacked out, as though suddenly shattered, as did the audio-system shortly afterward. There is reason to believe, however, that the sound communication system was eventually restored, and, according to some accounts, occasional reports (of an almost incredible nature) continue to be received, as the craft—which was heavily fueled for its return trip to earth—still blazes through the farther reaches of space.

Surely, despite the negative and rather disappointing aspects of the flight, there are at least two profitable lessons to be learned from it: (1) that the antiquated, intolerant attitude of the Agency, and of

Government generally, towards sexual freedom, can only cause individual repression which may at any time—and especially under the terrific tensions of space-flight—have a boomerang effect to the great disadvantage of all concerned, and (2) that there may well be, after all, an ancient wisdom in the old adage, *"Five's a crowd."*

Red Giant on Our Doorstep!

IDEA FOR A MUSICAL COMEDY

With title and credits we hear theme-tune "Fiasco!" (using the tune "Fiesta!") sung by Mexican guitar group in a tinny crooning style:

> "Fiasco! It's a holiday for everyone!
> Fiasco! Bringing happiness and joy!
> Etc."

The principal action takes place at Camp Trax in Guatemala where the Cuban invasion force is in training. Cuban invasion force is played by hundreds of *midgets*—with PETER LORRE as their leader —the midgets dressed in big Boy Scout hats, big guns, big packs, fierce mustachios, and mucho high-pitched gibbering (they're small but tough). The head of the CIA to be played by SLIM PICKENS, with aides WILLIAM BENDIX, HOSS WILLIAMS, and DAN BLOCKER. Also featured, GLADYS GEORGE, or similarly brittle slattern type, as the Red Cuban temptress after CIA data. And LENNY BRUCE as the friendly Camp Surgeon (*ostensibly* friendly, but actually in Red Castro hire) who receives large drug shipments by night—which he injects into the midgets' heads in a diabolic attempt to cripple invasion strength. None of the island Cubans are shown, except Castro himself (played by GROUCHO MARX OR ORSON WELLES) in fantastic orgy scenes. Action begins in Miami, at recruiting station, and ends in Bay of Pigs, with BRUCE (wearing two-way wrist radio) receiving direct instructions from Castro as to how to sink the supply ship. Midgets have become addicted to his drug, and constantly seek him out gesturing frantically at their heads. He continues to give injections even after they are in the water, often having to lean far out over the side of the ship to shoot the dope into their heads. A documentary type film, with SENATOR DIRKSON narration. DIRKSON concludes: "Well, as we've always said down in my home-state, 'If you can't beat 'em, *join* 'em!' Eh, folks? HAR! HAR! HAR!"

This would be a low-budget production. WILLIAM BENDIX and GROUCHO MARX are used here merely as types. There is reason to believe however that ORSON WELLES would not be unsympathetic towards such an undertaking and would work on deferment, as would, presumably, LENNY BRUCE. The purpose of the film would be to combat the notion of communism as an absolute, or as a Russian monopoly. Possibly even to suggest that there are instances of worse conduct.

Scandale at The Dumpling Shop

AT THE BEHEST of several irate American mothers, we recently paid a visit to one of New York's largest toy stores, The Dumpling Shop, to inspect their new line of baby-dolls—this being the source and object of the petition.

"It is quite unspeakable," wrote Mrs. Leyton-Reims of Westchester. "My club is taking action. May we count on *you?*"

It is, of course, a bit off the track for a freethought magazine like our *Realist* to become involved in controversy of this sort. Still, what's the use of it all if you can't take a stand occasionally, at least on matters of cultural importance. After all, these are serious times —East and West locked in dynamic struggle, our own culture faltering, indeed at times floundering, in a sea of cynicism and failing beliefs, youth desperately seeking values—so that it was with a heavy heart that we came away from The Dumpling Shop, after having seen the item in question, namely: the so-called *Little Cathy Curse Doll—Complete with Teeny Tampons.*

This "doll," we were blandly assured by the management, is merely a "logical follow-up" on last season's highly successful *Tina Tiny Tears—The Naughty Nappy Doll* ("She Cries Real Tears and Wets Her Beddy"). Whether or not it is a "logical follow-up" is, at least in our opinion, not the principal issue at hand; the principal issue is that of *taste*, of *responsibility*, and of *common decency*.

On these three counts we judge both The Dumpling Shop and the manufacturers of the *Little Cathy Curse Doll* to be in serious default. The lavish arrangements for the display of this so-called doll occupy a prominent section of The Dumpling Shop's smart fourth floor. Stretched overhead is a huge colorful circus-like banner which features a happy little girl holding the doll and exclaiming crossly: "Why, Cathy Curse, I *do* believe you're *staining!* I think *you'd* better have fresh panties and a teeny tampon!"

Certainly it would be naive in the extreme to raise shrill and pious protest against the simple abstractions of material greed and commercial exploitation which daily confront us—these are part and parcel of the system, dues of the freedom club and cheap at the price. Surely, however, we do have a right to ask: Have we really so depleted exploitation that it has come to this? And moreover, where then is it to end? One is forced to wonder, even to speculate with dread, *What next? Little Victor Vomit? Little Katy Ka-Ka? Don Diarrhea? Silly Sammy Shoot-Off?!!*

No, we cannot, *will not,* buy it. Our answer to Mrs. Leyton-Reims: Yes, you may *indeed* count on us. Our presses and our staff stand ready to shoulder a man-size burden in carrying your cause forward, which, by our lights, is also the cause of every right-thinking parent throughout this grand land.

Terry Southern Interviews a Faggot Male Nurse

LARRY M., 34 YEARS OLD, WHITE, born in Racine, Wisconsin, has lived in New York for nine years, and is presently employed as a ward attendant in one of the city's largest hospitals. The following is a verbatim transcript of an interview recorded there on March 7, 1965:

Q. Good. Well, let's see . . . now you've been a faggot male nurse for what—nine years, I believe?

A. Well, now, wait a *minute!* Ha-ha. I mean, look . . . well, I don't know what this *magazine* is you're from—the *Realist*, you said. I mean the copy you showed me and so on, but there was nothing about *that* kind of thing . . . I mean, ha, *I'm* not going to go along with *that* kind of thing!

Q. Oh well, listen, I didn't mean to be . . . well what do *you* say—"gay"? "Homosexual"?

A. Well, *gay*, yes, I mean *gay* is all right. *Homosexual*—yes, I'm not ashamed of it if that's what you mean.

Q. All right, now let me . . . well listen, what do you mean, "faggot" is . . . I mean you think "faggot" is what? . . . derisive?

A. *Derisive*, yes, it is derisive—*I* think it's derisive . . . I think it's derisive.

Q. Well, I didn't mean it that way—I assure you that . . . I was just trying to use words . . . you know, words of "high frequency incidence," as they say. I mean, semanticists and so on, that's what they say—that that's the word in currency—"faggot."

A. I know they do, I know they do, and it's probably . . . well, they're probably right, that that is the word they use. But, well, I didn't know, you know, exactly how *you*—well, you know, ha-ha. . . .

Q. But you really think "faggot" is *derisive*.

A. Well, I think . . . well, I *know*, I know for example that it's used that way.

Q. What, derisively?

A. Well, *derisively* . . . maybe not derisively, but *patronizing* . . . *condescending* . . . yes, condescendingly. Well, it's that . . . that kind of *tolerance* . . . you know? I mean *liberals* use it—the worse kind of so-called *liberal* uses it!

Q. Is that true? Well, what about a word like "queer"?

A. *"Queer"!* Oh well, ha! There you're talking about, I don't know what . . . I mean nobody would use a word like that except some kind of . . . of *lizard* or something.

Q. Yes, well I wouldn't use a word like that, like "queer" . . . or actually I wouldn't use a word like "fairy" either, or "pansy" . . . they just seem, I don't know, archaic or something. But what about "fruit"? I mean I think Lenny Bruce has made "fruit," you know to use the word "fruit," okay, don't you?

A. "Fruit"? Lenny Bruce used it? Well, Lenny Bruce . . . I mean Lenny Bruce uses these words and . . . well, what, you mean he used it instead of "gay"?

Q. Well, he used it, I don't know, he uses it some way, and . . . well, you know, it seemed to make it all right.

A. Yes, well . . . what, you mean he used it instead of "gay"?

Q. Yes, instead of "gay," instead of "faggot"—he uses "faggot," too, you know.

A. Yes, well some people, I mean some people can do that . . . they can do that and it isn't offensive.

Q. Yes, well that's the point—when I said "faggot" I didn't mean to be offensive.

A. Oh *I* know that . . . I *know* that now, that *you* didn't! But you see . . . well, the thing is you'd be surprised at the kind of people who *do*.

Q. What, here at the hospital?

A. At the hospital . . . well, everywhere, everywhere . . . yes, here at the hospital, yes, this is a kind of . . . of *cross-section* I guess you'd say.

Q. Well, listen, let's . . . I mean I'd like to ask you some questions about your work and so on, so why don't—

A. Well go, man, go, ha-ha . . . or *baby*—I don't know what to say . . . I mean you're not going to use our names or anything . . .

Q. Well, I'm not going to use *your* name. I mean, you know, isn't that the—

A. Well, that's the *thing*, yes, I mean I *can't* do that—you have no idea, I mean this is a very tough *state*, you can't just talk about these things with . . . with *immunity* . . . *impunity?* which is it? *You're* the writer. Ha-ha. *Are* you a writer?

Q. *Impunity* . . . you can't talk about them with *impunity.*

A. *You* didn't *an*-swer!

Q. What, about being a writer?

A. Yes! What do you write?

Q. Yes, well, listen, let *me* interview *you,* and then . . . *you* can interview *me.* Isn't that good?

A. Oh, ho-ho-ho . . .

Q. No, I mean what I'd like to do, you see, is be able to just put this straight down off the tape, without any editing or anything like that, and, well, if we get, you know, side-tracked . . . well, it's going to be all mixed up. You know what I mean?

A. Chrysler wouldn't like it?

Q. *Chrysler?*

A. Chrysler? Didn't you say *Chrysler?* Your boss!

Q. Oh, *Krassner* . . . yes, Paul *Krassner.*

A. *Krassner!* Yes, Paul Krassner—what's he like?

Q. Oh, well, listen, we can't . . . well, I'll tell you *one* thing about him, Paul Krassner, he's got this thing about *format* . . . you know? Tight and bright. "Let's keep it tight and bright!" he's always saying . . . and *that's* why we've *got* to stick to this one thing—you know, like *your* story . . . or I'll be in a real jam with Paul. Dig?

A. Do you call him "Paul"?

Q. Yes.

A. Ha-ha.

Q. What's wrong with that?

A. *Noth-ing, noth-ing!* Don't be so *touchy!*

Q. Well . . . let me ask you now what attracted you to this sort of work?

A. *People!* I love *people*—I love to *be* with them, and to *help* them. That's what hospital-work is—*helping people.*

Q. What about being a doctor, did that ever—

A. Oh no—no, no, I don't have the patience for that . . . for that sort of training. It's too . . . technical, and too, I don't know, *cold-blooded.* No, my approach is different . . . it's more intuitive, more instinctive, and more *direct*, much more *direct*—you see, I deal *directly* with my patient, and all the time . . . the doctor sees the patient, maybe five minutes a day—I see . . . well, I don't *see*, I'm *with*, that's the difference, I'm *with* my patient, all the time, as much as he needs me. The doctor has no . . . no *relationship* with the patients. I have *close* . . . *warm* . . . *wonderful, wonderful* relationships with my patients! They all love me, all of them—not all, no, I won't say that . . . there are some who, well, you know the kind, they don't *want* help, they don't know what love is—they *can't* love, well, you know the kind . . .

Q. You think they don't love you due to gayness?

A. Due to gayness? Ha, ha. Due to my gayness? Yes! No, I say yes *and* no! They don't like me . . . it's true some of them don't even *like* me—some of them *hate* me, and the feeling is mutual . . . well, I won't say that, I *pity* them—they don't like me because they're *afraid*—they're afraid of *love*, and they're afraid of *them-selves*—and this is especially true of the doctors.

Q. The *doctors?* The doctors don't like you?

A. The doctors, ha, ha . . . well, I don't get along with the doctors too well—our approaches are different, you see . . . I mean, they don't really *care* about the patient—and *they* know that I know it! And they're afraid—they know that my power . . . my *love*, is stronger, and they're *afraid* . . .

Q. What, for their jobs?

A. Or for their *souls!* Ha, ha.

Q. Well, surely some of the doctors like you—I can't see how you could stay on unless—

A. Oh *some* of the doctors, yes! The really, really good . . . well, *great* ones, do, yes—they appreciate my work and I appreciate theirs. We respect each other. But how many good doctors are there? One in a *billion?* Not to mention *great* doctors—which are practically non-existent!

Q. Well . . . I don't understand—do you mean there aren't any really good ones . . . or any that *like* you?

A. No! I *don't* mean that, I *don't* mean that. What *I* mean . . . Well, take Dr. Schweitzer . . . I've never met Dr. Schweitzer, but I think he must be a great doctor, and I think . . . well, I *know*, he would understand what I'm doing. And there are others, right here, not *great*, but good . . . the best . . . and they like me; they respect me.

Q. Well . . . let's see, how about—

A. Listen, don't get the idea that I'm giving a big *buildup* to the whole . . . well, whole *profession*, if you like, of hospital atten-dants—or male nurse, whatever . . . I mean, don't take me as a typical example by any means. I mean some of the others—well I wouldn't want to say.

Q. Why, what are they like?

A. Well, I'll tell you this much, it isn't because they like *people* they're there!

Q. What is it? Why is it?

A. Well, they're *sadists*, a lot of them—especially in the mental wards . . . *big, insensitive*—well, you've got no idea, what goes on in some of those wards—*animals*, like apes . . . big cruel apes! They just sit around waiting for someone to blow his stack so they can *slam* him!

Q. Really? Slam him?

A. That's what they call it—"slammin'." Somebody blows his stack and they yell "Slam him, Joe! Slam that nut!" What it *really* means, what it's *supposed* to mean is that you put him in the *slammer*, like, you know, in a padded-cell, and *slam* the door—but it means the subduing part too.

Q. And how do they do that?

A. How? Are you kidding? Any way they feel like. With their *fists*, if they can—that's what they really like . . . I mean the tough ones are proud of their reputations for never using the sap—you know, the leather thing . . . the black-jack. Or they may say "Big Joe had to use the sap!" which means that it was a *really* bad case if *Big Joe* had to use the sap! But of course a real *nut* is as strong as about four ordinary people.

Q. Well . . . but they aren't all like that, are they? Is that just the mental ward?

A. The mental ward. No, there's another kind, the exact opposite —not opposite, but completely different—they work in hospitals to be close to morphine, so they can get morphine. They couldn't care less about hitting anybody—they just sort of step aside . . . I guess hoping the guy will fall out the *window* or something. And when they have to sap him, they just tap him on the back of the head—no expression, nothing . . . they live in a world apart, some of them have terrible, terrible habits—I mean that would cost them two or three hundred dollars a *day* if they didn't work at the hospital.

Q. And they get morphine—how do they get it?

A. Oh well, they *get* it! Ha, ha, they *have* to get it—I mean they would *get* it if you . . . if you put it in a *safe* and dropped it to the bottom of the *ocean!* They're like Houdini when they go after *that*— nothing could stop them, *nothing!* I mean they don't even *worry* about *how* to get it—all they want is to be in the *vicinity* of it, because, if they *are*, they'll *get* it! And you know there's a lot of morphine in a big hospital.

Q. Well, what do you think . . . I mean, are they good at their work?

A. No! They're like zombies—no feeling, none at all . . . *they* can't help the patient. Why I have some *wonderful* relationships in the mental wards—but they don't care, about the patient, about anything . . . they don't even *speak* to anyone. Not to *me* anyway —*none* of them will even *speak* to me.

Q. But they must do their job . . .

A. Of course! They do their *job*. They make sure of *that*, that they do their *job!* Yes, that's true, they do their job and they do it very . . . well, very *thoroughly*—I mean, you see, they *cannot* afford to get fired, so . . . so they do their job very . . . very *well*, in a way. Very *careful* and *serious*—but never a *smile* or a kind word for anyone. Oh no, they're too serious! Ha! Well, I certainly wouldn't have them in *my* hospital. I can tell you that!

Q. What, you mean . . . well, do you think about that? About hospital administration?

A. Yes! That's what I'd *really* like to do—I'd like to organize *my own* hospital!

Q. What would you . . . would you have . . . an all-gay staff?

A. *What?* Ha-ha! *No-ooo!* Don't be *silly!* What an idea! Ha, ha, ha! An all-gay hospital! Well, who knows . . . maybe it *would* work out that way . . . who knows? I mean, one thing I *do* know, I would *not*, repeat *not*, use *women nurses!*

Q. You would not?

A. No! I would *not!* And I know what you're *thinking*, but I don't care, it isn't true, I would *definitely* not use them.

Q. Yes . . . well, why not?

A. Why not? For the very *simple* reason that a hospital . . . a *hospital* should be . . . clean . . . efficient . . . well-run! With an atmosphere of *love* and . . . human affection, human *warmth!* And care for the patient! People who care about the *patient!* And not just constant . . . *bitching* about having their *period!* Or *not* having their period! Or having their *menopause!* Or *not* having their menopause! Or washing their *hair!* Or *not* washing their hair! God!

Q. Is that—

A. Do *you* know . . . let me just say this . . . do *you* know that *nurses* . . . women *nurses*, are one *hell* of a lot more trouble than the patients are? That's *right*. They're *always* sick—*always* sick! If it isn't their *period*, it's something else. Something's wrong with their *breast!* Or their insides—ovaries! womb! uterus! vulva! tubes! And God knows what else! Christ, if I hear another *nurse* talk about her goddamn *tubes* . . . !

Q. Well—

A. I know, I know . . . I'm exaggerating. All right, all right, you're right . . . I am. *But* . . . *But!* . . . it's *only* an exaggeration. Do you follow? I mean it is *true* . . . it's *true,* but exaggerated. Right? Do you dig? And here's something else, and *this* is true—most nurses, almost *no* nurse, in fact, is *married* . . . they're sexually frustrated, and *bitter,* baby . . . bitter, bitter, bitter!

Q. Well, can't they make it with the doctors, or the patients? I mean—

A. Yes! Of course! Oh, they do, they do! With the doctors, patients, interns . . . *ward-boys, janitors—anybody!* Listen, I could tell you . . . well, that's why you can never *find* one of them! They're either . . . lying down in the rest-rooms, coddling their *period,* or they're off somewhere getting laid! In the . . . the *broom-*closet or someplace! Ha!

Q. Then you don't—

A. Oh listen, I've known some nice nurses, I don't say that . . . there's one *here,* right *here,* on this floor—day-nurse . . . a darling, perfectly darling little old lady—she's let's see, how old is [name] now . . . ? She's sixty . . . *four. Sixty-four* years old! And a *marvelous* nurse! Really. Marvelous sweet old lady! But, I mean, ha, ha, well, I don't mind telling you it's . . . well, it's a *rare* thing, a *very rare thing!*

Q. Yes, well—

A. But listen . . . just a minute—what did you say? Just before? You said *why* can't they make it with them? The patients and so on—is that what you said?

Q. Well, you said they were frustrated . . .

A. Well, but *that's* not going to change their . . . well, what kind of hospital is *that,* for heaven's sake! With the nurses getting laid all over the place! You think they *should* do that? Ha, ha, you . . . you've got some funny ideas about hospitals!

Q. I didn't say they *should* do that, I just wondered if they *did.*

A. And an all-*gay* hospital! Ha, ha! That's very *funny!*

Q. Well, you don't think that's . . . what, that isn't even *conceivable?*

A. Well, you couldn't get an all-gay *staff* to treat *only gay patients,* I can tell you that.

Q. But would it be *possible* to have an all-gay staff? I mean are there gay *janitors*, for example?

A. Oh, ho-ho! *Are* there!

Q. Well then, theoretically—

A. Ha, ha! Some of my best friends are gay janitors!

Q. Well, the point—

A. No, no, that was a *joke!*

Q. Yes, I realize that, I realize that. It's very funny.

A. Ho-ho! You didn't *laugh!*

Q. Well . . . I did really. I mean I *recognize* it as a joke. I acknowledge it as a joke. Ha, ha. How's that?

A. Ha, ha . . . Well, *you* have some funny ideas about hospitals, that's all I can say.

Q. I don't have any ideas about it—I wanted *you* to tell *me* about it. I mean we've . . . you've made certain generalizations, about doctors and so on, so I was asking about *that*.

A. About an all-gay hospital?

Q. Well, an all-gay *staff*, yes.

A. Well, it would be a damn *good* hospital, I can tell you that. Better than any there are *now*.

Q. Well, what about the . . . wouldn't the gay staff try to . . . try to take advantage of the non-gay patients? While they were asleep, or weakened or something?

A. Ha, ha! Well, I mean if you call love and . . . and—well, what do you mean "take *advantage* of"?

Q. Well, I don't know . . . it seems like they would.

A. Well, anyway, *one* thing—you could be sure of getting plenty of *attention!*

Q. Yes . . .

A. And I *do* mean *you!*

Q. Uh-huh . . .

A. Ha, ha! Now, now, don't take it so *person-ally!*

The Blood
of
a Wig

MY MOST OUTLANDISH DRUG EXPERIENCE, now that I think about it, didn't occur with beat Village or Harlem weirdos, but during a brief run with the ten-to-four Mad Ave crowd.

How it happened, this friend of mine who was working at *Lance* ("The Mag for Men") phoned me one morning—he knew I was strapped.

"One of the fiction editors is out with syph or something," he said. "You want to take his place for a while?"

I was still mostly asleep, so I tried to cool it by shooting a few incisive queries as to the nature of the gig—which he couldn't seem to follow.

"Well," he said finally, "you won't have to *do* anything, if that's what you mean." He had a sort of blunt and sullen way about him —John Fox his name was, an ex-Yalie and would-be writer who was constantly having to "put it back on the shelf," as he expressed it (blunt, sullen), and take one of these hot-shot Mad Ave jobs, and always for some odd reason—like at present, paying for his mom's analysis.

Anyway, I accepted the post, and now I had been working there about three weeks. It wasn't true, of course, what he'd said about not having to do anything—I mean the way he had talked I wouldn't even have to get out of bed—but after three weeks my routine was fairly smooth: up at ten, wash face, brush teeth, fresh shirt, dex, and make it. I had this transistor-shaver I'd copped for five off a junky-booster, so I would shave with it in the cab, and walk into the office at ten-thirty or so, dapper as Dan and hip as Harry. Then into my own small office, lock the door, and start stashing the return postage from the unsolicited mss. We would get an incredible amount of mss.—about two hundred a day—and these were divided into two categories: (1) those from agents, and (2) those that came in cold, straight from the author. The ratio was about 30 to 1, in favor of the latter—which formed a gigantic heap called "the shit pile," or (by the girl-readers) "the garbage dump." These always contained a lot of return postage—so right away I was able to supplement my weekly wage by seven or eight dollars a day in postage stamps. Everyone else considered the "shit pile" as something heinously repugnant, especially the sensitive girl ("garbage") readers, so it was a source of irritation and chagrin to my secretary when I first told her I wished to read "*all* unsolicited manuscripts and *no* manuscripts from agents."

John Fox found it quite incomprehensible.

"You must be out of your nut!" he said. "Ha! Wait until you try to read some of that crap in the shit pile!"

I explained however (and it was actually true in the beginning) that I had this theory about the existence of a *pure, primitive, folk-like* literature—which, if it did exist, could only turn up among the unsolicited mss. Or *weird*, something really *weird*, even insane, might turn up there—whereas I knew the stuff from the agents would be the same old predictably competent tripe. So, aside from stashing the stamps, I would read each of these shit-pile ms. very carefully—reading subtleties, insinuations, multilevel *entendre* into what was actually just a sort of flat, straightforward simplemindedness. I would think each was a put-on—a fresh and curious parody of some kind, and I would read on, and on, all the way to the end, waiting for the payoff . . . but, of course, that never happened, and I gradually began to revise my theory and to refine my method. By the second week, I was able to reject a ms. after reading the opening sentence, and by the third I could often reject on the basis of *title* alone—the principle being if an author would allow a blatantly dumbbell title, he was incapable of writing a story worth reading.

(This was thoroughly tested and proved before adopting.) Then instead of actually *reading* mss., I would spend hours, days really, just thinking, trying to refine and extend my method of blitz-rejection. I was able to take it a little farther, but not much. For example, any woman author who used "Mrs." in her name could be rejected out of hand—*unless* it was used with only one name, like "by Mrs. Carter," then it might be a weirdie. And again, any author using a middle initial or a "Jr." in his name, shoot it right back to him! I knew I was taking a chance with that one (because of Connell and Selby), but I figured what the hell, I could hardly afford to gear the sort of fast-moving synchro-mesh operation I had in mind to a couple of exceptions—which, after all, only went to prove the consarn rule, so to speak. Anyway, there it was, the end of the third week and the old job going smoothly enough, except that I had developed quite a little dexie habit by then—not actually a *habit*, of course, but a sort of very real dependence . . . having by nature a nocturnal metabolism whereby my day (pre-*Lance*) would ordinarily begin at three or four in the afternoon and finish at eight or nine in the morning. As a top staffer at *Lance*, however, I had to make other arrangements. Early on I had actually asked John Fox if it would be possible for me to come in at four and work until midnight.

"Are you out of your *nut?*" (That was his standard comeback). "Don't you know what's happening here? This is a *social* scene, man—these guys want to *see* you, they want to get to *know* you!"

"What are they, faggots?"

"No, they're not *faggots*," he said stoutly, but then seemed hard pressed to explain, and shrugged it off. "It's just that they don't have very much, you know, *to do*."

It was true in a way that no one seemed to actually *do* anything— except for the typists, of course, always typing away. But the guys just sort of hung out, or around, buzzing each other, sounding the chicks, that sort of thing.

The point is though that I had to make in by ten, or thereabouts. One reason for this was the "pre-lunch conference," which Hacker, or the "Old Man" (as, sure enough, the publisher was called), might decide to have on any given day. And so it came to pass that on this particular—Monday it was—morning, up promptly at nine-three-oh, wash face, brush teeth, fresh shirt, all as per usual, and reach for the dex . . . no dex, out of dex. This was especially inopportune because it was on top of two straight white and active nights, and it was somewhat as though an 8oo-pound bag, of loosely packed sand, began to settle slowly on the head. No panic, just immediate death from fatigue.

At Sheridan Square, where I usually got the taxi, I went into the drugstore. The first-shift pharmacist, naturally a guy I had never seen before, was on duty. He looked like an aging efficiency expert.

"Uh, I'd like to get some Dexamyl, please."

The pharmacist didn't say anything, just raised one hand to adjust his steel-rimmed glasses, and put the other one out for the prescription.

"It's on file here," I said, nodding toward the back.

"What name?" he wanted to know, then disappeared behind the glass partition, but very briefly indeed.

"Nope," he said, coming back, and was already looking over my shoulder to the next customer.

"Could you call Mr. Robbins?" I asked, "he can tell you about it." Of course this was simply whistling in the dark, since I was pretty sure Robbins, the night-shift man, didn't know me by name, but I had to keep the ball rolling.

"I'm not gonna wake Robbins at this hour—he'd blow his stack. Who's next?"

"Well, listen, can't you just *give* me a couple—I've, uh, got a long drive ahead."

"You can't get dexies without a script," he said, rather reproachfully, wrapping a box of Tampax for a teenybopper nifty behind me, "*you* know that."

"Okay, how about if I get the doctor to phone you?"

"Phone's up front," he said, and to the nifty: "That's seventy-nine."

The phone was under siege—one person using it, and about five waiting—all, for some weird reason, spade fags and prancing gay. Not that I give a damn about who uses the phone, it was just one of those absurd incongruities that seem so often to conspire to undo sanity in times of crisis. What the hell was going on? They were obviously together, very excited, chattering like magpies. Was it the Katherine Dunham contingent of male dancers? Stranded? Lost? Why out so early? One guy had a list of numbers in his hand the size of a small flag. I stood there for a moment, confused in point-less speculation, then left abruptly and hurried down West Fourth to the dinette. This was doubly to purpose, since not only is there a phone, but the place is frequented by all manner of heads, and a casual score might well be in order—though it was a bit early for the latter, granted.

And this did, in fact, prove to be the case. There was no one there whom I knew—and, worse still, halfway to the phone, I suddenly remembered my so-called doctor (Dr. Friedman, his name was) had gone to California on vacation a few days ago. Christ almighty! I sat down at the counter. This called for a quick think-through. Should I actually call him in California? Have him phone the drug-store from there? Quite a production for a couple of dex. I looked at my watch, it was just after ten. That meant just after seven in Los Angeles—Friedman would blow his stack. I decided to hell with it and ordered a cup of coffee. Then a remarkable thing happened. I had sat down next to a young man who now quite casually re-moved a small transparent silo-shaped vial from his pocket, and without so much as a glance in any direction, calmly tapped a couple of the belovedly familiar green-hearted darlings into his cupped hand, and tossed them off like two salted peanuts.

Deus ex machina!

"Uh, excuse me," I said, in the friendliest sort of way, "I just happened to notice you taking a couple of, ha ha, Dexamyl." And I proceeded to lay my story on him—while he, after one brief look of appraisal, sat listening, his eyes straight ahead, hands still on the counter, one of them half covering the magic vial. Finally he just nodded and shook out two more on the counter. "Have a ball," he said.

I reached the office about five minutes late for the big pre-lunch confab. John Fox made a face of mild disgust when I came in the conference room. He always seemed to consider my flaws as his responsibility since it was he who had recommended me for the post. Now he glanced uneasily at old Hacker, who was the publisher, editor-in-chief, etc. etc. A man of about fifty-five, he bore a striking resemblance to Edward G. Robinson—an image to which he gave further credence by frequently sitting in a squatlike manner, chewing an unlit cigar butt, and mouthing coarse expressions. He liked to characterize himself as a "tough old bastard," one of his favorite prefaces being: "I know most of you guys think I'm a *tough old bastard*, right? Well, maybe I am. In the quality-Lit game you *gotta* be tough!" And bla-bla-bla.

Anyway as I took my usual seat between Fox and Bert Katz, the feature editor, Old Hack looked at his watch, then back at me.

"Sorry," I mumbled.

"We're running a *magazine* here, young man, not a *whorehouse*."

"Right and double right," I parried crisply. Somehow Old Hack always brought out the schoolboy in me.

"If you want to be *late*," he continued, "be late at the *whorehouse*—and do it on your own time!"

Part of his design in remarks of this sort was to get a reaction from the two girls present—Maxine, his cutiepie private sec, and Miss Rogers, assistant to the art director—both of whom managed, as usual, a polite blush and half-lowered eyes for his benefit.

The next ten minutes were spent talking about whether to send our own exclusive third-rate photographer to Viet Nam or to use the rejects of a second-rate one who had just come back.

"Even with the rejects we could still run our *E.L. trade*," said Katz, referring to an italicized phrase *Exclusively Lance* which appeared under photographs and meant they were not being published elsewhere—though less through exclusivity, in my view, than general crappiness.

Without really resolving this, we went on to the subject of "Twiggy," the British fashion-model who had just arrived in New York and about whose boyish hair and bust-line raged a storm of controversy. What did it mean philosophically? Aesthetically? Did it signal a new trend? Should we adjust our center-spread requirements (traditionally 42–24–38) to meet current taste? Or was it simply a flash fad?

"Come next issue," said Hack, "we don't want to find ourselves holding the wrong end of the shit-stick, now do we?"

Everyone was quick to agree.

"Well, *I* think she's absolutely *delightful*," exclaimed Ronnie Rondell, the art director (prancing gay and proud of it), "she's so much more . . . sensitive-looking and . . . *delicate* than those awful . . . *milk-factories!*" He gave a little shiver of revulsion and looked around excitedly for corroboration.

Hack, who had a deep-rooted antifag streak, stared at him for a moment like he was some kind of weird lizard, and he seemed about to say something cruel and uncalled for to Ron, but then he suddenly turned on me instead.

"Well, Mister Whorehouse man, isn't it about time we heard from you? Got any ideas that might conceivably keep this operation out of the shithouse for another issue or two?"

"Yeah, well I've been thinking," I said, winging it completely, "I mean, Fox here and I had an idea for a series of interviews with unusual persons. . . ."

"Unusual *persons?*" he growled, "what the hell does that mean?"

"Well, you know, a whole new department, like a regular feature. Maybe call it, uh, 'Lance Visits. . . .' "

He was scowling, but he was also nodding vigorously. " 'Lance Visits. . . .' Yeh, yeh, you wantta gimme a fer instance?"

"Well, you know, like, uh, . . . 'Lance Visits a Typical Teenybopper'—cute teenybopper tells about cute teen-use of Saran Wrap as a contraceptive, etcetera . . . and uh, let's see . . . 'Lance Visits a Giant Spade Commie Bull-Dike' . . . 'Lance Visits the Author of *Masturbation Now!*', a really fun-guy."

Now that I was getting warmed up, I was aware that Fox, on my left, had raised a hand to his face and was slowly massaging it, mouth open, eyes closed. I didn't look at Hack, but I knew he had stopped nodding. I pressed on . . . "You see, it could become a sort of regular department, we could do a 'T.L.' on it . . . '*Another Exclusive Lance Visit.*' How about this one: 'Lance Visits a Cute

Junkie Hooker' . . . 'Lance Visits a Zany Ex-Nun Nympho' . . . 'Lance Visits the Fabulous Rose Chan, beautiful research and development technician for the so-called French Tickler . . ."

"Okay," said Hack, "how about *this* one: 'Lance Visits Lance,'— know where? Up shit-creek without a paddle! Because that's where we'd be if we tried any of that stuff." He shook his head in a lament of disgust and pity. "Jeez, that's some sense of humor you got, boy." Then he turned to Fox. "What rock you say you found him under? Jeez."

Fox, as per usual, made no discernible effort to defend me, simply pretended to suppress a yawn, eyes averted, continuing to doodle on his "Think Pad," as it was called, one of which lay by each of our ashtrays.

"Okay," said Hack, lighting a new cigar, "suppose *I* come up with an idea? I mean, I don't wantta *surprise* you guys, cause any *heart attacks* . . . by *me* coming up with an *idea*," he saying this with a benign serpent smile, then adding in grim significance, *"after twenty-seven years in this goddam game!"* He took a sip of water, as though trying to cool his irritation at being (as per usual) "the only slob around here who delivers." "Now let's just stroke this one for a while," he said, "and see if it gets stiff. Okay, lemme ask you a question: what's the hottest thing in mags at this time? What's raising all the stink and hullabaloo? The *Manchester* book, right? The suppressed passages, right?" He was referring, of course, to a highly publicized account of the assassination of President Kennedy —certain passages of which had allegedly been deleted. "Okay, now all this stink and hullabaloo—*I* don't like it, *you* don't like it. In the first place, it's infringement on freedom of the press. In the second, they've exaggerated it all out of proportion. I mean, what the hell was *in* those passages? See what I mean? All right, suppose we do a *takeoff* on those same passages?"

He gave me a slow look, eyes narrowed—ostensibly to protect them from his cigar smoke, but with a Mephistophelian effect. *He* knew that *I* knew that his "idea" was actually an idea I had gotten from Paul Krassner, editor of *The Realist,* a few evenings earlier, and had mentioned, *en passant* so to speak, at the last prelunch confab. He seemed to be wondering if I would crack. A test, like. I avoided his eyes, doodled on the "Think Pad." He exhaled in my direction, and continued:

"Know what I mean? Something *light*, something *zany*, kid the pants off the guys who suppressed it in the first place. A satire like. Get the slant?"

No one at the table seemed to. Except for Hack we were all in our thirties or early forties, and each had been hurt in some way by the President's death. It was not easy to imagine any particular "zaniness" in that regard.

Fox was the first to speak, somewhat painfully it seemed. "I'm, uh, not quite sure I follow," he said. "You mean it would be done in the style of the book?"

"Right," said Hack, "but get this, we don't say it *is* the real thing, we say it *purports* to be the real thing. And editorially we *challenge* the *authenticity* of it! Am I getting through to you?"

"Well, uh, yeah," said Fox, "but I'm not sure it can be, you know, uh, *funny*."

Hack shrugged. "So? *You're* not sure, *I'm* not sure. Nobody's sure it can be funny. We all take a crack at it—just stroke it a while and see if we get any jism—right?"

Right.

After work that evening I picked up a new Dexamyl prescription and stopped off at Sheridan Square to get it filled. Coming out of the drugstore, I paused momentarily to take in the scene. It was a fantastic evening—late spring evening, warm breeze promise of great summer evenings imminent—and teenies in minies floating by like ballerinas, young thighs flashing. Summer, I thought, will be the acid test for minies when it gets too warm for tights, bodystockings, that sort of thing. It should be quite an interesting phenomenon. On a surge of sex-dope impulse I decided to fall by the dinette and see if anything of special import was shaking, so to speak.

Curious that the first person I should see there, hunched over his coffee, frozen saintlike, black shades around his head as though a hippy crown of thorns, should be the young man who had given me the dex that very morning. I had the feeling he hadn't moved all day. But this wasn't true because he now had on a white linen suit and was sitting in a booth. He nodded in that brief formal way it is possible to nod and mean more than just hello. I sat down opposite him.

"I see you got yourself all straightened out," he said with a wan smile, nodding again, this time at my little paper bag with the pharmacy label on it.

I took out the vial of dex and popped a quick one, thinking to do a bit of the old creative Lit later on. Then I shook out four or five and gave them to the young man.

"Here's some interest."

"Anytime," he said, dropping them in his top pocket, and after a pause, "You ever in the mood for something beside dexies?"

"Like what?"

He shrugged, "Oh, you know," he said, raising a vague limp hand, then added with a smile, "I mean you know your moods better than I do."

During the next five minutes he proved to be the most acquisitive pusher, despite his tender years, I have ever encountered. His range was extensive—beginning with New Jersey pot, and ending with something called a "Frisco Speedball," a concoction of heroin and cocaine, with a touch of acid ("gives it a little color"). While we were sitting there, a veritable parade of his far-flung connections commenced, sauntering over, or past the booth, pausing just long enough to inquire if he wanted to score—for sleepers, leapers, creepers . . . acid in cubes, vials, capsules, tablets, powder . . . "hash, baby, it's black as O" . . . mushrooms, mescalin, buttons . . . cosanyl, codeine, coke . . . coke in crystals, coke in powder, coke that looked like karo syrup . . . red birds, yellow jackets, purple hearts . . . "liquid-O, it comes straight from Indochina, stamped right on the can" . . . and from time to time the young man ("Trick" he was called) would turn to me and say: "Got eyes?"

After committing to a modest (thirty dollars) score for crystals, and again for two ounces of what was purported to be 'Panamanian Green' ("It's 'one-poke pot', baby."), I declined further inducement. Then an extremely down-and-out type, a guy I had known before whose actual name was Rattman, but who was known with simple familiarity as "Rat," and even more familiarly, though somehow obscurely, as "The Rat-Prick Man," half staggered past the booth, clocked the acquisitive Trick, paused, moved uncertainly towards the booth, took a crumpled brown paper bag out of his coat pocket, and opened it to show.

"Trick," he muttered, almost without moving his lips, ". . . Trick, can you use any Lights? Two-bits for the bunch." We both looked in, on some commodity quite unrecognizable—tiny, dark cylinder-shaped capsules, sticky with a brown-black guk, flat on each end, and apparently made of plastic. There was about a handful of them. The young man made a weary face of distaste and annoyance.

"Man," he asked softly, plaintively, looking up at Rattman, *"when are you going to get buried?"*

But the latter, impervious, gave a soundless guffaw, and shuffled on.

"What," I wanted to know, "were those things?" asking this of the young man half in genuine interest, half in annoyance at not knowing. He shrugged, raised a vague wave of dismissal. "Lights they're called . . . they're used nicotine-filters. You know, those nicotine filters you put in a certain kind of cigarette holder."

"Used nicotine-filters? What do you do with them?"

"Well, you know, drop two or three in a cup of coffee—gives you a little buzz."

"A little *buzz?*" I said, "are you kidding? How about a little *cancer?* That's all tar and nicotine in there, isn't it?"

"Yeah, well, you know . . ." he chuckled dryly, "anything for kicks. Right?"

Right, right, right.

And it was just about then he sprung it—first giving me his look of odd appraisal, then the sigh, the tired smile, the haltering deference: "Listen, man . . . you ever made red-split?"

"I beg your pardon?"

"Yeah, you know—*the blood of a wig.*"

"No," I said, not really understanding, "I don't believe I have."

"Well, it's something else, baby, I can tell you that."

"Uh, well, *what* did you call it—I'm not sure I understood. . . ."

" 'Red-split,' man, it's called 'red-split'—it's schizo-juice . . . *blood* . . . the blood of a wig."

"Oh, I see." I had, in fact, read about it in a recent article in the *Times*—how they had shot up a bunch of volunteer prisoners (very normal, healthy guys, of course) with the blood of schizophrenia patients—and the effect had been quite pronounced . . . in some cases, manic; in other cases, depressive—about 50/50 as I recalled.

"But that can be a big bring-down, can't it?"

He shook his head somberly. "Not with *this* juice it can't. You know who this is out of?" Then he revealed the source—Chin Lee, it was, a famous East Village resident, a Chinese symbolist poet, who was presently residing at Bellevue in a straightjacket. "Nobody," he said, "and I mean *nobody*, baby, has gone anywhere but *up, up, up* on *this* taste!"

I thought that it might be an interesting experience, but using caution as my watchword (the *Times* article had been very sketchy) I had to know more about this so-called red-split, blood of a wig. "Well, how long does it, uh, you know, *last?*"

He seemed a little vague about that—almost to the point of resenting the question. "It's a *trip*, man—four hours, six if you're lucky. It all depends. It's a question of *combination*—how your blood makes it with his, you dig?" He paused and gave me a very straight look. "I'll tell you this much, baby, it *cuts acid and STP* . . . " He nodded vigorously. "That's right, cuts both them. *Back, down,* and *sideways.*"

"Really?"

He must have felt he was getting a bit too loquacious, a bit too much on the old hard-sell side, because then he just cooled it, and nodded. "That's right," he said, so soft and serious that it wasn't really audible.

"How much?" I asked, finally, uncertain of any other approach.

"I'll level with you," he said, "I've got this connection—a ward attendant . . . you know, a male nurse . . . has, what you might call *access* to the hospital pharmacy . . . does a little trading with the guards on the fifth floor—that's where the *monstro*-wigs are—'High Five' it's called. That's where Chin Lee's at. Anyway, he's operating at cost right now—I mean, he'll cop as much M, or whatever other hard-shit he can, from the pharmacy, then he'll go up to High Five and trade for the juice—you know, just fresh, straight, uncut wig-juice—90 c.c.'s, that's the regular hit, about an ounce, I guess . . . I mean, that's what they hit the wigs for, a 90 c.c. syringeful, then they cap the spike and put the whole outfit in an insulated wrapper. Like it's supposed to stay at body temperature, you dig? They're very strict about that—about how much they tap the wig for, and about keeping it fresh and warm, that sort of thing. Which is okay, because that's the trip—90 c.c.'s, 'piping hot,' as they say." He gave a tired little laugh at the curious image. "Anyway the point is, he never knows in front what the *price* will be, my friend doesn't, because he never knows what kind of M score he'll make. I mean like if he scores for half-a-bill of M, then that's what he charges for the split, you dig?"

To me, with my Mad Ave savvy, this seemed fairly illogical.

"Can't he hold out on the High Five guys?" I asked, ". . . you know, tell them he only got half what he really got, and save it for later?"

He shrugged, almost unhappily. "He's a very ethical guy," he said, "I mean like he's pretty weird. He's not really interested in narcotics, just *changes*. I mean, like he lets *them* do the count on the M—they tell him how much it's worth and that's what he charges for the split."

"That *is* weird," I agreed.

"Yeah, well it's like a new market, you know. I mean there's no established price yet, he's trying to develop a clientele—can you make half-a-bill?"

While I pondered, he smiled his brave tired smile, and said: "There's one thing about the cat, being so ethical and all—he'll never burn you."

So in the end it was agreed, and he went off to complete the arrangements.

The effect of red-split was "as advertised" so to speak—in this case, quite gleeful. Sense-derangementwise, it was unlike acid in that it was not a question of the "Essential I" having new insights, but of becoming a different person entirely. So that in a way there was nothing very scary about it, just extremely weird, and as it turned out, somewhat mischievous (Chin Lee, incidentally, was not merely a great wig, but also a great wag). At about six in the morning I started to work on the alleged "Manchester passages." Krassner might be cross, I thought, but what the hell, you can't copyright an idea. Also I intended to give him full and ample credit. "Darn good exposure for Paul" I mused benignly, taking up the old magic quill.

The first few passages were fairly innocuous, the emphasis being on a style indentical to that of the work in question. Towards the end of Chapter Six, however, I really started cooking: ". . . wan, and wholly bereft, she steals away from the others, moving trancelike towards the darkened rear-compartment where the casket rests. She enters, and a whispery circle of light shrouds her bowed head as she closes the door behind her and leans against it. Slowly she raises her eyes and takes a solemn step forward. She gasps, and is literally slammed back against the door by the sheer impact of the outrageous horror confronting her: i.e., the hulking Texan silhouette at the casket, its lid half raised, and he hunching bestially, his coarse animal member thrusting into the casket, and indeed into the neck-wound itself.

"*Great God*," she cries, "how heinous! It must be a case of . . . of . . . *NECK*-ROPHILIA!"

I finished at about ten, dexed, and made it to the office. I went directly into Fox's cubicle (the "Lair" it was called).

"You know," I began, lending the inflection a childlike candor, "I could be wrong but I think I've *got* it," and I handled him the ms.

"Got what?" he countered dryly, "the clap?"

"You know, that Manchester thing we discussed at the last pre-lunch confab." While he read, I paced about, flapped my arms in a gesture of uncertainty and humble doubt. "Oh, it may need a little tightening up, brightening up, granted, but I hope you'll agree that the *essence* is there."

For a while he didn't speak, just sat with his head resting on one hand staring down at the last page. Finally he raised his eyes; his eyes were always somehow sad.

"You really *are* out of your nut, aren't you?"

"Sorry, John," I said. "Don't follow."

He looked back at the ms., moved his hands a little away from it as though it were a poisonous thing. Then he spoke with great seriousness:

"I think you ought to have your head examined."

"My *head* is swell," I said, and wished to elaborate, "my *head* . . ." but suddenly I felt very weary. I had evidently hit on a cow sacred even to the cynical Fox.

"Look," he said, "I'm not a *prude* or anything like that, but this . . ."—he touched the ms. with a cough which seemed to stifle a retch— . . . "I mean, *this* is the most . . . *grotesque* . . . *obscene* . . . well, I'd rather not even discuss it. Frankly, I think you're in very real need of psychiatric attention."

"Do you think Hack will go for it?" I asked in perfect frankness.

Fox averted his eyes and began to drum his fingers on the desk.

"Look, uh, I've got quite a bit of work to do this morning, so, you know, if you don't mind. . . ."

"Gone too far, have I, Fox? Is that it? Maybe you're missing the point of the thing—ever consider that?"

"Listen," said Fox stoutly, lips tightened, one finger raised in accusation, "you show this . . . *this thing* to anybody else, you're liable to get a *big smack in the kisser!*" There was an unmistakable heat and resentment in his tone—a sort of controlled hysteria.

"How do you know I'm not from the C.I.A.?" I asked quietly.

"How do *you* know this isn't a *test?*" I gave him a shrewd narrow look of appraisal. "Isn't it just possible, Fox, that this quasi-indignation of yours is, in point of fact, simply an *act?* A *farce?* A *charade?* An *act*, in short, to *save your own skin!?!*"

He had succeeded in putting me on the defensive. But now, steeped in Chink poet cunning, I had decided that an offense was the best defense, and so plunged ahead. "Isn't it true, Fox, that in this parable you see certain underlying homosexual tendencies which you unhappily recognize in yourself? Tendencies, I say, which to confront would bring you to the very brink of, 'fear and trembling,' so to speak." I was counting on the Kierkegaard allusion to bring him to his senses.

"You crazy son of a bitch," he said flatly, rising behind his desk, hands clenching and unclenching. He actually seemed to be moving towards me in some weird menacing way. It was then I changed my tack. "Well listen," I said, "what would you say if I told you that it wasn't actually *me* who did that, but a Chinese poet? Probably a Commie . . . an insane Commie-fag-spade-Chinese poet. Then we could view it objectively, right?"

Fox, now crazed with his own righteous adrenalin, and somewhat encouraged by my lolling helplessly in the chair, played his indignation to the hilt.

"Okay, Buster," he said, towering above me, "keep talking, but make it good."

"Well, uh, let's see now. . . ." So I begin to tell him about my experience with the red-split. And speaking in a slow, deliberate, very serious way, I managed to cool him. And then I told him about an insight I had gained into Viet Nam, Cassius Clay, Chessman, the Rosenbergs, and all sorts of interesting things. He couldn't believe it. But, of course, no one ever really does—do they?